Will their love be strong enough to keep them alive and get them back to Earth?

Finding one's psi-mate is something every Sandarian hopes for, but when Ian Cavacent accidentally starts the bonding process with the Earthling, Dani, he has to fight his desire with every ounce of his being. If the process is completed, it means both political and financial suicide for Ian and his family.

A natural klutz, Dani somehow always manages to land on her feet and win her mixed martial arts matches. At home on Cat Island, her balance is thrown when bazillionaire Ian takes notice. Unfortunately some Torog aliens also take notice, sending her life spiraling out of control and into Ian's arms. But Dani isn't the type of woman to let alien voodoo decide her future or her mate…no matter how gorgeous the man is or how much pleasure he gives her.

For centuries the Cavacents have mined Earth for a precious element, carnium, while protecting the planet from other alien species. Thanks to the Torogs, Dani and Ian must flee to Sandaria. As Dani learns to use her newfound psi powers, the empire crumbles around them.

Visit us at www.kensingtonbooks.com

Books by Sabine Priestley

Alien Attachments
Alien Attachments
Rebellion

Published by Kensington Publishing Corporation

Alien Attachments

Alien Attachments

Sabine Priestley

LYRICAL PRESS
Kensington Publishing Corp.
www.kensingtonbooks.com

LYRICAL PRESS BOOKS are published by
Kensington Publishing Corp.
119 West 40th Street
New York, NY 10018

All Kensington titles, imprints, and distributed lines are available at special quantity discounts for bulk purchases for sales promotion, premiums, fund-raising, educational, or institutional use.

Special book excerpts or customized printings can also be created to fit specific needs. For details, write or phone the office of the Kensington Sales Manager: Kensington Publishing Corp., 119 West 40th Street, New York, NY 10018. Attn. Sales Department. Phone: 1-800-221-2647.

Lyrical Press and Lyrical Press logo Reg. U.S. Pat. & TM Off.

First Electronic Edition: August 2014
eISBN-13: 978-1-61650-566-0
eISBN-10: 1-61650-566-4

First Print Edition: August 2014
ISBN-13: 978-1-61650-582-0
ISBN-10: 1-61650-582-6

To Justin, Sabrina, and Sebastian. (Extra kudos to Sebastian for coming up with the title.) To my mom, who never doubted me. To Melanie Sherwood and Ted Reynolds, the best critique partners, who saw this book all the way through. Finally, to all lovers of my little genre, Science Fiction Romance. I hope you enjoy it.

Chapter 1

A dark-skinned male and a tall blond female danced around each other, bamboo sticks at the ready, waiting for an opening. Sitting on the warm iron bleachers above, Ian Cavacent leaned forward in anticipation. The old warehouse on Cat Island doubled as many things. Tonight, it hosted the weekly mixed fight competition. The popular event drew crowds from as far away as Nassau. Humans jostled for a seat or stood in groups around the improvised, oversized boxing ring. The target of his interest was the blond woman. He'd come to watch her for the past few weeks. A friend of his human support agent, Jared, she fascinated him. He had a rule to avoid women on the island, but there was something about this one. She intrigued him. And not for the usual reasons, either. Yes, she was pretty, beautiful even, but there was more to it than that.

Jared slid into the seat next to him and handed him a beer. "Dani said you were stalking her."

"I don't stalk." Ian took the plastic cup. "Besides, I wasn't aware she knew I was here."

"Yeah, she told me that too."

Ian took a long pull on the beer. "There's just something odd about her. Maybe it's the way she moves. Her motions aren't practiced, she's constantly off balance, and yet she pulls in win after win. If I didn't know better, I'd say the fights were rigged."

The crowd quieted, and tension rose as the timer ticked down to zero.

Below, the two continued their dance, circling each other. The man lunged and Dani twirled with an awkward step, but still managed to dodge the swing of the bamboo. Sweat dripped into the cleavage of her sports bra and down the small of her back, leaving a dark stain in the fabric. She parried left and right. As usual, her maneuvers were halting and lacked grace.

Ian winced when Jared erupted in one of his booming sneezes. Dani shot an annoyed glance their way. Big mistake. In that fraction of a second, her opponent swung his bamboo. The jagged tip grazed the skin below her left eye before slamming into her wrist. The impact pushed her over the edge. She ducked, nearly fell over, spun around and in a surprisingly fluid movement, sent her opponent's stick flying. The crowd erupted with cheers and jeers for both sides. Money changed hands and the tension evaporated. The two opponents approached each other. Cradling her wrist, Dani declined a handshake. They shared some good-natured words before they left the floor.

Ian's powerful psi allowed him to see a purple mist radiating from her injuries. "That's going to hurt," Ian said.

"Dammit," Jared mumbled, grabbing one of his ever-present tissues. "Can you tell how bad it is?"

"Not yet."

"Well"—Ian swallowed the dregs of his beer—"she may have won, but she's going to be out of commission for awhile. She's not going to be happy with you."

"Yep." Jared wiped his nose. "I best go down and apologize. Come with me? She knows you've been watching. Be kind of weird at this point not to say hello."

A wave of anticipation washed over him. Aside from his three support agents, he limited his involvement with humans to the occasional short-lived affair off the island. Yet his reaction to spending time with this woman surprised him.

"You know I prefer to keep my involvement with humans away from here." Still, he was tempted. On the verge of changing his mind, he sensed a pending communication. "Hold on, incoming message from Marco." Marco was the Earth Protector, or EP, currently on duty. He waited a beat for it to arrive.

We got company, boss. His com relayed the message.

"Apologies are going to have to wait. Someone's paying Earth a visit." Ian said.

Jared followed him out the back door.

* * * *

Dani wiped the sweat from her brow and followed Dugo out of the fight area. Bazillionaire Ian Cavacent and her friend Jared were leaving out the back. Ian always kept to himself, and as far as she knew, never fraternized with the locals except Jared. His recent interest in her sparked an explosion of fantasies. Even better, he seemed the type who would be okay with a "nothing complicated" scenario. And he was hot. Seriously hot, hence the fantasies. She'd love to get him in front of her camera…and a few other places. Those wavy blond locks and smoky green eyes. *Yum. Why haven't you contacted me, Mr. Cavacent?*

Dugo interrupted her musings. "Someone needs to tell Jared to take his allergy meds." He nodded toward her arm. "You okay?"

"I'll be fine." She gave him a good-natured nudge with her other elbow. "You almost got me there."

He took a hand towel off the supplies table and handed it to her. "You're bleeding."

The medic came over and applied antibiotic ointment and a butterfly bandage to her cheek. "You should have that looked at."

"I will," Dani said.

Dugo tossed the towel in the laundry bin. "Glad I missed your eye. Seriously, man. I didn't see you comin'."

"And that's the way it's done," Dani said with all the swagger she could muster. Which was a lot, even with the pain radiating from her wrist.

Dugo laughed. "So what do you say? Have a drink with me?"

"Dugo…"

"Hey," he said, shrugging. "I never see you with no one here. You fly around the world and take your pictures, but this is home. Why you not date anyone?"

"Who says I don't?" Dani could tell by his stance he wasn't buying it. Didn't matter, he didn't have to. It was her business. "Gotta go. Catch ya next time."

Chapter 2

The following day, after a swim along the beach, Ian sat on a barstool across from Jared. Two additional members of his EP team sat on either side of him. They were like night and day. Armond Nolde, white-haired albino, and Marco Dar, dark and swarthy.

"That was no accident last night, boss," Marco said.

"I know." Ian motioned for Jared to pour them some drinks.

After leaving Dani's match, they'd ported off world to the base where their fighters were kept. Humans had no idea their little planet was the focus of increasingly frequent alien attention. It was the EP's job to keep it that way. Last night Torogs attempted to land. During their interception, a team hired by Councilman Gordat Prayda fired on Ian's ship. The Torogs fled, and Prayda's goons claimed mechanical failure of their equipment.

Mechanical failure, like hell. Politics on Sandaria had become increasingly perilous.

Jared poured beers for the three Sandarians and wiped down the already-clean counter.

"Aside from the obvious," the albino Armond said, reaching back to tighten his ubiquitous pony tail, "I find it disturbing Councilman Prayda appears to believe the accidental death of Lord Cavacent's heir and only child would go unpunished."

Armond had a point. "I talked with my father after the incursion last night. He agrees the increase in Torog activity is concerning, but thinks we should stay quiet about the attack on me. The fewer waves we make right now, the better. Let's just try and avoid any further contact with Councilman Prayda's pets."

Marco rapidly tapped his beer glass. "If you'd just let me blast that *crag* last night—"

"The emperor's guards would be all over us," Armond finished.

Ian sensed Marco's rising anger at Armond. The two rarely saw eye to eye. "At ease." Ian slid Marco's beer away from his tapping finger. He used his psi to calm the man. *I've told you before to stop letting him get under your skin.*

Marco's psi wasn't strong enough to broadcast his thoughts but the release of tension in his shoulders as he took a long pull on his beer was enough for Ian.

Jared, who'd been listening to the exchange, leaned against the bar. "Trouble in paradise?"

Marco snorted.

Ian ignored the reaction and addressed Jared. "Let's just say the empire is a little unstable right now." The concern on Jared's face was clear. "Don't worry too much. Earth shouldn't be involved. Aside from you and the Papallos, Earth can remain blissfully ignorant of the existence of aliens."

Closer to his father's age, Jared bore the appearance of a scruffy old sea captain. He'd worked with his father before Ian took over.

"Where's the new kid?" Jared asked, pouring some mixed nuts into a bowl.

Grinning, Marco grabbed a handful of nuts and shook his head.

"She's getting settled," Ian said. "Has some more unpacking to do. You'll meet her later."

"Marco here said she's height-challenged," Jared said.

Marco held his hand out below shoulder height. It wasn't much, given that he was sitting. "She's a little spitfire."

"Five-foot-four," Ian said.

"With her boots on," Armond added.

Jared raised a bushy eyebrow.

"Just wait till you catch her in action," Ian said. "Unbelievably fast and knows how to use her size to her advantage. Oh, and she's got blazing red hair."

"I have got to see this." Jared blew his nose and shook his head. "You three over six-foot, and Little Red Riding Hood."

Ian laughed. "An odd picture all right. It works, though. She nailed the trial and has total psi-control over her ship. Never once went to manual."

"So, what do you think the Torogs were coming for?" Jared asked.

"The usual," Ian said. "Hunting humans or going after carnium."

Jared stacked more glasses behind the bar. "That's the stuff you use to go all faster than light, right?"

Ian found Jared's vernacular to be a continuing source of entertainment. "Been taking notes?"

"I work for aliens. I'm always taking notes." Jared leaned back against the bar and crossed his arms. "Third time this week Torogs have hit our radar. What's going on?"

"I wish we knew," Ian said.

Jared remained silent for a moment. "You know, boss. I don't like the idea of Earth not having you guys around. Don't go gettin' yourself killed."

"I don't plan to. My father thinks the emperor doesn't have long. The problem is, no one knows who or what will take his place. Until we know that, we just have to ride it out." Ian's psi registered the approaching vehicle before he heard the crunch of tires on the crushed-shell gravel outside. Desire pulsed through him. "Well, well. Looks like we've got company. Sounds like Ms. Standich herself." Ian took a beat to enjoy the sensations she induced.

"She the one you're stalking?" Marco said.

Ian scowled at him. "I'm not stalking her."

"Whatever you say, boss." Marco pointed a finger at Jared. "He said it."

Jared plucked a nut out of the dish and flicked it at Marco.

The nut stopped in mid air, a few inches from Marco's face and spun around for a moment. Marco flicked his finger. The nut shot through the air and bounced off Jared's head, causing him to burst out laughing.

A moment later, the massive wood plank that made up the front entrance creaked open grudgingly. Sand scraped against the floor. The sliding doors at the back of the bar stood wide open, and the cross breeze pulled at Dani's blond hair as she struggled with the weight.

"When," she said, clutching a white hat and beach bag, "are you going to fix this thing?" She held her right wrist close to her chest. Slipping through the opening, she turned to use her rear to push the beast closed. She gave a mighty shove with her ass. The door gave more than expected and she let out a short squeak as she tried to regain her balance.

Graceful as always, Ian thought.

"Thanks for your help last night, by the way." Dani glared at Jared.

Ian stifled a laugh.

Waves of purple radiated from her arm and the left side of her face. She wore large, dark sunglasses that hid the injury to her eye, but her wrist was visibly bruised and swollen.

Jared rushed around the bar and gave the door a shove. "What can I say? My allergies never stop. You gotta learn not to be distracted."

"Hold it in next time."

"Sure, kid." Jared kicked at the bottom of the door, which finally clicked shut.

Ian was surprised by the obvious closeness of the relationship, but then he never stuck around when locals came into the bar. Until now.

"So?" Dani said, placing her bag and hat on a bar stool not far from Ian and his EPs. "When are you going to fix that thing?"

"Fix it? Why? Keeps the tourists down to a minimum."

"You own a bar on the beach. Aren't you supposed to want tourists?"

Jared shrugged. "I'm good with the ones I get from the hotel"—he indicated a path leading up a slight hill—"and the few wanderers."

Dani gazed at the beach beyond the small patio and sighed. "You do have a slice of heaven here."

Jared poured some nuts into a bowl and slid them across to her. "I don't think you've formally met my friends here." He indicated the team. "This is Armond, Marco and 'course you know about Ian. Guys, this here is Dani."

They exchanged greetings and Dani focused on Ian. "Been enjoying my fights, Mr. Cavacent?" She smiled with her striking blue eyes.

Jared coughed loudly.

Ian was sure the word "stalker" was buried in the cough somewhere. He decided to ease up on his usual role of arrogant millionaire. He needed to find out why she captivated him so. "Call me Ian, and yes, I have been enjoying your fights. You have an unusual technique."

Dani scoffed. "Lack thereof, you mean." She removed her sunglasses and revealed a nasty gash below her left eye. Dark bruises surrounded the puffy wound.

"Ouch." Jared leaned in for a closer inspection. "At least you won."

Dani set the glasses down. "Yeah, well it's going to be awhile before I can compete again. I figure you owe me some drinks in the meantime."

"Suppose that's only fair."

Fascinating purple swirls worked their way up to her shoulder and out from her cheek. The color was deep and rich, meaning she was in a great deal of pain. That, or she had an unusually high tolerance for it.

Dani dug around her bag with her left hand and pulled out an insulated Tervis cup. "Rum and coke, please." She slid the cup over to Jared.

"Want some ice for that wrist? And maybe your face?" he asked.

"No, thanks."

Jared set her drink down while she gathered up her bag and put her sunglasses back on.

"Why thank you kindly, sir," she said with an exaggerated southern accent. "I always rely upon the kindness of strangers."

Jared bowed. "Anything for you, Miss Scarlett."

"Boys." She gave a nod and headed for the path leading to the hotel pool. Ian waited until she was out of earshot. "She moves like a cat."

The men watched as she tripped and sloshed her drink onto the path.

"A clumsy cat," Marco said, finishing his beer. "That's it for me. I can't take this humidity. I'll check in with you later, boss." He stood. "Thanks, Jared."

"I too, have had enough of this damp climate of yours." Armond said, getting to his feet. "I'll report in this evening." He followed Marco out.

Jared sneezed. "That's why you selected this place, isn't it?"

Ian didn't answer, just grinned. "How long have you known her?" He indicated the direction Dani had taken.

"Years," Jared said around his tissue. "Her aunt took her in when her parents died in a plane crash. She was only fifteen or sixteen at the time. I used to let her sweep up around the bar in exchange for sodas. Got the feeling she needed the company. Anyway, auntie spends most of her time in New York these days. Dani keeps the house going when she's not off freelancing for Vogue or some other slick rag."

"Journalist?"

"Photographer. She's good too, if you like that sort of thing." Jared wiped his nose again. "Personally, I prefer landscapes and animals to pretty humans." Jared popped a few peanuts into his mouth. "She's in pain."

"That woman, my friend, is in a world of hurt," Ian agreed.

"Think maybe you could help her out?"

Ian finished off his beer. "You know how I am about getting involved with locals."

"She's good people, boss. Besides you don't have to get involved." Jared made quotes with his fingers around the last words. "I've never seen her with anyone. Losing your folks at such a young age, I suppose it can mess you up. Just tell her you know some techniques to help with the pain."

Ian cast another look at the retreating woman. "Why are you so concerned? Is there something I should know about you two?"

Jared harrumphed and crossed his arms. "I'm old enough to be her dad."

"So?"

"I'll admit, I have a soft spot for her, but it's more like a daughter. Like I said, she's good people."

Ian couldn't deny his attraction to her, and he was curious to see if he could figure out why he found her so appealing. Probably those blue eyes. *I'll talk to her for a while. She'll have nothing to say, and I'll get her out of my system.* "Fine. But just enough to ease her pain. I can't do more, obviously."

"Obviously. Thanks, boss. Hey, when you get back, I'll buy you a beer."

"That's real generous, considering I own the place."

Jared chuckled and ate another handful of peanuts.

* * * *

Dani had finally gotten herself situated on the raft, her drink within reach on the deck, when she noticed Ian heading her way. A deep thrill rippled through her and she bit her lip. The pool area was empty except an old couple eating ice cream at the far end.

Ian sat next to her cup, and dangled his legs in the water. Nice, muscular legs.

"Hello again," he said.

"Ian." Dani nodded in greeting.

"I'm guessing you're in a fair amount of pain right now."

"Nothing I can't handle." Where was he going with this?

"If you're interested, I'm proficient in an ancient Chinese art of pain management."

Dani tilted her hat to get a better view. "Seriously?" She'd heard some lines in her time, but that had to be the cheesiest.

"Seriously." He shrugged and took a sip of her drink.

Dani huffed and scowled at him. "You better not drink it all or you'll have to get me another one." His smoky green eyes were an intriguing contrast to his olive skin. The way he looked at her made her body tingle. "How exactly does this Chinese voodoo work?"

Ian pushed off the side and into the water with a smile on his face. "Certain places on the body can be manipulated to ease pain and do other things like lower blood pressure." He stood next to her, causing a slight wake to bob the raft up and down.

"Hmm…I don't know."

"Really? Jared's worried about you and I promised I'd help."

Dani glanced back toward the bar. She couldn't see Jared from here, but she knew he'd be worried. It's what he did under all that gruffness. When she looked back, she found Ian's gaze had shifted to somewhere south of her eyes. A flood of pleasure washed over her at the thought of his lips on her breast.

She cleared her throat.

Ian smiled at her with a crooked grin.

The thrill from earlier boiled over to something far less manageable. *Wow. This is some serious attraction.* "Um, precisely where and how will you be manipulating me?"

Ian laughed. "I assure you my intentions are honorable."

Well, that was disappointing. She tilted her head. If he didn't feel the same attraction right now, she'd eat her bikini. "Go ahead then. Let's see what you can do." She pulled her hat down over her face and leaned back.

The raft rocked in the water as he moved behind her. He lightly touched her injured arm sending a zap of euphoria through her. *Wow.*

His fingers slowly trailed up each of her arms and the tension in her core rose with it. As he reached the base of her neck, she said a little prayer he'd be open to a friends-with-benefits situation. His hands settled on her shoulder muscles and pressed harder. A bolt of pleasure shot through her. *This is insane.* She couldn't slow her breathing. He was no where near her private bits, yet it was as if...

Ian ran his thumbs up the cords in her neck.

She caught her breath as the intensity increased. *No way.* Her body tensed as pleasure exploded, leaving her motionless as the incredible sensation rolled outward to her fingers and toes. *Holy shit.*

* * * *

Ian drew his fingers along the top of Dani's shoulders, enjoying the buzz her silky smooth skin created.

Her body shivered, causing his psi to ripple through him. *Interesting.*

He gently probed along the muscles to find the right spot.

Dani let out a long sigh and relaxed into his hands.

He found it odd he'd have such intense chemistry with a human. He closed his eyes and reached out with his psi. Her cheek possessed only a flesh wound so he dampened the nerve endings to stop the pain. Next he moved to her wrist where he found a hairline fracture. He focused his psi and mended the bone, leaving most of the bruised tissue and muscle, but again dampened the nerve endings. A minute passed before Ian realized something was off. His psi buzzed with an energy he'd never experienced before.

Dani's breathing quickened.

He was about to let go when a blast of psi tore into him. The sheer force was astonishing. He nearly flung her behind him, before he realized it *was* her.

Not possible. Humans don't have psi. Unable to resist, he explored further. Like a Sandarian child, her psi was unrefined and clearly not under control. He should let go, but like a moth to a flame, he delved deeper. And deeper still. The magnitude floored him. She could very well be as strong as he.

This had the potential to change everything. If people on his planet found out, his family could lose all rights to this world. Rights to both the carnium and their protectorship of Earth. Humans could never defend themselves against the aliens who would come looking for an easy grab at the coveted mineral. With the unrest of the empire, it might be years before another protectorship could be effectively established and agreed upon. By then, Goddess knew, how much damage would have been done.

A human with psi. It made no sense. His family had been protecting Earth for generations. Never had a human been found with psi. He'd been with a number of women, and never had there been an inkling. He needed to discuss this with his father. He began to pull back. As though in response to his leaving, her psi pulsed and pleasure unlike anything he'd ever imagined washed though him. His body and psi buzzed with the intense energy. Stronger and stronger it grew. He drew a deep breath, riding the wave of pure ecstasy.

Almost as if—*Holy Goddess.* Ian slammed the connection closed and staggered back. His heart pounded in his chest. He stared at his hands as though they belonged to someone else. *My psi-mate?* The pleasure slowly subsided. He wanted more, needed more. *Mother Goddess help me.*

Chairs scrapped across the pool deck and snapped him out of his reverie. He threw a glance over his shoulder. The old couple prepared to leave. The man winked at Ian, then said something to the woman that made her laugh.

He returned his attention to Dani. She inhaled quickly as if she'd been holding her breath. He stood a moment longer, torn between staying, because he wanted to, and returning to Sandaria to talk with his father. Duty won. He whirled around, slicing through the water.

She called after him but he didn't respond.

What did I just do?

* * * *

Dani coughed as water splashed over her face from Ian's abrupt departure. She jerked to a sitting position. She'd been momentarily paralyzed, and it freaked her out. The movement sent pulses of pleasure rippling through her. *Holy crap, that was amazing.* "Hey, what was that? Ian?" She spun around to find him nearly at the steps. "Ian!"

He bolted out of the water and headed back to the bar, dripping wet.

The photographer in her couldn't help but analyze the scene. *Damn, he does wet really well.* Dani wiped the water from her eyes and looked around for her hat. *Crap.* She reached over and plucked the soggy mess off the surface of the water. Plopping it on her head, she sighed as the waterlogged rim flopped over her face. *Great.* She shook the hat out a few times and stopped mid-swing.

What the... Slowly, she put the hat back on her head and held up her injured hand. She flexed her fingers and bent her wrist back and forth. The tendons were stiff and still looked like hell, but there was no pain. Swinging her legs off the lounge, she slid into the waist-deep water. Submerging her hand, she drew her palm back and forth under the surface. Still no pain. *What in the world did he do?*

Dani got out of the pool, gathered up her bag and drink and hurried down the path after him. She flexed her pain-free wrist the whole way.

Jared stood behind the bar, filling salt shakers.

"Where'd Ian go?"

"Said he had to run."

"Yeah, literally. I want to talk to him about this pressure point thing." Dani sat across from him.

"Pressure point?"

"You know, the pain thing."

"Oh yeah, how'd it go? Pretty cool, huh?" Jared screwed the lid on a shaker.

"I guess. I mean the results are great. Unbelievable really, but the effect—" Dani stopped herself. What was she going to do? Tell Jared she'd just had some freak pleasure event? As if. "I just can't believe how effective this pressure point thing is." She slid her empty cup over to Jared. "Can I have another rum and coke, please? Mr. Personality sloshed water in mine."

Jared put down the shaker. "Sure. I take it you're feeling better?" He rinsed out the Tervis cup and made another drink.

"I'll say. He's got a nice touch, I'll give him that." *There's an understatement.* "But as soon as he finished, he bolted from the pool. Swamped me with his wake. Got my new hat wet."

"Really?"

"Yeah, and check this out." Dani held up her wrist and twisted it around. "What the—even the bruising is going away now, look."

Jared leaned in for a closer inspection and frowned. His eyes moved from her wrist to her face. "Take your glasses off, Dani."

She did as he asked.

"Oh, dear."

"What? What's wrong?" She reached up and probed the gash under her eye. The skin felt like a month-old scar. "Jared, what's going on?"

* * * *

Ian walked across the expensive, plush carpet of his father's study on Sandaria. He'd thrown on a pair of jeans and a shirt left unbuttoned, before using the portal to his home planet.

Not exactly dressed for the occasion. He couldn't wrap his head around a human with psi, but couldn't deny it, either. Nor the effect she'd had on him. His psi still buzzed. He ran a hand through his hair and sighed. This was as impossible as it was true.

Windows spanned the back wall, a perfect frame for the summer storm raging outside. Clouds swirled around like multi-colored paint in a mixer. They spun side by side but never blended, their chemical compositions too different to merge. Light from the tempest threw soft hues of purple and green across every surface. This time of year you could set your watch by their arrival, but in another month their chaos would hit randomly.

Ian reached out with his psi. His father wasn't near or was blocking. He approached a large desk by the windows and activated the com with his psi. A holographic screen appeared in front of him.

"What can I help you with, your lordship?" a female computerized voice asked.

"I need to see my father."

After a pause the voice continued, "I am unable to locate Lord Cavacent. I will connect you with the house staff."

The screen flashed and Samuel, the head servant, appeared. The portly man stood in the kitchen, no doubt sampling the evening's meal.

"Your lordship! What can I do for you?" He straightened his shirt, pausing when he took in Ian's appearance.

"I need to speak to my father. Please locate him for me, Samuel. I'll be here in his study."

"Certainly, sir. Is everything all right, sir?"

"Everything is fine," he lied. "Let me know if you have trouble finding him." He disconnected before Samuel asked any more questions.

The clouds whirled in their violent dance outside. He found the storms energizing and missed them when he was on Earth. He sensed his father's approach a moment before he entered the room.

Rucon Cavacent entered with an air of authority befitting a major lord on Sandaria. He raised a brow as he took in Ian's attire. "What is it, son?" He walked over to the bar and poured them both an Oban. Ian had made sure to stock his father's favorite whisky from Earth.

Rucon added ice and brought the drinks over. "Someone kick sand in your face?"

"More like psi." Ian took the drink. His father's psi brushed across his own.

"You're a mess. What happened?"

"I was…exposed to very powerful and completely raw psi. No restraint whatsoever. It—"

"Raw psi?"

Ian held his father's gaze. "From a human."

Rucon's glass halted halfway to his lips. An odd expression crossed his face. "That's not possible, son." His hand trembled when he took a drink.

Ian sensed his father's conflicting emotions. They were far more powerful than he'd expected. "A friend of Jared's showed up at the bar," he continued. "She had some minor injuries, and Jared asked if I would help her with the pain."

"Surely you didn't?" His father's tone said far more than his words.

Ian held his ground. "She means a great deal to him. He's never asked for anything before. A moderate amount of healing wouldn't hurt."

"And just how did you explain this little hands-on event?"

"Chinese pressure points."

Rucon made a grunting noise Ian couldn't interpret.

"Regardless, it worked. I connected and sent a small amount of energy. I was almost done when it happened. Father, she possesses a massive psychic ability. Possibly stronger than my own."

Rucon frowned. "I doubt that. You are the strongest in generations."

Ian wasn't so sure. "I'm fairly certain she's not aware of it. It's more of a subconscious thing. Which, come to think of it"—Ian nodded and paced by the window—"would explain a lot. That's got to be how she wins."

"Wins what?" Rucon asked, sounding distracted.

"Mixed fights. She wins all the time, but obviously has no training. She's got to be using her psi."

Rucon joined Ian at the window and watched the storm. "Nothing else happened? When you connected?" Rucon searched his son's face.

"Nothing." Ian didn't know if his father bought it or not. Ultimately, it didn't matter. Bonding with a human would be political, and ultimately, financial suicide for the Cavacent clan.

Rucon's shoulders relaxed. "We need to step up our move to Earth. I think I'm close to getting the support of the Supreme Commander."

This was news. "And our rights to the carnium?"

"We're negotiating. I should be able to secure at least a percentage. When I have the go ahead, we'll need to move quickly. Ian,"—his father looked pained—"life will be easier there. We will be further removed from politics, whatever they turn out to be."

"I can't imagine a worse political environment than this."

"Agreed. In the meantime stay away from this woman. And don't say anything. To anyone. If Councilman Prayda finds out humans have psi, he'll have the emperor revoke our protectorship. We'll lose everything before we break free. That cannot happen."

Many factions within the empire wanted to get their hands on Earth's resources, and protecting its inhabitants wouldn't be a priority. The Cavacents' biggest advantage was they had protected the planet for over two hundred years, and kept humans largely safe and ignorant of their mining operations. Their history on Earth gave them a reasonable claim to residency. But they couldn't move until the emperor was taken down, or it would be seen as treason. They walked a fine line as they readied for a new order in the galaxy.

Rucon returned to business, but was still pale. "Any further activity with Torogs?"

"Not since last night."

"Keep your eyes open. Let me know if you need more agents."

"I will."

"How's the new recruit working out?"

"Surprisingly well, given her size."

"Which is?"

"Small."

"So is your mother and I wouldn't mess with her. Speaking of your mother, you'd best go clean up and say hello before you return to Earth. I'll inform her you're here."

Ian rubbed his neck and nodded. It had been a few weeks since he'd been back. If his mother found he'd come home without seeing her, there would be hell to pay. "All right." He turned to go, but Rucon stopped him.

"Remember, don't mention this. Not even to her. She's rather fond of that blue planet of yours. I don't want to upset her."

Chapter 3

Dani looked up at the sound of the door scraping across the sandy floor. For a split second she thought it might be Ian. She shifted her weight on the barstool and threw a quick smile at the two men who entered. The smile faded fast. They were the ugliest dudes she'd ever seen and they moved… wrong. Leather criss-crossed their torsos over pasty gray skin.

Leather? Who wears leather in the Bahamas? The hair at the back of her neck prickled, and she had an overwhelming urge to run. They stood there and stared at her. She stared back.

"Hey Jared, you've got customers," she called out.

Her voice startled them. Without taking their eyes off her, weird clicks and croaks came out of their bulbous lips.

What the hell?

Jared came out of the back room clutching a tissue. He froze as the two men came around the bar into full view.

No way. The two had decidedly round torsos and were dressed identically. Under the leather straps, a matching leather skirt fell just above the knee. Or where the knee should be. Instead, they had some sort of ball joint. Reality did a strange shift to the left when she noticed that below the joint were fleshy stumps, slightly padded on the bottom. *No feet.* Her head spun. *Handicapped?* She tried to figure the odds of two people having the same mutation when Jared reached behind the bar, pulled out a sawed-off shotgun, and fired. One shot each, to the center of their chest.

"Jared!" She flew off her seat. "Oh my God, what did you do?"

"Get in the back, Dani, now. Move!" Jared shouted.

Dani bolted the short distance around the bar.

The two guys lay on the floor but weren't dead. They oozed blue goo and stank like nothing she'd ever smelled before, a combination of skunk and sweetness. *Ewww.* They struggled to get up, screeching and clicking.

She backed away and Jared shoved her through the door to the storeroom. He stepped next to her and slapped the side of the doorframe. A faint click and the opening was gone, replaced by what looked to be solid metal.

"Holy shit, what just happened?" Dani touched the cool metal surface. She turned around, not sure where to go or what to do. The shelves were lined with bottles of liquor and bags of pretzels and peanuts. A small fan in the corner stirred the humid air.

"What happened to the door? Did you see the legs on those guys? They have no feet, Jared. And those knees? And you shot them." She struggled to make sense of it all.

Jared faced the far wall, hands flat on the wood paneling. He worked his hands up, then back down again along the surface.

Dani frowned. "Jared?"

He continued his strange behavior.

"What"—Dani took a few steps forward—"are you doing?"

"Sorry Dani, no time to explain. Those two are gonna be pissed. We need to get to the villa. I don't think they can get in here, but I'm not hanging around to find out."

"Pissed? Dude, they're gonna be dead." She rubbed her face. "We should call 911. Except, wait. You shot them for no reason. Oh, this is so not good. Those have to be some kind of prosthetic legs. Why'd you shoot them Jared?" She kept replaying the scene over and over in her head. Images flashed back and forth from the way the guys were shaped to the fact Jared shot them. *Oh my God. They bleed blue goo.* Nothing made sense.

"They're fine, Dani, trust me. This is a normal gun. Won't do much but slow 'em down and piss 'em off."

"A normal gun? As opposed to what? An abnormal gun? Do you know those guys?" Dani grabbed fists full of hair and pulled. The pain helped to clear her head.

"Not personally. But I know their kind. Not very bright but wicked strong."

"Their kind?"

Jared moved faster and cussed like a sailor as he slapped the wall harder. An opening appeared so fast he almost fell into the void. "Gotcha," he said, and turned back to her.

"Oh, this just keeps getting better and better. Why don't I have my camera?" She inched closer to the opening, craning her neck to get a better view.

Dim, gray walls, about twenty feet across with a fourteen-foot ceiling. She took another step and peered around the corner. Light from the storeroom showed a large, slightly oval tunnel leading off to the right. Jared stepped in and Dani caught his sigh of relief as a row of lights came on overhead. More rows switched on farther along the tunnel, one after another, until they curved up and out of sight.

"What is this? The Bat Cave?"

Jared motioned for her to follow.

She looked over her shoulder at the metal door. "So...long creepy tunnel or two creepy whatever they are back in the bar. Any other options?"

"Not unless you know how to summon an EP," Jared replied. He nodded toward the tunnel while fiddling with his phone.

She was about to ask what an EP was when a muffled bang from the door made her jump.

The adage "Better the devil you know, than the one you don't" didn't give her any warm fuzzies. Jared waited for her. He may not be who she thought he was, but he had to be better than the two in the bar. She motioned toward the opening. "You sure this thing isn't going to close on me? Slice me in half?"

"No, but it might leave you behind if you don't get moving."

Dani scowled at him. "Excuse me, what happened to nice Jared?" She held her breath and stepped into the tunnel.

"He's busy keeping us alive." Jared slapped the side of the opening a few times before finding the right spot. She winced a little when the door flashed closed.

"You think those guys were going to kill us? Why?" The air smelled fresh and slightly metallic, not dank and stale like she'd expected.

Jared continued tapping the screen on his cell phone. "Because it's what they do."

"Don't think you're going to get much of a signal in here."

"Signals fine, he's just not answering."

"He?" Dani scanned the empty space they stood in.

"Ian."

"Ian Cavacent?"

"Yes Dani, Ian."

Jared tried the number again. "Shit. Right, well either something is wrong at the villa or he's gone"—Jared glanced at her—"out."

"Out?"

"Yes, out." He pocketed the phone, crossed the tunnel and started slapping the far wall.

She knew the routine by now.

"Can I help?"

"No. Won't open for you."

"Seriously? Another secret door? Where's this one go to? Oz?"

"Nowhere, it's what's inside I'm after."

"You ever heard of 'X marks the spot'? Given the trouble you had getting into this place, I think an X would come in real handy." Dani wondered if now would be a good time to panic, when, once again, a door flashed into existence and a room appeared. Not a room, a garage. She really should have been more surprised. Maybe she'd used up all her shock for the day. A rectangular shape glided out of the space. Like a pontoon boat without the pontoons, it stopped a few feet in front of her. A larger vehicle remained parked inside. She backed up a few steps. Disbelief trickled down her spine as she inspected the hovering vehicle. No wheels and no noise. Not really a car—no roof, only inward facing seats around the edges.

She raised her right hand. The swelling was gone. She twisted her wrist back and forth. No pain. *Maybe the Chinese voodoo Ian did to me is causing me to hallucinate. I'm probably still floating in the frickin' pool right now.*

"Hover craft, I presume?" she asked, deciding the science fiction theme worked as good as any.

"They call them cruisers."

"Of course they do. Who's they? And why is this tunnel connected to your bar?" Her voice echoed around them.

"Hold on a sec," Jared replied. He placed his hand on the wall again and found the spot on the third try. The door to the garage disappeared.

Dani's gaze followed the lights into the distance and up to who knew where. She turned back to the cruiser.

Jared hurried around the vehicle and held a door open for her.

"Thanks, but, after you."

He hopped inside and took a seat. The craft barely moved. She stepped forward, put her hands on either side of the opening and jumped in, landing as hard as possible. Her flip-flops slapped against the metal surface. Still, virtually no motion registered in the cruiser. She grabbed hold of the rail and flung her weight from side to side. Although it didn't feel as if they were sitting on the ground, it was more stable than free floating.

Jared laughed. "I did that the first time I got in too. 'Course, that was after I tried to push it into the wall. Amazing, huh?"

"How does this work?" Dani sat next to Jared. As soon as her bum hit the cushion, they shot off down the tunnel. She let out a short squeal and grabbed the seat cushions. Her pulse shot up a notch. "Are you steering? Where are the seat belts?" she managed to croak out.

"Autopilot. Don't worry, it's perfectly safe."

"You do realize those are some seriously famous last words, don't you? Hindenburg? Titanic? Ring a bell?" She forced a smile, hoped it looked better than it felt, and tried to relax. *So not happening.* She decided to settle for breathing and watched the walls fly past. They were smooth, like someone had melted out the core, which, as far as she knew, wasn't possible. Then again, floating cars weren't possible either. Her swimsuit cover billowed up from the breeze so she let go of the seat long enough to tuck the gauzy fabric between her legs. "You mentioned summoning something."

Jared hesitated a moment. "Guess the cat's out of the bag now. Be kind of hard to explain this vehicle. Not to mention the gents at the bar. We need an EP. Stands for Earth Protector."

"Earth Protector? You're kidding right?"

"No. Pretty much what it sounds like. Cliche as it may be, we are not alone in the universe."

Dani held Jared's gaze. She'd heard what he said, but couldn't process the words. They sat on her brain like little beings, patiently waiting to be let in. *Knock, knock.* Dani let out a nervous laugh. *Maybe if I ignore them, they'll go away.* Jared didn't blink. *Or maybe not.*

"So you're not an EP?"

"Nah, I'm human, just like you. I'm what they call a Support Agent, or SA for short. I do what I can for Ian and the other EPs, but I'm based with Ian."

"So you're a spy."

"Support agent, not secret agent," Jared said. "Although, we are a secret."

"You're a spy for aliens."

"Stop it. It's not like that."

"Wow," Dani said, letting it go. "Ian is an alien? As in E.T.?" Dani's fingers ached from gripping the seat cushion. She forced herself to let go. She remembered his smoky green eyes and the touch of his fingers on her shoulders and neck. Something similar to, but oh so different than fear, shot through her. *What did you do to me?* "And here I was, ready to buy into the whole Chinese pressure points voodoo crap. Not so much, huh?"

Jared shook his head, grinning. "Not so much. Though, I'm surprised how far he went with you."

"How did you know——" She broke off when she realized he was talking about her healed wounds. "Pretty amazing stuff." *To say the least.*

"He was only supposed to help with the pain. Not sure what's up."

The cruiser had none of the usual sensations when riding in a vehicle. No hum of the engine or vibrations from the contact between ground and car, and yet the tunnel sped by uncomfortably fast. She closed her eyes for a few seconds, the only clue they were moving was the breeze causing her hair to swirl around her face. She reached up and wiped some strands out of her mouth. Jared sat so nonchalantly wiping his nose, he might as well have been on his couch at home, watching TV. She changed the rhythm her fingers tapped out and thought about all the science fiction movies she'd watched.

"Okay, so, Ian—does he look like he looks?"

"What?"

"You know, is he really some ten-armed slimy thing wearing a fake skin?"

Jared laughed. "I'm pretty sure what you see is what you get with these guys."

"How many are there?"

"If you mean EPs, there's four. Just got a new one in fact. Haven't met her yet myself."

"Got a new one, huh? What did he do? Pick her up at an alien yard sale?"

"Ha, ha," Jared said.

Dani jumped as the cruiser made a slight course adjustment. "So what do you do?"

"Anything I can. Help them blend in and provide human cover when necessary. And always keep my eyes open. Did you get a good look at those boys back at the bar?"

"Yeah. The funky legs and blue blood?" She flashed back to the bar. "And their arms too, now that I think about it. Who are those guys?"

"They're aliens. Not nice aliens, either."

"Clearly not related to Ian. I mean, he's hot, even by *Vanity Fair* standards."

Jared looked up from his phone and grinned. "The boys in the bar are Torogs. They aren't supposed to be here."

"What do they want?"

"Generally, they come for two reasons. First, there's a mineral they want here called carnium. They use it in FTL ships—"

"Whoa, wait." Dani lifted her hand. "FTL? As in 'Faster Than Light?'"

"That's the one." Jared said. "How else do you think they'd get here? The other reason is for sport."

"What kind of sport? Basketball?" Dani pretended to make a hoop shot.

Jared shook his head. "Very funny. More like hunting."

Dani bit the side of her lip before saying, "I get the feeling they don't hunt animals."

"Depends. Do you consider humans to be animals?"

"Some."

"Yeah." Jared chuckled. "Fortunately for us, the Cavacents like our people as well as our planet. The Sandarians are happy to let them keep the peace as long as they can mine the FTL mineral. Overall it's a good thing for us because...*War of the Worlds*? It could happen. I don't know all the details but I get the impression we humans would be in a heap of trouble without the Cavacents around. Apparently some distant relative of Ian's was awarded Earth Protectorate for some great deed in the empire's military."

"And now we have an empire." Dani's head started to spin.

"An empire, a Galactic Trade Organization they call the GTO, and some kind of council. Gets complicated. I'm still sorting it out. What I do know is things aren't going well."

"What do you mean?"

"I mean the empire isn't a peaceful place right now."

Dani rubbed her temples then fingered the scar below her eye. There was barely a trace of the gash she'd had less than an hour ago. She looked at Jared, then at the tunnel flying by. *I must be hallucinating. It's the only answer.*

"It's all real," Jared said as though reading her mind.

"Why are you answering all my questions? Isn't this top secret or something?"

Jared took his time to reply. "There are a number of humans who know about the EPs and Sandaria. I trust you."

"What if Ian doesn't?"

"Then you'll forget everything I've said." He went back to inspecting his phone.

"Just like in the movies, huh?"

"Just like in the movies."

A loud boom echoed down the tunnel from the direction of the bar. They exchanged a glance and Jared punched a few numbers into his phone. "We're okay for now."

Dani leaned over to see his screen. It showed a live cam feed from the back room of the bar. The alien dudes just blew something up. As the smoke cleared, she got a good view of them.

"Those guys are seriously freaky." She couldn't turn away. Like driving by a car crash, she had to watch. The way their arms and legs moved was totally wrong. The bottom part of their legs could move in any direction. The squishy bit at the end reminded her of a camel's foot. "That is so unbelievably bizarre, Jared. It doesn't look like they should be able to stand."

She leaned closer. "Their arms have the same weird joint, don't they?"

"Yeah, not quite the same range of motion though. And they only have three fingers and an opposing digit."

Dani shook her head. "You shot them and they seem fine now."

"They regenerate fast. You basically have to take out the brains to kill them, but you need more power than an Earth gun."

Dani burst into nervous laughter. "Ha! They're zombie creepoids. Zomboids! Unbelievable."

"Kinda interesting when you think about it. Makes ya wonder how many of our legends and horror stories are based on actual events. These critters and others have been visiting Earth for hundreds of years."

"Makes sense," Dani said.

The zomboids were staying put for now but they'd done a number on the room. Shattered bottles and shredded bags of pretzels littered the small space.

"Trust me, you don't want to get anywhere near those boys. They're slow at first. Their reflexes aren't great from a stand still but once they get moving, watch out."

Dani resisted the urge to pull her hair again. She'd end up bald at this rate.

Jared leaned forward and put a hand on her shoulder. "Your reality changed today. Going to take time for all this to sink in."

"That's for sure. It's exciting, though. I feel like a kid being told there really is a Santa Claus." Dani sat back and closed her eyes. *I hope you're looking down on this from somewhere, Dad. You were right. Aliens are real.* They ascended an incline but the cruiser stayed level. She turned, looked over the back, and gasped. This was no small rise. "So where is our great Earth Protector? Don't see much protecting going on. Aside from you, of course. Thank you very much by the way." She gave him a heartfelt grin.

"I wish I knew where he was, and you're welcome." They both winced as another boom echoed around them. Jared glanced at his phone and frowned. "We're still good but I'm starting to wonder how long that's going to last."

"How can you tell?"

Jared's display showed thick, gray smoke. "The door has sensors. If it's breached, an alarm will go off here." He nodded at his device.

"Nice."

"Time to call in some reinforcements." Jared tapped his screen a few times. Although now she paid attention, it wasn't your average smart phone. Whoever was on the other end, picked up almost immediately.

"We've got company on the island," Jared said. "They're trying to enter the tunnel from the bar." Jared listened for a moment before nodding his head. "That's right. We're almost at the door to the compound and Ian is MIA."

There was a pause while the person, or alien, on the other end talked. "Okay. Thanks." Jared hung up. "Help will be at the villa in a few minutes."

"Good thing they're close by. How many live on the Cat?"

"Only Ian. That was Marco. His base is in New Zealand. He just needs to get dressed before heading over."

"New Zealand?"

Jared nodded, watching her.

She held his gaze, nodded back, and decided to say nothing. Clearly, she had a lot to learn. The craft slowed and the ground leveled off. Ahead, stood a circular door that was shaped like a bank vault. In the center was a smaller, human-sized entrance.

"Does this lead to Ian's backyard or something?" Dani asked.

"Nope, right into the central hallway. Kind of a foyer without a front door."

"He built his villa into the hillside?"

"They're kinda big on tunnels. Makes sense for them. It's a good way to get around the planet and they use them for mining the carnium stuff I told you about."

The cruiser glided to a stop not more than five feet from the door.

Jared got up and nearly dropped the phone when it emitted an obnoxious sound. He pressed a button, silencing the noise. His face said it all. "We're gonna have company kid, those Torogs are almost as fast as the cruiser here. Let's go." He leapt down and ran to the center door.

Dani followed him out, trying to stay calm. Jared searched for the elusive spot to open the door. As usual, there was no X.

Odd, increasingly loud, sucking noises came from the tunnel behind them. Goosebumps spread across her body. She turned to keep an eye on the tunnel.

"Jared, they're coming. Please hurry." She shot him a glance. He frantically slapped around the edges. Nothing happened so he cursed and tried the other side.

"Ah shit, Jared. Where's the frickin' X? The one that marks the spot, remember?" Her voice came out like a squeak.

"That would compromise security, kid."

"How? You said it wouldn't work for me."

"Yeah, well it's just because—because—" Jared kept slapping the wall by the door. "I don't know why. Ask Ian." Sweat dripped down his forehead.

"Oh, I'll ask him all right." The sucking sound got louder and Dani's fear mounted. *Get a grip. Mad is better than panicked. It's just another match...against aliens...no problem.* Dani shook out her arms and bounced on her toes. She pictured herself back at the gym, getting ready for a fight. *Time to get mad.* She kicked off her flip-flops and continued her warm-up.

Pluck, pluck, pluck. The Torogs were moving fast when they crested the rise, but slowed when they caught sight of Dani and Jared. They emitted clicking and squeaking sounds as they made their way forward. Their squidgy feet worked like suction cups, allowing them to climb the hill and accounted for the odd sounds.

"They're here," Dani said.

Jared stepped in front of her, arms out.

Like that's going to happen. She stepped around him.

"Very gallant of you Jared but I'm not letting you face these zomboids alone. I know how to fight, remember? And thanks to some alien magic, I'm feeling pretty good right now." Dani whipped her wrist around a few times, made a fist, and jumped into a fighting stance. "Ha!"

Jared grimaced. "Fine, but don't let them get a hold of you." He appeared calm except for the sweat trickling down his temple. The tunnel was comfortably cool. She rolled up her sleeves and tucked the top of her cover-up into the back of her bikini bottoms. *Never thought I'd be dressed like this in a fight.* She stole another peek at Jared. "And here I thought you were this sweet old bar dog, living a peaceful life of island bliss."

"Who you calling old?"

Dani laughed. She had a major adrenaline rush going. There was a time in Brazil when some jerk tried to steal her camera gear. She'd taken him out in less than a minute, but the high lasted for weeks.

You can face fear, or feel it, her dad used to say. She shook out her arms. *Feel it, and it eats you alive. Face it, and you get to kick some ugly alien butt. Okay, he never said that. I wonder if they even have butts.* She gave another laugh and pondered the question. The leather covered their midsection and she wasn't about to ask.

The two aliens moved together. The bizarre sounds getting louder and faster the closer they came. Their eyes had no pupils—only black orbs.

Dani had the uncomfortable feeling they focused on her. She slid into a standard defense position and contemplated where and how to hit the creeps. Her heart pounded. "Jared, get to the door. You have to get it open." Her voice came out low and calm. This was her zen before a fight. Her body was strung tight, every nerve on edge. Her mind focused on nothing but her opponent.

The Torogs lunged.

Dani spun and lashed out with a kick. Her heel connected with the closest alien's head. Her foot squished in an inch or so before hitting bone.

Eww. Remembering Jared's advice, she moved left to avoid capture only to find herself swept up in a crushing embrace. *Oh, God. They're behind us.*

* * * *

Dani's feet dangled above the ground. The zomboids in front of her sailed backward through the air, arms and legs flailing, screech intensity at maximum. The door to the tunnel flashed closed. *We're inside.* She tried to slow her breathing, waiting for the adrenaline to wear off. She peered down to find a massive arm around her waist. A matching arm surrounded Jared, who was squeezed in next to her. He looked as surprised as she felt.

The arm appeared human, and they were still breathing. Good sign.

The grip loosened, and they slid to the floor. Dani took a tentative step forward and turned around.

She remembered him from the bar. Tall dark and swarthy. He stood at least as tall as Ian, but was built like a house. Where Ian was long and lean, this one was wide and buff. Dark hair fell over his brown eyes, and he grinned like a kid at Christmas.

Jared straightened out his rumpled shirt, not that it made any difference. "Boy am I glad to see you. I was starting to get worried. Thought maybe you'd gone AWOL too. Just in time, thanks."

"You're welcome. Always glad to be of assistance. I see we have company." He turned to her. "Dani, wasn't it?"

She untucked her cover-up and smoothed the flimsy material over her thighs. "Yes, and your name again?"

He stuck his hand out. "Marco. Marco Dar, at your service."

His hands were enormous and nicely warm. "Nice to meet you."

Instead of letting go, he pulled and kissed her on each cheek.

Jared laughed. "Easy, boy. Dani got caught in the middle of our Torog visit, so she's in the know."

"That's great," Marco said, still clutching her hand. "Let me assume the responsibilities for our absent host and welcome you to Cat Island Villa." He kissed the back of her hand, twice, before letting go.

Serious overkill, but when they looked like this, who cared? Dani gave him her best smile. "Thank you, it's nice to meet you too. Really nice, given the whole life saving thing." She jumped a little as a muffled sound came from the direction of the door. "Should we be worried about that?"

"Nah, that thing is impregnable," Marco said, digging around in his pocket. He pulled out a phone like Jared's, and keyed in a code. The screen showed the other side of the door.

The aliens stood about ten feet back, both looking at a device the larger one gripped in its three-fingered hand. The alien pressed something and after a short pause another boom echoed through the hall. Marco knitted his brows. "Looks like they got a new toy."

"How did you manage to grab us and send them flying at the same time?" Dani asked, not even trying to hide her admiration.

"It's a little thing called psi, darlin'." Marco continued to peer at the phone. "I can show you the embrace part again if you'd like." Marco took a step forward, a come hither grin on his face.

Dani stepped back. "That's okay, I—"

"What the hell is she doing here?" They all jumped at Ian's voice. The vibrations coursed through her like thunder off canyon walls. He walked toward them, dressed in a black button-up shirt and black jeans.

Euro style boots completed the look and Dani wished, again, she could get him in front of a camera. Especially with those boots—Mark Nason, or some brand like it. She had a thing for boots.

He covered the distance between them in a few strides. "Marco, report."

"Yes, sir. Received a call from Jared approximately five minutes ago. Bar under attack and you MIA. Sorry, boss, that's verbatim." Marco stretched his neck and scratched behind his ear while inspecting the walls nearby.

"I was off site. Continue," Ian said, with no further explanation.

"Right. Well I found these two about to be Torog food, backed up against the entry. Jared seemed to be having trouble opening the door."

"No kidding," Dani said. All the pent up fear and anxiety exploded inside of her. "Have you guys ever heard of 'X marks the spot'? Seriously, it's a brilliant little thing. Lets you know *where* the spot is that *opens the door.* Jared and I almost died. Twice. No X. He says it compromises security." Dani pointed at Ian. "I say it might just save our butts."

Shit, there I go again. She covered her mouth with her hand.

Jared exploded into an ear-splitting sneeze and busied himself with a tissue. Marco now seemed intensely interested in the ceiling.

"Sorry," Dani said. "Didn't mean to go off like that." She peered down at her cover up and wished for clothes. And shoes. She shuffled her bare feet.

Ian wore a barely suppressed grin.

Like the plucked string of a guitar, her body vibrated from the connection, hummed with such intensity she thought she might lose her vertical position in the world. *Okay, take a deep breath and chill.* She concentrated on Jared who appeared simultaneously nervous and amused. She poked him in the ribs with her elbow. "What? I said I was sorry."

"The security of this villa," Ian said, crossing his arms, "is none of your business."

"My life is my business, thank you very much." She crossed her arms and returned his stare. *He thinks this is funny.* She bit back a number of further retorts *she* thought would be funny and decided to let it go.

Ian addressed Jared. "Care to tell me how she came to be here?"

Jared cleared his throat. "Wasn't an option short of letting her die. The Torogs showed up at the bar shortly after you left. I shot them point blank in front of her. We locked ourselves in the back room and took the tunnel to get here. Kinda had to explain some stuff, what with the cruiser and all." Jared stood taller and gave a nod in her direction. "She handled everything fine, and I trust her."

Marco took a step closer to Dani. "She's going to have to stay here till we find out what's got the Torogs all fired up."

Ian sighed and ran a hand through those blond waves of his.

"My apologies," she said. "I realize I'm here without an invitation, or clothes, but I didn't exactly ask to come."

He laughed then, which surprised them all. "I know. Sorry for my poor manners, I—"

A massive boom echoed through the hall, coming from the tunnel.

"You absolutely sure we don't have to worry about that?" she asked Marco. Before anyone answered, the sound of splintering wood came from the left. Moving as one, Ian and Marco bolted for a small room off the hall.

Dani and Jared followed them. The back wall of the small space was covered in monitors displaying multiple views. There was the wreck of a storeroom back at Jared's Place, the empty bar, and numerous angles of the villa they were in now.

Marco tapped a display with the Torogs in the tunnel. "They have a new toy, boss. I was just checking it out when you arrived." He pointed to another screen, displaying a large wooden door. Flowers in pots adorned either side, and vines hung from an arbor around the area she assumed was the front entrance.

Seven Torogs lurked ten feet from the entrance as one of them pointed a small device at the door. Another ear splintering crash reverberated from farther inside the villa.

Marco turned to Ian. "Whatever that weapon is, there's a delay before they can fire again."

Ian leaned closer to the monitor. "We need to get our hands on one of those."

"I'm on it," Marco said. "The empire is going to decimate them for this."

"The empire is going to hell in a hand basket, as our human friends would say." Ian leaned closer to the monitor. "They wouldn't have tried this, even a few years ago." The images on the screens changed, showing different rooms and exterior views.

"They're inside the shield range," Marco said, studying his phone. "Should we activate the perimeter to keep more from getting in?"

Ian shook his head. "We do that, they can't leave."

The sound of shattering glass came from some place close. One of the monitors showed a large dining room. And Torogs. They were climbing, or more accurately, falling through a shattered window. They weren't built for climbing, so the whole thing was almost comical.

"Marco"—Ian pushed out of the chair—"we're compromised, clear the tunnel, now."

Marco typed something on a keyboard and hit enter. "Ready, boss."

Ian nodded and concentrated on his phone.

Less than a second later came another boom, this one different. An odd vibration tingled her bare feet and she grimaced as pressure swelled inside her ears.

On the monitor, the Torogs in the tunnel flew impossibly fast down the steep incline, away from the villa.

"Move," Ian growled.

Marco grabbed Dani by the upper arm and they ran back to the tunnel entrance. She glanced back. Ian held his right palm a few inches from the door to the room with the monitors. A solid wall took its place.

Guess they don't need an X.

Marco opened the door to the tunnel and she and Jared hurried through after him.

Dani waited for the Torogs to reappear. Her feet twinged with more of the muffled booms that had sent the zomboids fleeing in the first place. They must be herding them back to the bar. The next explosion created a hot blast of air.

Ian sprinted down the hall. Steps away from the tunnel entrance, a red beam tore though his upper arm. Blood sprayed in all directions as he pivoted through the door, landing hard on his back.

Dani's heart slammed into her chest as time slowed to a crawl.

Marco sealed the door. Both he and Jared were next to Ian before Dani fully registered what happened.

She stepped forward, half afraid of what she'd find. "Is he okay?" A thick trail of blood oozed from the closed door to Ian. The smell of burnt flesh made her nauseous. Of course, he wasn't okay. Stupid question. So much blood. The laser must have hit an artery. A wave of concern bordering on panic enveloped her. She held her stomach and leaned against the wall to stabilize herself. She'd seen her share of nasty injuries from mixed fights, but nothing like this.

Marco lay one hand on Ian's chest and the other on the shoulder above the wound. He spoke in hushed tones, then closed his eyes and fell silent.

Jared got up and came over to Dani. "He's going to be okay. Marco needs a few minutes with him before we go."

"How could he be okay? Look around, there's blood everywhere."

Jared squeezed her arm. "He's going to be fine. Remember your wrist and the voodoo? Marco can heal too. He's not as powerful, can't completely heal him, but he can make it safe for Ian to travel."

Marco's body weaved slightly as he hovered over Ian.

Something tugged at the corner of her mind. She had an unreasonable urge to kneel next to Marco and help, which was insane. She couldn't do anything.

Jared retrieved a first aid box out of a small compartment at the rear of the cruiser and sat down.

Dani took a seat next to him. "Aren't you going to take the kit to him?"

"In a minute. He needs to finish what he can."

It must have only been three or four minutes, but it seemed like forever before Ian sat up. Marco, who'd been kneeling the whole time, moved to stand but wobbled over and sat down hard. Jared shot out of the cruiser and knelt between the two men. He talked to Marco as he pulled out gauze pads and medical tape for Ian. Marco shook his head and attempted to stand again, this time successfully.

Dani hurried over, careful not to slip on any blood. She tried to ignore the smell of burnt flesh. "Can I help? Do anything?"

Marco weaved a little as he answered. "Nope, we're all good. Healing isn't exactly my strong point. I have to use a lot of psi energy, but I'll be fine. We'll both be fine, won't we boss?"

"I'll be better when I get my hands on those putrid *crags*," Ian said.

Jared cut the sleeve off Ian's shirt, applied a thick wad of medical pads, and wrapped gauze around his arm.

Ian seemed a little shaky when he got to his feet, but his voice remained strong. He glanced down at the bandage. "Good job, you two." He turned toward the cruiser, then stopped abruptly at the sound of a massive boom coming from the other side of the door. Marco stepped to his side and the two men shared a look.

"Let's move," Ian said. "I don't know what that thing is, but we're going to find out."

Dani stepped into the cruiser and sat next to Jared. She struggled to make sense of everything. She wanted to ask more about psi, but Ian stepped in and took the seat a across from her. Their eyes met and that reverb hit again. She liked it. A lot.

He grinned. "You've had an interesting day. How you holding up?"

His acknowledgment of everything she'd been through, even though he sat there nearly bleeding to death, made her want to cry. Which was stupid. She sat up a little straighter and smiled back at him. "Definitely one for the record books. I'm good. Any chance of getting some clothes where we're going?"

"I'll see what I can do." He pulled his phone from the non-bloody side of his shirt. The bloodstain on his arm bandage had stopped growing.

Marco jumped in and sat a few seats down from her. The cruiser took off like before. Halfway back to the bar, they slowed to a stop. The cruiser turned to the right and an opening appeared at the flick of Marco's hand. As they sped down another tunnel, Dani glanced back to find the opening had vanished.

Ian talked to someone on his phone in hushed tones. She heard him say her name and glanced up as he scanned her body from head to toe. "Size eight?"

"Yeah. Maybe a ten on top," Dani said.

He winked at her and relayed the information to the person on the phone.

Marco chuckled and muttered something about a ten on top.

Dani crossed her arms and glared at him.

"Sorry," he said. "Just kinda cute the way you said that. You know, being a perfect ten and all. Cuz, you are in my book."

Jared rolled his eyes, but kept quiet.

It was impossible not to like the man. When he smiled, which he did often, he looked like an overgrown kid with a new puppy.

Dani willed the tension out of her shoulders and smiled back. "It's okay. I'm just a little stressed right now. Where are we going?"

"Como," Marco replied. "We'll get some good food. Oh, and we have a new EP. Wait till you meet her."

Dani was about to ask where Como was when she looked up and registered two things: first, no one was looking where they were going, and second, they were about to slam into a solid wall. She screamed and threw herself to the floor to brace for impact.

Chapter 4

Dani lifted her head, heart pounding, and swept some hair off her face. The heat of Ian's body registered through the thin fabric of her cover-up, and she buzzed with the crazy energy he caused. He knelt next to her in a protective stance. All three men looked for the cause of her scream. She winced as a fresh drop of blood oozed from the bandage on Ian's arm.

"You okay?" he asked, getting back to his seat, but holding her gaze.

She reached for the med kit and pulled herself up next to him.

He was inches from her face. His breath smelled of something spicy. She tore her gaze away and pulled some pads from the kit. They were still in the tunnel, but now the solid wall lay behind them. "I thought..." She swung her head around and turned back to face him. He was so close. She folded the gauze into squares. "We were headed for a wall just now. I swear," she whispered.

Marco's laughter echoed off the walls, breaking the spell.

She added more pads to absorb the fresh blood.

"Need some help?" Jared asked, handing her the roll of gauze.

Dani started with surprise. She hadn't given any conscious thought to what she was doing. Heat rushed to her cheeks. This obviously wasn't her job. She took the roll from Jared anyway. Might as well finish. Ian's presence permeated her senses. "Sorry about that," she said to no one in particular as she rolled the gauze over the pads.

"It's all right," Ian said. "We should have warned you."

Every glance into his eyes increased the amazing buzz coursing through her. Her eyes slid to his lips. She wanted to run her fingers across them, to taste them. *For crying out loud, get a grip.* She sat up straight. "Jared, do you have any—"

"Here." He held out scissors.

She took them, cut the gauze and gave them back. She tucked the end into the top of the bandage and tried to ignore what the touch of his skin was doing to her. "That should hold you." She moved back to her original seat. Her blood pounded in her ears. She was so turned on, she had to force herself to slow her breathing and not look at him. The hum inside dimmed to a manageable level with the distance between them. Ian leaned back and closed his eyes.

She paused a second to take in the long lashes resting on his cheeks, before looking at the tunnel fly by. Bandaging Ian's arm like that was weird, even for her. It had been a completely automatic response.

Marco plopped down next to her. "The tunnels aren't directly connected unless it's a short distance, like from Jared's bar to Ian's villa. For longer distances, we install portals to connect the ends. What you saw was the portal, not a solid wall. I can see how that could give you quite a fright. How about a hug to make you feel better?" Marco's eyebrows bounced.

Dani patted his arm. "Thanks big guy, but I'm good. I just thought we were going to be bugs on a windshield."

Ian opened his eyes at the chirp of his phone. "Ria's waiting for us," he said, grunting a little as he slipped the phone back into his shirt pocket. "Marco, call Armond and have him meet us there. We'll contact my father after we've briefed the team. We need to find out why the Torogs have gone rogue."

The end of the tunnel appeared, nearly identical to the one on Cat Island. The same kind of metal door opened and the cruiser came to a stop. A petite redheaded woman came out to greet them. She wore the female version of the EP's attire. Black jeans, black button-up shirt and killer boots.

They piled out of the cruiser. The redhead stood at attention and seemed to resist the urge to salute.

"Commander," she said, grasping her hands behind her back. "Sir, you didn't mention you were injured."

"Must have slipped my mind. I'll need you to finish the healing." He turned to Jared. "Ria, this is my SA, Jared."

Jared took her hand with enthusiasm. "Heard all about ya. Though, got to say, it's hard to believe half of it. No insult intended, mind."

"None taken," Ria said. "And don't worry, you'll believe it soon enough."

Marco let out a laugh. "She's not kidding. Small packages, man. Small packages."

Dani liked the woman instantly and smiled when Ian introduced them next.

"This is the guest I mentioned. See that she gets clothes and anything else she needs."

"Yes, sir." Ria held out her hand. "Welcome to my humble abode."

Dani was impressed by the redhead's grip. Ria glanced down at Dani's bare feet. "Size nine? Ten?"

"Nine," Dani said.

"Ian mentioned clothes. I figured you might be needing some shoes as well."

Ian rolled his eyes. "Just get her what she needs."

The group headed for the door and Ria fell in beside Dani. "Gina, one of my SAs is already in town getting you clothes. I'll give her a call about the shoes size."

"Thank you," Dani said. "I've never wanted to get out of a swim suit so much in my life. So, uh, any chance of getting some boots like yours? Happy to pay. Those are awesome."

Ria laughed. "There's a local guy who makes them. I'll see if he's got your size." Ria hurried up next to Ian. "Your room is ready, sir. I can finish your healing whenever you'd like. I think sooner rather than later would be best."

"Agreed," Ian said. "And stop with the 'sir.'"

They filed inside and Marco closed the hefty door behind them with flick of his hand.

Dani remembered being a kid and trying to move books and bend forks with her mind. Nothing ever happened, but these guys had some magic. She wondered what else they could do as she took in her new surroundings. The entryway stood about the same size as Cat Island, but where the island villa had all white and sophisticated beach decor, this was Mediterranean all the way. Marble floors with rich browns and reds complimented an array of artwork. The floor was cool to her bare feet as they walked the length of the large hall.

At the base of a wide staircase Ian turned to Ria and said, "Give me five, then meet me in my room to take care of this arm."

"Yes, s—um, sure. Five minutes."

"Let Ria know if you need anything, okay?" he said to Dani.

"I will. Thanks." That familiar buzz caressed her insides as he held her gaze. Just as it was getting really good, he turned away and the sensation disappeared like so much smoke. Ria escorted them into a large sitting room. Glass doors stood opened to a patio that overlooked a lake.

Dani approached the doors with a growing sense of wonder. Across the lake stood a rustic village nestled at the base of the mountains. A tall church spire to the right and an ancient castle peaked out above the green trees.

"You've got to be kidding me. You said Como but"—she turned to Jared—"*Lago* Como? We're in Italy?" She couldn't quite believe her eyes. "That's Varenna and Castle Vezio over there, isn't it?"

Ria stood next to her. "You've been here before I take it?"

"Yes, a number of times for photo shoots. I love this place."

Ria put her hands in her back pockets. "It is beautiful from what I've seen so far. Don't know if they told you, but I'm new to the team and this"—Ria made a sweeping gesture with her arm—"is my base on Earth. It's going to be rough, but I think I can handle the accommodations."

"Your base on Earth," Dani repeated. "That sounds unbelievably bizarre. Just as bizarre as getting from the Bahamas to Italy in ten minutes, or whatever it was."

Jared took up the position to her left. "Closer to eight if you want to be exact. Don't worry. You'll get used to the whole alien thing faster than you think."

Ria checked her watch. "Gina should be here soon with your clothes. Her husband Battista is around here some place. They've been with the villa forever. Wonderful people, you'll love them. Jared, you probably know your way around here better than I do, so please make yourself comfortable."

Ria turned to Marco. "Ian should be ready for me now. I'll take care of his arm. Can you grab some food and bring it to the library?"

"Yes, ma'am. I'll meet you there," Marco said, heading down a hallway off the main foyer.

"I'll see you two later," Ria said with a wave.

Dani sat on the arm of an oversized chair and took in the view. "Amazing."

"You're tellin' me," Jared said. "I never would have guessed."

Dani looked over to find Jared watching Ria leave. "Guessed what?"

"Ria," Jared said, pulling a tissue out of his shirt pocket. "Did you see her?"

"Of course I saw her. She seems nice." Dani said.

"Well sure, nice in a little doll kind of way." Jared crossed his arms and chuckled. "Hard to believe she can hold her own in a fight."

"Never underestimate your opponent, my friend." Dani shrugged and returned to the view. "So, we must be in Bellagio, right?"

"Correct. We're on the back side from the port where the ferries come and go. Wait 'till you see it at night. I don't know how long we're staying, but stairs over there"—Jared pointed off to the left outside—"lead to the pool and farther down to a private beach complete with boat and dock."

"These Cavacents sure like their creature comforts, don't they?" Dani opened her mouth to comment further when footsteps echoed from the hallway that led to the tunnel.

"Ah, sounds like Armond is here," Jared said.

"He's the tall blond one, right?"

"Yep. Technically, he's an albino. Come on, I'll introduce you properly before they get started." Jared led her to the hall they'd come in. "Armond. You remember Dani."

The man was striking. Easily the tallest of the three male EPs. His skin was nearly translucent and complimented his eerily pale blue eyes. His long white hair lay in a ponytail at his back. Unlike Ian and Marco, he reeked formality. It wasn't just his standard EP attire of black jeans and button up shirt, and more amazing boots. Everything about him screamed formal, making Dani feel, once again, seriously underdressed.

Armond nodded at Jared and gave Dani the once over. He offered Dani a stiff handshake before excusing himself to meet the others in the library.

"He's...interesting."

"He's a bit full of himself," Jared said under his breath, "but he's wicked smart."

"I heard that," Armond's voice came from around the corner.

"I know ya did," Jared called back. "Great hearing too." He winked at her.

"Are all Sandarians so flipping gorgeous? Any one of them could be on the cover of *GQ* or *Cosmo*."

"I don't know, to tell ya the truth. I've only met the EPs and Ian's folks a time or two. They're good looking enough." Jared scratched his chin. "Good question."

Just then a short, stout Italian woman came in from the direction of the kitchen, which smelled heavenly. Dani's stomach growled. Probably because she hadn't eaten in hours. The woman rattled on in Italian into her cell phone as she grappled with a large number of bags. Parcels hung looped over her arms and shoulders. Jared rushed over and took the assorted items from her, one by one, trying not to dislodge her phone. She winked at Jared and they managed to get everything on the large dining room table. As soon as she'd finished her call, she erupted in a loud cry. "Jared! Is so good to see you." She gave Jared a big hug and kissed him on both cheeks.

"And this must be Ms. Dani, yes? I hope so because it seems to me she is the same size Signor Ian had me get clothes for." The woman smiled at Dani.

"Yes, this is Dani Standich. Dani, I'd like you to meet Gina Papallo."

Gina gave Dani the same hug and kisses as Jared, as though they were old friends. "Welcome my dear! I have so much for you. Come, let me show you to your room. You can get cleaned up and try on some of the pretty clothes, yes? I got you some sandals. Ms. Ria says you like the boots. I call senior Cali. We'll see what he has for you."

"Thank you so much. I hate to be a pain, but could I grab a bite to eat first? Must be low blood sugar or something, I go from zero to starving in a heartbeat."

"Of course." Gina slapped her forehead. "I am so sorry. I should have asked. Yes, please come with me. I'll show you the kitchen. I'm making a wonderful Italian stew for dinner. Perhaps you would like some bread and butter for now?" She turned to Jared as they were leaving the room. "Come on Jared, I know you're always ready for food."

"Darn straight. I could eat a horse."

"Funny Americans. I'm afraid bread will have to do."

The bread was divine. Dani was placing her empty plate in the dishwasher when raised voices came from the great room. The EPs had been in the library for fifteen minutes or so, and something had them riled. She took Jared's plate and put it next to her own, then followed him out of the kitchen. The EPs were gathered in the entry hall, their voices urgent. Ian had on clean clothes. She lingered a moment on the boots, then up to his arm. He moved like nothing had happened and there didn't appear to be any bandages under his sleeve. Dani marveled at the implications of such a powerful healing ability.

The photographer in her couldn't help but appreciate the good looks of the team. Ria was definitely the odd woman out, but somehow she had a presence all her own. This group would photograph well and she wished again for her camera.

Marco nodded greetings before jogging off to the tunnel door. Armond ignored them.

"Call me the second you know anything," Ian said.

Ria placed her hands on her hips. "I don't understand. It worked fine this morning."

"Let's just hope Marco's is working," Ian said as he turned to Jared. "Armond and Ria's portals aren't functioning. Marco's checking his."

"What does that mean, boss?" Jared said.

Ian ran a hand through his hair. "We're not entirely sure. Communication with Sandaria is down, which implies the main portal on Cat Island isn't functioning. It shouldn't do that unless there've been four portal moves within an hour. No one has used it since this morning. Armond, your experience with the Portal Masters makes you the expert. Any idea?"

"I'm afraid I have nothing further to add at this time."

"Right," Dani said, obviously having nothing to add herself. "I'm going to go get cleaned up and try on some clothes."

* * * *

By the time Dani showered and tried on all the clothes Gina had purchased for her, it was half past six. She settled on jeans and a white button up shirt, with small frills that ran all the way around the neck. She didn't usually do frills, but decided the effect wasn't half bad. She put her damp hair in a loose ponytail, slipped on some strappy sandals, and headed downstairs to the great room. Marco and Armond were back and they looked grim. She reached the bottom of the stairs and stopped.

Marco's face brightened when he caught sight of her. "Dani! Come and join us."

Dani glanced at Ian. "Is that okay? If this is a meeting or something…"

"You're fine. Come on in," Ian said. "You're looking better."

"Better?" Marco said, "Don't you know beautiful when you see it, boss?" He patted the cushion next to him eagerly.

Dani sidestepped the couch and selected a chair facing the windows.

Marco pressed his bear paw sized hand over his heart as though he'd been stabbed.

"Nothing personal, Marco, I just want to enjoy the view. It's beautiful."

Dani buzzed inside. She threw Ian a sideways glance and found him watching her. She was seriously attracted to the man. He seemed like the type that liked to keep his relationships casual. She liked casual. Casual was safe. Then again, he was an alien. Which left all sorts of questions bouncing around her head. In his swimsuit, everything appeared normal, but the interesting bits in his trunks were still a mystery. The more time she spent with him, the more she wondered. Especially with the crazy chemistry between them. No one had affected her so physically before.

Gina entered from the kitchen wiping her hands on a dishtowel. "Dinner will be ready at eight o'clock, Signor Ian. Italian stew for us tonight."

Murmurs of appreciation spread around the room, and Ian thanked her.

The Italian woman made her way over to Dani and fingered the ruffle of her collar. "Ah, so lovely. Is good fit, *si*?"

"Yes. Thank you." Dani liked the portly woman. She smelled of bread and pasta. The grandmother Dani never had.

A moment later, a large burly Italian entered from the kitchen, putting something in his mouth.

"*Oy,*" Gina shouted. "That better not be my bread for supper."

The man feigned shock. "How could you ask such a thing?" he said around a mouthful, before swallowing.

Gina wagged a finger at him. "Dani," she said, "this is my Battista. When he's not helping to save the world, he's getting in the way around the villa and eating all the food before dinnertime. Please feel free to ask for anything you need."

Battista came around the chair and Dani stood to meet him. He took her hand and kissed the back. His eyes crinkled when he smiled, and as with his wife, she liked him immediately.

"Ah, *bellissima*, you are so pretty. And so tall. Anything at all you need, you ask, *si*?"

Marco cleared his throat. "She'll ask you, *after* she asks me, right darlin'?"

Dani grinned.

Jared came over and gave Battista a pat on the back. "You're looking good old man."

"Bah, who are you calling old? You beach dog."

"I think you mean, beach bum," Dani said.

"Bum? But that is a bottom, no? Ha! Jared, you are a beach bottom!" Battista laughed his way back to the kitchen.

Dani pondered the comfy chair, but what she really needed was a walk. So much had happened today, and the EPs were back to discussing possible solutions. "Hey Jared, want to go for a walk? Bellagio is beautiful at night."

"Not much I can do here," Jared said. "What do you say, boss?"

"Go for it," Ian said. "Make sure you stay together. And don't be late. Trust me, you don't want to miss Gina's cooking." Ian shot her his wicked grin, sparking that odd buzz.

"So I've heard." She took a moment to enjoy the buzz before turning to go. "We'll catch you guys in a while."

Jared led her across the sitting room to a large foyer. Ten-foot, double wooden doors graced the entryway. A massive Morano glass chandelier hung over the marble tiled floor. They walked out into a balmy summer night. The air smelled of the lake and greenery. A brick wall, covered in lush vines, guarded the villa. A wrought iron gate stood open at the end of the drive. They strolled through and crossed a narrow road.

Dani inhaled deeply. "It smells so different from Cat Island. Normally you'd spend eight hours on a plane before making the transition."

On the far side, a narrow alley angled over a small crest then back down to the village.

"Can you imagine if everyone in the world had the ability to get around so fast? It would change everything. Talk about a global economy."

"Might well destroy everything too," Jared said. "Extremists could take terrorism to a whole new level."

"Yeah, always the bad with the good, huh?"

They continued to follow the alley in companionable silence until they reached an intersection at the top. Directly ahead, the soft glow of the village radiated over the rooftops as the path led down to the port where the ferries disgorged their tourists and locals. They continued across the small clearing when a soft plucking sound came from the alley to their left. The hair on her arms stood straight up, as Jared swung out his arm to stop her.

"You have got to be kidding me," Dani said in a low whisper.

Jared held his finger to his lips and pulled out his phone. They listened, still as statues.

Pluck, pluck.

Jared hit a button, and three short beeps sounded. He grabbed her upper arm and propelled her to the right.

Dani stumbled and glared at him. "What do you think you're doing?"

"Get up the alley. I'll hold them off till Ian and the others get here. They'll find us by my phone." He put the phone back in his pocket and pulled out a gun about the size of a small banana. He'd shot the others with a sawed off shotgun, what was this tiny thing supposed to do?

"Jared, you can't be serious. You might as well spit at them. Come with me, come on." She tugged at his sleeve, but he wouldn't budge.

"Don't worry. This here is a little alien technology, compliments of our friends. Ian gave it to me when you were upstairs. Now, move already. Nothing you can do without a weapon, and I only got the one. Get up the alley and out of sight."

Dani hesitated, but he had a point. She turned to go.

"Dani."

"Yeah?"

"Stay close. The gang will be here in a few minutes."

"I'll stay close all right."

The plucking sounds came louder and faster as a Torog crested the hill. Heart pounding, Dani sprinted up the alley. Ahead and to the left she spied a turnoff. An unfamiliar zing echoed down the alley, and Dani glanced back. The small gun shot a red beam directly into the Torog's skull. The alien fell backward as a mass of brain matter spilled onto the bricks. Dani stopped, but another Torog went for Jared, who took aim and fired. *Shit, how many are there?*

Her heart raced as she took off again, rounded the corner, stumbled, and plowed head first into the stinking chest of a Torog.

No! Panic shot through her as she turned to get away.

Massive arms encircled her. The alien jerked her up and spun her around, holding her back pinned against its body. The stench of its breath and skin was putrid. The creature placed its hand over her open mouth, and she tasted the acidic and slightly tangy skin. Bile rose in her throat and silence fell over the alley. Dani struggled, but it was no use. Incredibly strong, the more she struggled, the harder the rancid thing squeezed until she couldn't breath. Stars danced in front of her eyes as she silently cried out.

* * * *

The emergency signal blared from all the phones at once. Ian checked the GPS. "They're at the intersection on the way to town. Move."

The four blasted out the door and ran across the street to the alley. The sound of Jared's gun buzzed over their footfalls. They crested the hill to find Jared standing over two dead Torogs. "Took you long enough." Jared lowered his arms, shaking slightly.

"Where's Dani?" Ian scanned the clearing. "Jared, where the frack is Dani?" He spun around and froze as her psi slammed into him. Like when they were in the pool, he sensed everything she did. The crushing weight and stench of a Torog as it dragged her up the alley enraged him. He bolted up the passage, turned the corner, and fired. The Torog's head exploded, covering Dani in blue blood and brain matter. Ian closed the distance between them. Both fear and shock were in her eyes.

The creature's arms still circled Dani's body as it fell backward. Ian lunged forward and grabbed Dani's shoulders. She was soaked and slippery, so he grabbed handfuls of her collar and pulled against the dead weight. Finally, as its body relaxed, the arms slipped down Dani's side and its bowels released their contents at her feet.

Her skin was pale and her eyes wide. She stood looking at him, wild-eyed, dripping bits and pieces of Torog.

Ria and Jared rounded the corner, breathing heavily. Dani swayed slightly.

"Where's Armond and Marco?" Ian asked, ready to catch her if she fell.

"Couple of locals heard the commotion. Armond is working his magic while Marco keeps watch. Clean-up crew is on the way."

Dani stepped away from the mess at her feet, pulling herself away from Ian's hold. She was covered in reeking blue liquid and bits of matter. Ria hurried to her side.

"She's in shock," said Ian. "Get her back to the villa and clean her up." He wiped his hands off on his shirt.

Dani shook her head. "No. I'm not. I'm not in shock." The look she gave him was one of mixed fear and anger. "You shot me. Or at me. You didn't even look, you just turned the corner and fired."

"Dani," Ria said.

"No!" Dani pointed a finger at Ian. "I am not expendable, do you hear me? I may be a lowly human, but you can't just shoot us because we're in the way." Dani wiped some slimy matter off her face and flung the pulpy stuff to the ground.

"Don't be absurd," Ian said.

"Absurd?" She waived her hand, flinging more excess matter over the carcass. "That could be me spread out all over there."

Ignoring the blood, Ria took hold of her upper arm. "It's all right, Dani. Ian is amazingly accurate. We all are. Remember, we're not human. He'd never hurt anyone on accident."

Ian's eyes narrowed. "Is your mouth always ahead of your brain? I saved your life. You're welcome." He turned to Jared who stood frozen to the spot. "Get her back to the villa. Take Ria and Marco with you. Armond and I will wait for the clean-up crew and make sure we don't have any more guests."

"Sure, boss," Jared said, coming back to life.

"Ria," Ian said, "put the shields up around the villa. Do it now. Have Armond and Marco do the same to their bases. This makes no sense. I don't know what they're doing or why but we're in lockdown as of now."

Ian turned to Dani. "I'm sorry about your clothes."

"My clothes?" Dani said with a heavy dose of sarcasm.

"Yes," Ian said, finally losing his temper. "Your clothes. Because from what I can see, the rest of you is perfect. I mean fine. You're just fine."

Ian turned and waived his hand in dismissal. He needed to check the alley to make sure there were no other humans around.

"He's sorry about my clothes?" Dani said as they left. "And now he walks away? I swear Jared, he didn't even aim. He just fired. The only reason I'm alive is pure luck."

"Settle down, Dani," Jared said. "Ian Cavacent doesn't do luck. This is all new to you, give it some time."

"Come on," Ria added, "let's get you cleaned up. No offense, but you stink."

Dani made a puffing sound but didn't argue.

Ian waited until their voices faded before returning to the alley entrance. He watched them walk down to where Marco and Armond stood near the Torog bodies. Armond would be able to redirect any humans that came upon them. He'd erase their memory for a few minutes and send them in another direction. When they figured out something was off, he and these stinking Torogs would be gone. Armond's ability to erase human memories was a psi skill he'd never heard of, let alone seen before. One of many oddities about the albino.

He couldn't help but watch the swing of Dani's hips as she turned the corner. He blew out a breath and paced, pondering the last few minutes. He'd not only sensed her presence and reacted without thought, he'd *been in her head*. Not good. Instinct solely to protect her, regardless of danger to himself or the others. It was inexcusable and completely out of character.

The unmistakable whining sound of the cloaked cleanup crew arriving echoed up the alley. Only in emergencies were these vehicles used. They may be invisible but they were solid mass. Too much risk of exposure to use frequently.

Ian slapped both palms against the wall in front of him and leaned in, feeling the warmth of the stone. What if she was, in fact, perfect? Perfect for him. He knew it was true.

He pushed off the wall and gave a short laugh. *Unbelievable. I find a psi-mate and she's human. Frack.*

Chapter 5

After scrubbing herself raw in the shower, Dani put on another set of clothes. She opted for a black pullover and jeans this time. Not knowing what else to do, she left the putrid blood- and brain-splattered clothes in the shower. She washed her trembling hands for the fourth time and looked in the mirror. Her wet blond hair dripped down her shirt and framed her unnaturally pale face. Pulling her hair to the side, she leaned forward and squeezed excess water into the sink. *Have I lost it? Was I really attacked by aliens? Twice?* Not liking what she saw in the mirror, she left the bathroom and sat on the massive four-poster bed. She wished her parents were still alive so she could call them. The tears came without warning, and she let them fall.

A knock at the door made her jump. She grabbed a handful of tissues from the nightstand and blew her nose. "Come in."

Ria entered carrying an awesome pair of boots. She took in the situation, closed the door, set the boots down, and sat next to Dani on the bed. She leaned in and wrapped her arms around Dani's shoulders.

"Sorry," Dani said, fighting back more tears. "Everything's just... catching up with me."

"Gee, I wonder why? Let's see, within the last eight hours or so you've learned there are aliens protecting Earth. That they can travel back and forth from planet to planet and have all kinds of bizarre technology. You learned some of them are butt ugly, stink, and keep trying to kill you. Oh, and then there's being covered with alien blood and brains. Yeah. Really can't see what your problem is."

Dani smiled through her tears.

"You big baby," Ria said.

Dani reached for another tissue and wiped her eyes and blew her nose. "Speaking of blood and brains, I wasn't sure what to do with the clothes, so I left them in the shower."

"Ah, hence the lingering Eau De Torog," Ria said. "Pretty disgusting don't you think?"

"Those zomboids are rancid, even before you get to the brains. Not too smart are they?"

Ria gave one last squeeze and sat up. "Not the workers, no." She put her feet on the lower bed rail with her elbows on her knees. "The Torog's society is built on three classes: politicians, engineers and workers. The guys you've been seeing are all workers. They're either soldiers or the laborers of their society. The workers are dumb as doornails but strong. The engineers are responsible for the Torog's science, and the brains behind their advancing technology. They tend to stay on the ships or their home planet. The politicians are the only ones that communicate with other races. They're relatively new to the GTO, which is why this is all so strange. They're breaking all kinds of rules here."

"Interesting," Dani said. She mimicked Ria's position. The smaller woman looked like a child next to her. "I'm amazed at how much you EPs resemble humans. I mean for being aliens and all."

"Actually, we're pretty much genetically identical, except for the psi. There's lots of speculation about the similarities. No one knows why some planets don't have psi. Most people think we all share a common seed somehow, but no one can agree on who or what seeded multiple planets with the same DNA."

"Multiple planets?" Dani asked.

"Sure. There's dozens of worlds with our genetics. Quite a few completely alien worlds too, of course, like the Torog's, but the Sandarian Empire is ruled by beings that look like you, me, and the boys."

"Wow." Dani rubbed her temples.

"Is anything else bothering you? As if all this wasn't enough."

Dani dabbed the tissue to her eyes. "My Dad would've loved this. He was always reading science fiction and going on about how unlikely it is that humans are the only intelligent beings in the universe, let alone the most advanced."

Ria touched Dani's hand. "Would have loved?"

"My parents were killed in a plane crash when I was fifteen. My aunt took me in. That's how I ended up on Cat Island. She never had any children though, and didn't really know what to do with a teenager. Don't get me wrong, she's great, but not too affectionate."

"I'm so sorry. I can't imagine losing my parents. If you ever need an ear or just want some company, promise you'll let me know, okay?"

"Thanks, Ria. Same goes for you, although I don't think there's much I could do to help you."

"Are you kidding? Girl time! Gina's wonderful, but she's older, and from what I've seen so far, has a ton of friends and family around. Being close to my age, you give me a better perspective of Earth girls. Deal?"

"Now, that I can do. Deal."

Ria slid off the bed. "Before I go, any boyfriends or anyone you need to call?"

"No. I prefer to keep my relationships uncomplicated."

Ria paused a moment before continuing. "You want to go downstairs? I'll get Battista to get rid of those clothes and air the place out for you."

"Sure, sorry about freaking out earlier." Dani stood. "I saw Ian come around the corner and there was no pause. No 'taking in the situation.' He just fired and hit the Torog millimeters from my head."

Ria turned to face her. "Dani, we're not like you. You do mixed fights and you're good at it, right?"

Dani nodded.

"So you understand how important both accuracy and reflexes are. We are so much faster than humans. We assess the situation and move before you know what's going on. Millimeters is a foot for us. Maybe two."

"You don't think he was careless?"

"No way. Ian is anything but careless. Besides"—Ria gave her a gentle nudge—"I think he likes you."

The butterflies in her stomach stirred. "Ha, pretty sure I put an end to that."

"He understands," Ria said. "You've been through a lot. Don't worry about it."

"I'll try, and thanks."

"That's what friends are for, right?"

"Right. So," Dani said, eyeing the boots, "those for me?"

Ria grinned and reached down for the black leather boots. "They're a little big for me. Not custom made, but they're a size nine. Edwardo stretches out the leather before he makes his shoes so it's like slipping into a pair of old favorites. Here, try them on."

Dani took the boots and inspected them. Slightly pointed toe and a two-inch heel with a zipper up the side. The bottoms were rubber with some serious tread. They were calf height, with intricate designs stitched into the leather. She grabbed a pair of socks and slipped them on. "Wow," she said, taking a stroll around the room. "These rock. Thank you."

"My pleasure, friend. My pleasure."

Dani was in a much better mood as they left the room.

Downstairs they found Battista and Gina serving drinks from the bar in the corner. The rest of the group were scattered around the room, some sitting, some standing. Ian paced in front of the windows and raised his glass to her when she entered. Dani accepted a wine from Gina and went over to him. He stopped his pacing and leaned against the windowsill, ankles crossed as she approached.

"I want to apologize for earlier." Dani toyed with the stem of her wine glass. "I was out of line. You saved my life and I bit your head off. I'm sorry."

"It's all right. I probably would have done the same thing in your shoes. Which are nice, by the way." Ian glanced at her boots.

"These are amazing. What do I owe you for all of this?"

"Nothing. Don't worry about it."

Clearly the man wasn't lacking for money so she was okay with that. "Thanks. I'll try and keep my brain ahead of my mouth from now on." Dani laughed. "Although I haven't had much luck with that so far."

Ian chuckled in a quiet, private manner. It warmed her insides. She liked the feeling of complicity with this man.

Apology complete, she stepped over and eased into her favorite chair.

Armond, who sat brooding across the room, broke the silence. "Anyone care to guess the odds of Torogs being in Bellagio by chance?"

"Zero," Ria said. "Question is, are they following us somehow, or did they stake out the portal? And if so, are they lurking around all the portals? Do they even know where they all are?"

"Good questions," Ian said. "I don't see how they could know. But even if they do, why? Why are they pursuing us? All they've ever done is try to sneak in and out again. This will cost them their membership in the GTO for sure. What could possibly be worth that?"

"Maybe they've decided to change the game," Marco said. "Instead of hunting humans, they're hunting EPs."

"Too high a price to pay for a little sport," Armond said. "No, it must be something else."

Marco mimicked Armond in a high-pitched voice. "Must be something else."

"Easy, Marco," Ian said in warning. He swirled the ice around his glass, brows drawn together. His hand stopped halfway to his mouth. "Hunting. That's it. But not to kill. To capture."

Ian stared at Dani, which as usual caused an array of interesting sensations.

"What?" she asked.

"I'm not sure." Ian pushed off the windowsill. "You thanked me for saving you, but did I?" He nodded his head, talking faster now. "Something was off about the alley situation. I couldn't put my finger on it."

Dani snickered. "You mean besides me being covered in alien innards?"

"Yeah, besides that." Ian grinned. "When I rounded the corner, the Torog wasn't trying to kill you. You'd have been dead long before I got there. No, it was dragging you up the alley. Alive. They're after you, Dani."

Now everyone stared at her. "That's crazy. What would they want with me?" she asked.

Ian shook his head. "No idea, but we've got to get the off-world portal working again. Everyone have their bases shielded?"

The EPs all nodded.

"Good, keep them up," Ian said. "If I'd had them up on Cat Island, we wouldn't be here now."

Jared leaned forward on a plush chair. "You had no way to know, boss. They've never been to the island before."

"Like Marco said, it's a new game. Just wish we knew what we were playing." Ian finished his drink. "It's been a long day. We'll prep tonight and head out first thing tomorrow."

"Where to?" Marco asked.

"Obviously," Armond said, as though Marco was a child, "Cat Island. That's where the main portal is. That's where the problem is."

Marco glared at the albino.

"He's right," Ian said. "We need to get the portal open."

Marco leaned back on the couch and took a long drink of his beer.

Wanting to diffuse the mood, Dani asked, "How do they work exactly? The portals."

Marco livened up and sat his drink down. "Portal Masters make them. It's pretty amazing stuff. They're powered by psi. Anyone with psi can use the portals, but they can't create them. There are limits too. Like the amount of mass that can be moved and the number of times in an hour they can be used."

"If they're broken," Dani said, "then why did the one in the tunnel work? You said that was a portal."

"It is, but the portals in the tunnels are terrestrial and independent. They stand alone and only go from one end to another. The off-world portals, however, are all tied together via the main one on Cat Island."

"How many tunnels are there?"

"Enough," Ian said, clearly not wanting to say more.

Dani pushed a little further. "So, you can travel around the world, but you can't leave?"

"Pretty much," Ian said.

"What if the Torogs destroyed the main portal?" Dani asked.

The EPs all shook their heads.

"You could bomb the place, burn it to the ground. Only Portal Masters can remove a portal," Ian said.

Dani swung her feet around to drape over the arm of the chair so she faced the group. "If it's so impervious, how did the Torogs break it?"

Armond scowled at her, which was the most emotion she'd seen from the guy yet. "They can't break it."

"But, you just said—"

"Only psi-abled Sandarians are Portal Masters." Armond stood abruptly. "I don't know what they've done, or how. All we know is that the main portal is down."

If she didn't know better, she'd swear Armond looked spooked.

"Is there anyway," Ian asked, "for a non Portal Master to affect a portal?"

"Nothing in my training would lead me to believe so," Armond replied.

Ian put his drink down. "Is anyone due back on Sandaria for any reason? Expecting or expected to make any calls?"

Ria, Armond and Marco shook their heads.

"Then it could be days," Ian said, "before anyone realizes the portals are down. We'll get into the villa through the caves."

"What about Dani?" Ria asked.

"She comes with us. Everyone does. Until we know why they're doing what they're doing, we assume vulnerability across the board. Come on, we have some work to do tonight." Ian walked behind the couch to a built-in cabinet on the far wall. He waived his palm near the surface. A large, floor-to-ceiling panel slid sideways into the wall. The others got up and gathered round.

Dani peered in and whistled. Along the back hung row after row of what she assumed were weapons. She recognized the small gun that Jared had in the alley. "Very *Men in Black*, guys," she said.

Jared laughed. "Very. I call this one here the cricket," he said, palming the small gun.

Ian reached in and retrieved another one of the crickets. He handed it to Jared and nodded at Dani. "Take her to the sim room and teach her how to use this." He turned to Gina. "You good?"

"*Si*, Signor. I practice with Battista, many days." The woman was all business now, and showed no sign of the easygoing grandmother figure from before.

Dani followed Jared back to the tunnel. He moved to open the door when she put a hand on his arm.

"Wait, you sure there aren't any Torogs in there?" she asked.

"They can't use the tunnel portals," Jared answered.

"Why not?"

"First, because the shield is active. Second, because they don't know where the access points are. That's part of the whole 'no X to mark the spot' thing. Like the door to our garage back at the bar. You have to know where it is."

"And they got into the tunnel on the Cat because they already knew where we were."

"That's right."

"Okay, how did they get to Bellagio then?"

"They have their own means of getting around Earth. They generally use small, cloaked vehicles. Slower than our tunnels, but faster than any Earth craft."

"Wow. Aliens among us. All those crackpots with crazy stories."

"Not all crazy." Jared opened the tunnel and they made their way to another, smaller door. He pressed his palm to a pad on the left and an opening appeared.

"The speed of these doors freaks me out," Dani said.

Jared chuckled. "I know what you mean."

Once they stepped inside, lights popped on, illuminating a massive room. It was entirely grey and completely empty. The space was fifty or more yards in each direction and at least thirty feet high.

"This is cheery," Dani said.

Jared let go with a typically explosive sneeze that echoed around the space.

"Bless you."

He mumbled something into a tissue and closed the door. On the wall adjacent, he fiddled with a console. Classic red, ringed targets appeared at different heights and distances, spread throughout the room.

Dani squinted at the closest one. "Is that real?" She walked up to the three dimensional target and reached out to touch it. Her hand went right through. "Holograms," she said smiling.

"It gets better. Check this out," Jared said, turning a dial on the console. Colors on the orb intensified.

"Touch it again," Jared said.

The target now had the consistency of a plastic ball. "Un. Believable."

"You ain't seen nothin' yet. Come on back, let's get started." He turned the dial back and the target returned to hologram form.

Dani returned to Jared's side. He reached into his pocket, pulled out the two crickets and handed one to her, demonstrating how to hold the weapon.

"The safety is here, on the butt," he said, pressing his finger on a small green patch.

Dani did the same, but nothing happened.

"Hold on, I have to key the laser to your DNA." Jared placed his finger on the green patch on her gun then nodded for her to put her finger next to his. A low whirring sound emanated from the gun and it vibrated in her hand. Jared let go, and she held the gun in firing position.

"Not bad," Jared said. "Now let's see how good a shot you are." He aimed and fired at the nearest target. An almost imperceptible whine came from the gun and a red beam shot out the front. A black spot appeared to the left of center.

"Wasn't this a lot louder in the alley?" Dani asked.

"I had it set to kill then. We're in training mode."

"Ah." Taking aim, she pulled the trigger. "Bull's-eye! Yes!" Dani dropped her arm to her side and smiled at Jared. The gun continued its whirring.

"Aaahh!" Jared jumped back a good three feet and stared at his foot, a shocked expression on his face. The tip of his boot remained next to Dani.

"Oh my god, Jared are you okay? Where are your toes? Please tell me you have your toes." Dani frantically kicked at the piece of shoe left behind. *No blood, no toes.* She looked at Jared.

"They're fine," he said, still looking at his now open-toed shoe. "Must've used the wrong setting. Can I see that?" He motioned for the gun.

Dani handed it over gladly.

"Well," Jared said, changing a setting on the side. "That could have been worse. It wasn't set to kill, but it wasn't on train either."

"Thank, God. I am sooo sorry. I didn't know it was still firing." She looked again at Jared's toeless boot. "Seriously though, where are your toes? You really are human, right?"

Jared mumbled something under his breath.

"What?" Dani said.

"Bunions. All right?? I have bunions so I wear my shoes big. Now, do you want to tell me how someone who wins as many fights as you do, can be so clumsy?"

Dani shrugged. "It's a gift?"

"Well, watch it, will you?" Jared stepped back another two feet. "Keep going till you get to the last target. The beam is active for two seconds. Got that? Two seconds." He didn't wait for an answer. "You'll need to press the trigger again after that."

Dani aimed and fired. She had to adjust as the targets got further away, but managed to nail most of them with increasing accuracy.

"This place is great," Dani said, aiming at the last target.

"Okay, now let's try some moving targets." Jared pushed another button on the wall, and the space came to life. Virtual Torogs and other creatures darted in all directions.

"No way, this totally rocks!" She laughed and fired away, blasting body parts off anything in sight.

Thirty minutes later Dani's arms ached.

"Okay Annie Oakley, you're good to go. Put your finger back here." He demonstrated. "Feel the nub?"

Dani placed her finger on her own gun and found the little bump. "Yep."

"Now press it. It will cycle through the two levels."

Dani repeated his actions. "Got it."

"Remember, green is training mode. It's useless if you're in trouble. Now press and hold and the light will go off… Good, you're locked and set."

"That was downright therapeutic. I feel so much better now," she said, handing the weapon to Jared.

"You hold on to it. And try not to kill anything that looks human."

"Ha, ha. Very funny."

Jared patted her on the back. "Well done. Come on, I need to scare me up some new shoes."

Chapter 6

Dani and Jared found the others in the dining room. A vast array of weapons from the wall, and items she didn't recognize, were laid out on the table. Large backpacks lay open and the EPs sorted through the devices, selecting what they wanted.

"How'd it go?" Ria asked.

"Great," Jared replied. "Aside from a minor alteration to my footwear."

The group glanced down at Jared's feet.

"Nice," Marco said.

Dani ran a finger along the edge of the table. "That was amazing."

"The sim room is great, isn't it?" Ria stuffed another mystery item into her pack. "I can spend hours in there. Did you show her the alien attack mode, Jared?"

"Oh, yeah. She stayed alive for almost ten minutes on her first try."

Marco let out a whistle.

"Wow," Ria said. "Way to go girl." She gave Dani a high five and a questioning look.

Dani let out a nervous laugh. "I'm sure that's nothing compared to what you guys do."

Ian held her gaze a moment. That pleasurable buzz rippled through her and she could have sworn his eyes flashed green. A not-so-subtle reminder, perhaps, that he wasn't human.

He smiled at her. Then, like a switch being flicked, the buzz disappeared. He looked away, and continued sorting and stuffing items into the pack.

What is that buzz he gives me? Alien foreplay? The thought of what might come after the warm-up made her heart skip a beat. Would she do it? With an alien? *If it's anything like at the pool...hell yes.*

Gina interrupted her thoughts when she came out of the kitchen. "All right everyone. I have dinner ready in ten minutes. Signor Ian, can we move the toys from the table please? Or would you prefer to eat in the kitchen?"

"Let's keep it simple. Everyone can serve themselves in the kitchen."

"*Si,* Signor. I will get the plates ready." Gina smiled at Dani. "You are hungry now, yes?"

An image of blue stew with unidentifiable matter floating on the surface assaulted her senses. The smell of Torog was real enough to make her gag. "I'm sorry, I couldn't possibly eat. I think I'll just turn in."

Ria came to her side. "I had Battista put a backpack on your bed. Pack a few days worth of clothes in there, okay? No telling what we're going to need."

"Sure."

Ria gave her a hug and returned to the table.

"Ms. Dani, if you get hungry later, you will help yourself in the kitchen, yes?" Gina said walking over for a warm embrace.

"I will. Thank you, Gina." The older woman smelled of Italian herbs.

Marco and Jared called goodnight, while Armond remained silent. Ian came around and pulled her aside. The warmth of his touch both soothed and aroused.

"I'm really sorry you got sucked into all this. I don't know why they're after you, but don't worry. We'll keep you safe, I promise."

The buzz he gave her started up again only to evaporate just as quickly. Dani tilted her head and caught another flash of green in his emerald eyes.

"Thank you," she said, more convinced now that he controlled that delicious feeling. She left them to their work.

When she reached her room, she did as instructed and packed her bag. In the drawer with underwear and socks, she found a soft white cotton shift and robe. The gown was quite short, with the robe falling a few inches above the knee. She gave Gina a mental thank you, and put them on before getting ready for bed. She could never figure out how women slept in long nightgowns. She'd tried a few times, but always found herself tied in knots, and panicking. Her mother used to love long nightgowns and flowing robes. She crawled into bed and stifled tears as thoughts of a Christmas long ago drifted into her mind. She dozed off with the image of her mother twirling around in front of their Christmas tree, the red silk of her robe billowing out around her. That was their last Christmas together.

* * * *

The Torog wrapped putrid arms around Dani's waist and squeezed. Her breath wouldn't come and pain ripped through her stomach.

Dani shot up, heart pounding. She glanced around and let out a sigh when she remembered where she was and realized she'd been dreaming. The pain was real however. Her stomach growled and reminded her she hadn't eaten dinner. She slipped out of bed, threw on her robe, and headed for the door.

I may never eat stew again, but more bread sounds good. Dani made her way downstairs, and padded silently across the foyer to the kitchen. The Papallo's quarters were off the other end of the large room so she skipped the light. Moonlight filtered in through bay windows, surrounding a small dining area. It was enough. She retrieved a plate and pulled a loaf of bread from the bread box on the counter. She dug around the fridge and found some butter and some fizzy water. Not caring about calories for once, she slathered on the butter and closed her eyes as the freshly baked bread worked magic in her mouth. Each swallow easing her hunger and washing away the day's fatigue. She finished the large piece of bread and stood contemplating another.

"Still hungry?" Ian's voice startled her.

Or was it Ian? Something wasn't right about his voice. She licked her fingers and finished the job with a napkin, tossing it on the counter.

"Ian?" He sounded different, but she knew it was him. The strange tingling sensation he caused pulsed through her. She held her breath a beat and let it wash over. A small groan of pleasure escaped her lips. She searched the kitchen, her eyes settling on the dark space between two of the bay windows by the small dining table. "How long have you been there?"

Ian leaned forward out of the shadows. The side of his face illuminated by moonlight gave him an unreal appearance. He picked up an empty plate and stood.

Dani's heart raced as he came closer in nothing but a tee shirt and jeans. His bare feet silent on the tile.

"Awhile. I couldn't sleep." His voice sounded husky and low, much more than usual. It played on her emotions, confusing and exciting her. A wave of pleasure radiated from her core.

Ian stepped past her, his arm brushing against her sleeve. Behind her, she heard the sound of his plate clink against the granite counter. She nearly jumped when his hot breath caressed the side of her neck.

"Don't let me stop you. You're obviously hungry."

The way he emphasized the last word made her shiver and her stomach flip-flop. She turned to face him, their bodies inches apart. He trailed a finger down her arm from shoulder to wrist, then took her hand in his and raised it to his mouth. "No more pain?" His lips pressed against her palm.

Her knees almost buckled when a thrill shot through her, causing an involuntary shudder. "Ian—" Her voice caught, and she cleared her throat. "What are you doing?"

Ian inhaled deeply as he closed the gap between them. "I'm giving in, Dani. You want me to, don't you?" One hand slid around her waist, the other trailing up her arm to stroke the line of her jaw.

Waves of pleasure rolled out from his touch. Hot moisture pooled between her legs. Ian's eyes were impossibly vivid, the greenest she'd ever seen, and right before her, they began to glow.

Oh, shit. Dani took a slow, shaky breath. She stood in the arms of an alien and this was the point of no return. Did she want to?

His thumb brushed her lower lip.

The heat in her grew.

"Dani?"

He said her name in a rumbling growl that reverberated deep inside. She tingled everywhere.

Leaning forward, his mouth brushed her ear. "I'll leave if you want me to, just say the word."

He kissed her neck, tentatively, questioningly. The heat of his lips melted any resolve she may have harbored. The thought of him leaving her now, in this state, was unbearable. Aroused on every level, she reached her arms around his neck and pressed against him.

This must be a dream. She moaned as he nipped his way down her neck causing little sparks of pain. Her entire body rippled with the effect. *If I wake up now, I'm killing the person responsible.*

In one smooth movement, Ian scooped her into his arms. His eyes burned brighter than ever, their light visible on her robe. Her nipples were painfully hard and she was ready for him in every way. Impossibly fast, he carried her out of the kitchen, up the stairs, and pushed open the door to his suite. He closed the door and set her down. Soft carpet caressed the soles of her feet, her senses in overdrive. She slid her hands up his chest and around his neck. She stared into his luminous alien eyes as he leaned down and kissed her. Gentle at first, still questioning, his tongue parted her lips. The kiss became fervent as his hands explored the contours of her body, and his erection pressed against her. She needed desperately to touch him everywhere, to feel his skin on hers. As though reading her mind, he stepped back. She swayed slightly when he peeled off his shirt. His muscled body beautiful in the soft light of the moon streaming in from the window.

She untied her robe, dropped it to the floor and pulled her gown over her head, leaving her in a cotton bikini, wet with her desire. Ian took his time as he drank her in from head to toe.

He paused at her breasts, his eyes a flash of green, and a wave of pleasure so intense she couldn't breath, washed over her. Helpless, she leaned against the door, eyes closed, and let the sensation reign—like an orgasm, but not limited to her loins. Something pulsed outside of her body. *How is this possible?* Dani tried to make sense of what was happening when it stopped as quickly as it started. *No, no, no.* She moaned, wanting more. She opened her eyes to find Ian removing his jeans.

A moment of panic flashed through her when she remembered he wasn't human. What if he wasn't…the same down there? She held her gaze on the floor, afraid to look.

He stepped closer.

She lifted her head. *Oh yes.* He was definitely normal there, but…was there such a thing as too big?

"Not between us," Ian said.

"How—"

"Shh, I'm glad you like what you see." His voice, so deep and strange, resonated within her. Her breath caught and her back arched when he bent down and took her nipple in his mouth, biting to the point of pain. He picked her up again and carried her to the bed. He laid her down and removed her panties with his teeth, while his hands wreaked havoc with her breasts, then thighs. The energy between them grew as the tempo increased.

Something built up inside her. Sexual yes, but more. On the verge of an orgasm, another burst of pure pleasure coursed through her. It was paralyzing. So similar yet so different from the orgasms she knew. She somehow experienced the space beyond her body. *What is this?* She opened her eyes, and again the feeling vanished, leaving her with an overwhelming sense of frustration.

"Oh, God. Ian, that's you, I know it is. Don't stop, please." Dani ached for completion.

Ian growled and moved on top of her. He rested on his elbows as his erection played over her abdomen. He bit and nibbled her neck and ear.

Sounds and moans escaped her without warning. "Ian, please." She lifted her pelvis and rubbed against him. A look of sadness swept across his face and the word *"human"* slid into her mind. The pain that word caused him hit her physically, and she froze, confused. The green of his eyes intensified, held her captive.

He shook his head and the look of pity turned into one of mischievous desire. A grin pulled at the corner of his mouth as he growled again. The sound sparked another wave of desire. It started between her legs and rolled over her head. Again, she floated in a sea of unimaginable pleasure, so much more than physical. When it stopped, all too soon, Dani hiked up her knees and wrapped her legs round his waist. She reached down to guide him in. He obliged, filling her completely. Every cell in her body responded. It was a thrill unlike any she had ever known and, with it, came an absolute inability to speak. Something outside her responded while he slid in and out, faster and faster. Pleasure flooded over her as the sensation echoed throughout, body and soul.

His pace quickened and the pleasure narrowed its focus. The intensity increased, exquisite, but it wasn't the same as before. *He's holding back.* Her body responded by matching his rhythm, and taking it up a notch. Faster, they moved until the orgasm took her by force and rolled over her again and again. The thrill ran down her legs and up into her belly.

And yet, out of reach but so close…something. Something more— something she needed. They came to a stop and their heartbeats slowed. Ian lowered his head next to hers, his breath hot on her shoulder.

"Oh Dani, that was close." His voice was back to normal.

"I don't know about you," Dani laughed "but I got a lot more than close."

He brushed the hair away from her eyes. His own back to their brilliant but non-glowing color. "You are so beautiful."

Dani studied his face. "Why do you look so sad?"

He smiled then. "Not sad, darling, sated."

"I'll say."

Ian slid out of her and lay next to her body. One hand propping up his head and the other tracing her curves. The sensation tickled and made goose bumps spread over her. He laughed and pulled the sheet up to her belly button. He cupped a breast and toyed with her nipple.

"Not fair," she said.

"Earth has a saying here, about love and war?"

Dani laughed. "Yeah, 'All's fair in love and war.'"

He leaned over and kissed her. Sweet and slow. Again she thought she sensed sadness but wasn't sure why. Their lips parted and he lay next to her, one arm across her chest.

She'd just had the best sex of her life with an alien. Her head swam. What next? Relationships never lasted with her. She wondered how he'd feel about a friends-with-benefits scenario. She knew how she'd feel.

She turned to face him.

"I should probably get back to my room. I really need a few hours of sleep."

He let out a long sigh. "I'll walk you."

* * * *

Ian kissed her one last time and closed her bedroom door. He smelled her on his fingers and inhaled deeply. He took his time returning to his room. There would be no more sleep for him tonight.

This was a mess. An achingly beautiful mess. *She is the perfect mate. Perfect and impossible in equal measure.*

The empire was ruled and fueled by pure bloodlines. As an only child he had a duty to continue the line. To mate with a Sandarian of equal status.

The thought of hiding her origins crossed his mind, only to be replaced by a vision of the massive birds of prey from Dortan. They took down creatures twice their size. Gordat Prayda would find out. Ian knew it to be fact. He would find out and destroy the Cavacent family.

They couldn't hide a bond so he couldn't be intimate with her again. His gut clenched at the thought.

If only she were Sandarian. He closed the door to his room behind him and leaned against the cool surface of the door.

In the morning he'd have Armond erase her memory of their night together. It meant telling Armond about her psi, but he saw no choice. All she'd remember is a peaceful night's sleep, and all he had to do was stay away from her.

He leaned his head against the door, the same place she'd stood before. She'd wondered if he was too big for her, and he told her nothing was too big between them. He was wrong. He pushed off the door. It was time to shower. Time to erase her smell and her taste. Time to get to work and forget about things he couldn't have.

Chapter 7

Dani entered the kitchen the next morning to find she was the last one down. The EPs sat at the table where Ian had watched her the night before. A bolt of desire shot through her at the memory. *I could sure handle a replay.*

Jared and Battista stood around the center island drinking coffee while Gina worked the stove. Dani smiled, and called out "morning" to the room in general. She couldn't help but wonder if any of them had seen or heard her and Ian.

Gina scooped a mound of scrambled eggs onto a plate. "*Ciao bellezza,* how are you this morning? You sleep well I hope?"

"Um, yeah, I slept fine." Heat rose to her face and she kept her back to the table.

"Come. Do you want some eggs and toast? Ham and bacon are over there." She pointed to where Jared and Battista stood around a granite island. "You better hurry. Those two, they don't eat. They inhale."

Dani's stomach answered for her and she took the offered plate. "Thank you." She went over and stood next to Jared, helping herself to both ham and a slice of bacon.

Jared poured some orange juice and slid the glass over to her. "How ya doin'? Feeling better this morning?"

"Yeah. I think I just needed some rest."

Ian and his team finished up their food and carried their dishes to the sink. He and Armond approached her as she finished her eggs. "Are you ready to go?" Ian asked.

"Sure," she said, swallowing her food. "Let me run up and grab my bag."

"Great. Bring it downstairs and meet us in the library. Armond has an idea about why the Torogs might be after you. He only needs a few minutes to check something out."

"No problem. I'll be right back." Dani put her plate with the others and headed for her room.

* * * *

Downstairs, Ian and Armond waited in the library. The room was smaller than his on Cat Island but well appointed with dark mahogany bookcases, which filled the walls from floor to ceiling. An enormous fireplace took up most of one wall and was surrounded by overstuffed leather furniture. The fire pit was Ria's portal and currently useless. He sat in one of the chairs and Armond on one side of the couch.

"Are you sure?" Armond said.

"I'm sure. I have no excuse for last night and you no doubt understand the sensitive nature of the situation."

"Indeed." Armond leaned forward, elbows on his knees. "Do you think perhaps it would be better to simply…remove the situation entirely?"

The look in Armond's eyes told Ian he understood all too well the implications of a human with psi.

"No. She is not to be harmed. None of this is her fault. I simply need to try and put this woman's life back to normal. When this is all over, we can discuss erasing her memory of us entirely. For now, let's just remove the complication I created last night."

Armond nodded but didn't appear convinced. "It may not work. She's not Sandarian, but if she has psi, I may not be able to erase her memory."

Ian hadn't thought of that. "We have to try."

Dani knocked on the door a few moments later.

"Come in," Ian called. "Please, have a seat." He motioned to the spot next to Armond. "Armond needs to connect with you. To see if he can find anything the Torogs might be picking up on."

"Connect?"

She sounded more than a little nervous.

"It's all right. Just a light touch, skin on skin."

"Yes," Armond said. "I can detect any unusual…activity."

Ian mentally kicked himself for not going over what to tell her. Armond had the tact of a Sandarian street peddler. "Please," he said. "It won't take a minute and we need to get going."

Dani sat perched on the edge of the couch.

"Give me your hand," Armond said.

Dani gave a nervous laugh. "Sure, if you give it back."

Ian smiled, but as usual, Armond just stared.

"Oh, for Pete's sake, here." Dani stuck her hand out.

Armond placed her hand in his open palm and took her wrist with his other hand. "Relax."

Ian nodded his assent. The albino closed his eyes, inhaled deeply, and appeared to simply stop breathing.

Ian glanced at his watch. It was ten till seven. He wanted to get going and get this over with. He resisted the urge to move, and remained still and silent.

Armond abruptly let go of the wrist and dropped Dani's hand. "I see nothing here that would attract attention. I need a word with Ian. Close the door behind you."

"That's it?" Dani asked Ian.

"Guess so." Ian stood and reached out to help her up. He walked her to the door. "Don't mind him. Manners aren't exactly his strong point."

"Yeah, I got that. See you in a bit?"

"Be right there." Ian closed the door behind her and listened as she walked away.

"Well?" He asked Armond.

"No. She's unusually strong. Like you." Armond stood and waited.

Ian wanted to say he'd already figured that out, but held his tongue. It was clear Armond was not happy about having failed his assigned task. He would have found the albino's discomfort with his failure funny if not for the ramifications.

"You can't erase her memory at all."

"Correct."

Damn. He hadn't counted on this. Last night in the kitchen he'd known the moment her feet touched the floor in the room above. With each step, something inside woke and grew stronger. He sat in the shadows and watched her. The seconds passed and his psi energy increased with each tick. His body hummed with it. He knew bonding could produce such an effect but he never imagined he wouldn't be able to control it. *I couldn't resist her last night any more than I could stop breathing now.* Ian knew how to face his fears in battle, but this was something else. *I have to stay away from her. And I need her to help.*

Chapter 8

Dani left the library to find Ria coming back from the tunnel. "Hey, Sunshine," Ria said. "Cruisers all loaded. The boys coming?"

"I guess. Armond said he needed to talk to Ian. So, back to Cat Island, huh?"

Ria searched her face.

Dani hoped it didn't show a tenth of the fear that threatened to overwhelm her.

"You worried about the Torogs?"

"You think?" Dani smiled. "This gets more and more like a cheesy fantasy flick every day. We're on a quest to somehow mend a magic portal, and blocking our way are nasty, smelly, alien creatures. I assume we have a plan?"

Ria laughed. "It's going to be okay. We've been monitoring the villa and there only seems to be one Torog left. He's in the library with the portal, so odds are he's a guard. The library doubles as Ian's office and he's got another way in, so yeah, we have a plan."

"Why only one Torog?"

"No idea and we can't be certain. There are some small pockets not visible on the cams, but you couldn't hide many there. All we have to do is get the portal open."

"What if they attack again?"

"Worst case scenario, we take you through and you get to see Sandaria."

Dani thought of her dad and grinned. "Let's do that."

Their chat was interrupted when Ian and Armond blew out of the library and called the team to action.

No one spoke much on the ride to Cat Island but the energy was intense. The EPs fiddled with their devices, and constantly monitored the video feeds from the villa. Gina and Battista huddled together and talked in hushed tones. Jared spent the time messing with his phone, and was it her imagination, or was Ian avoiding her? He hadn't looked at her once since the library.

Dani wrung her hands in her lap. The portal approached and a flush of embarrassment ran through her at the thought of her earlier reaction. The surface shimmered, resembling a wall of standing water. There was a slight tug when they passed through, then they were on the other side. A few minutes later they stopped at the entry to the main tunnel.

"All clear?" Ian asked.

"I got nothing," Marco said. The others confirmed. The portal opened and they turned right and headed for Jared's bar.

Dani tapped Jared on the knee. "Aren't we going to the villa?"

"Ian's got a back door, so to speak. For emergencies."

"What self-respecting alien wouldn't?"

They shared a smile before pulling to a stop by the garage. Dani whistled at the massive hole where the door used to be. The storeroom beyond lay in rubble. Broken bottles and a blanket of soot covered everything. They grabbed their bags and filed out.

"Jared, I'm so sorry about this place." Dani picked her way through the debris.

"Hold it, Dani." Ian's voice played on her nerves. "Marco. Armond. Check it out," he said.

She stepped aside to allow the EPs to pass.

Jared came up next to her and surveyed the mess. "It's just stuff. Stuff can be replaced."

"All clear," Armond called back.

Ria gave Dani's arm a squeeze and passed by them into the bar.

Dani followed, patting her pocket where the gun rested. Jared spoke to Ian behind her.

"I called my brother. He put a 'closed for vacation' sign on the bar. The Hummers you wanted are out front and the keys should be in the usual place."

"Good work."

Everyone filed into the bar area which remained intact.

Dani glanced around, glad to see the Torog's blood gone. Soft moonlight filtered in through the windows. She shook her head. "From dawn to the dead of night, in a matter of minutes."

"You get used to it," Jared said.

"You keep saying that."

Jared found the keys and tossed a set to Ian. He bounced the other in the palm of his hand and stood next to Dani. "You okay?" he asked.

She blew out a long breath and nodded.

Ian cleared his throat. "You four wait here," he said to the humans. The EPs went outside to check the surroundings.

Dani took the opportunity to stretch her muscles.

Battista attempted to mimic her movements with a comical effect.

Gina slapped his arm.

Dani laughed at the portly Italian. "It's a routine I do before a fight. Helps me focus. I wish I knew what we were going to find at the villa."

"We'll know soon enough," Jared said.

Battista gave up on Dani's stretches. "A more interesting question is why are they after our Dani?"

"He's right you know," Gina said. "They kill instantly. Dragging you off like Signior Ian described. That is not heard of." The older woman gave Dani a thoughtful expression. "You no worry. We won't let you out of our sight, *bambina.*"

Normally Dani wouldn't be concerned, but her circumstances had become far from normal. "Thanks."

Ria pushed open the front door. "We're good to go. I'm riding with you guys. Jared, you drive."

"Got it," he said, and tossed the keys into the air one last time.

Dani motioned for Gina to go first, but the Italian paused. "What is it that makes you smile little one?"

"You. Dear, sweet, Italian lady right at home packing heat."

"Packing heat?"

"Oh, um, a gun. A very deadly gun."

"Ah, *si.* Is no mistake, I would kill an alien in a heartbeat if it threatened my family or our team."

Dani nodded. "I don't doubt it. Glad you're here."

Gina turned to Battista. "Did you hear? I have heat."

Battista laughed and said something in Italian that made Gina blush.

As they filed through the heavy door, Dani scanned the lot for her car. Someone had put the top up.

Jared followed behind. "My brother locked her up. Old Barrel can hot-wire anything."

"Thanks," she said. "I didn't even think about it. Or the house. I should call—"

"Already taken care of," Jared said and winked. "Part of our job remember? Make the protectors invisible."

"Right." Dani's boots crushed the white shells of the parking lot as they headed for the far corner. It was empty. "Where are we going?"

Ria put her hand out to slow their pace. "Another step and…here." Out of nowhere a black Humvee appeared.

"Whoa." Dani stopped, looked around and backed up a step. The Hummer and the others disappeared from sight. She stepped forward and there they were.

Battista chuckled as he held the door open for Gina.

"Okay, that's cool," Dani said, duly impressed.

Ria pulled open the second row door and motioned for Dani to climb in. Dani took the middle seat between Battista and Gina, as she was a bit smaller than they were. Jared got in and started the engine, which was nearly silent. A GPS screen showed both vehicles in a Google Earth map. Out the window there was only the parking lot. She gave a silent greeting to her father who, she knew, would be jubilant right now.

Unbidden, her thoughts turned to the previous night. Deep inside a thrill ignited, like the down bit on a roller coaster. *He's thinking about me.* She tried not to be bothered that he was keeping her at arms length. Probably just focused on the job.

The Hummer turned off on to a barely discernable road and drove another five minutes through thick brush. Jared used the GPS screen to keep a safe distance from the other vehicle. The trip was slow going, but they made it without mishap. They parked underneath a group of trees. Moonlight dappled the ground, filtered from the leaves above. Ian led them to a large boulder formation. He raised his hand, and the now ubiquitous magic panel appeared. The EPs gathered around, blocking Dani's view.

"What are they looking at?" Dani asked Jared.

"They're checking the tunnel. Make sure it hasn't been breached."

Dani strained her neck to get a better look.

Ria stepped aside to let her see. "This tunnel goes to the library where the portal is. Like I said, the entrance is concealed, but we can't be too careful."

Apparently satisfied, Ian opened the door. As with its larger cousins, the lights switched on, starting with the ones closest to them and continuing up the smooth, grey walls. The tunnel itself was smaller. Much smaller.

Not good. Dani followed Ria into the narrow space. The ceiling was no more than seven feet, which made the EPs appear even taller. She tried to concentrate on the fact the tunnel was well lit. *Light is good.* The walls seemed to close in on them when Marco sealed the door, and her gut wrenched. *Breathe, just breathe.* They made their way forward. The air was cool and slightly damp. Fifty feet or so from the end of the tunnel,

Ian pulled them to a stop. He waved his hand along the side of the wall, opening a door to a small room. The space was empty except for some crates labeled in French.

Jared took a closer look. "Boss, you have a seven thousand square foot villa and a wine cellar."

Ian grinned. "I also have parents who help themselves. This is my special stash."

Dani found the thought of Ian's parents somehow disconcerting.

Ian swung his backpack off and motioned for the others to do the same. The EPs selected an assortment of weapons then put the packs next to the crates.

"I want you four to stay out of sight in the storeroom until we dispose of the Torog, and make sure he's alone," Ian said.

Panic flared through her and she resisted the urge to run screaming back toward the Hummers. "No." Dani backed up a few steps. "No. Sorry but no. That room is really small, and I've seen how hard it can be to open these doors without that psi stuff because you can't find the bloody spot, and I'm not getting stuck in there and—"

"And you'll do as you're told," Ian snapped.

She glared at him. "Look, you jerk—"

"Hold on." Ria stepped between the two. "Dani, are you claustrophobic?"

Dani nodded. "This tunnel is about my limit."

Armond burst out laughing. The sound surprised her. He didn't say much. He was generally rude and she'd never heard him laugh. He folded his arms across his chest. "You must admit it's humorous."

"Must not," she said.

"Jared told us you excel in mixed fights," Armond said, "and you lasted ten minutes in the alien attack sim. On your first try. But you won't get into a little room with three highly trained Earth Support Agents?"

"Not to mention the wine," Jared added.

"Do not touch the wine," Ian said.

Dani wrapped her arms around herself. "Not happening. No way."

"Ria, take care of that." Ian pointed at Dani. He checked his phone again and walked over to the tunnel's end.

I'm a "that" now? Dani bit back a few choice words and turned to Ria. "What are you going to do?" She backed up another step.

Ria smiled and closed the gap between them. "Don't worry. It's the same as healing someone. I take your fear away, that's all. We're friends remember? I would never hurt you."

Dani frowned. "Healing. You mean like what Ian did in the pool?"

"In the pool?" Ria repeated.

"Yeah, Ian did something. Healed my wrist and my face."

"Really? That's interesting." Ria glanced over to where the boys stood discussing the Torog. "Then I guess it's exactly like that." She turned her gaze back to Dani. "What do you say?"

"Okay, but am I going to remember it this time?"

"You didn't remember?" Ria's eyebrows knitted closer together.

"I remember he did something, but I kinda blanked out during. Snapped out of it when Mr. Personality over there took off and swamped me."

"That's really odd. Look, let's talk about this later. Right now, we need to hurry." She took Dani's hand in hers and closed her eyes.

The tension melted away, replaced by a familiar tingling sensation. She glanced at the little room. *No fear.* She let out a sigh while her body tried to adjust to the previous adrenalin levels.

"Wait, Ria!" Everyone jumped when Ian's voice boomed through the tunnel. The EPs scanned the tunnel for danger. Ian covered the distance between them impossibly fast.

What's up with him? Dani stifled a laugh. The others looked around, searching for a threat. *Who cares? Alien voodoo totally rocks.*

Ria dropped Dani's hand and backed up. "Ian." She whipped around and let out a squeak when she found him directly behind her.

"Ian she's—"

"I know Ria." He ran a hand threw his disheveled blond hair.

"But that's—"

"I know, Ria."

"But that means—"

"Ria. I know," he growled. "We're not discussing this now. Not with anyone. Clear?"

Ria looked at Dani like she'd grown a second head. "Yes, sir."

Ian took Dani by the upper arm. " Now, if you don't mind." He propelled her toward the small room. "We've wasted enough time here."

Dani stumbled and grinned. "You guys sure have some amazing skills." She gave Ian a prolonged stare. Pleasure rippled through her and she didn't fight it. "Sure. Lock me up. You could probably put me *in* one of those crates right now and it wouldn't bother me." She took a step toward Ian. "You"—she poked a finger in his chest—"could do anything to me and it wouldn't bother me."

Ria cast her a another strange look, which didn't bother her either. She spun around before Ian could respond and walked into the tiny room. She leaned against the far wall next to the others with her arms crossed.

"Lock us up, Captain," Dani said, giving Ian a salute.

Ian flicked a wrist toward the opening and the door flashed shut.

"What was that all about?" Jared asked.

"I dunno. Something between Ian and Ria," Dani said with a shrug.

* * * *

Ian stomped over to the concealed entrance and ignored the questioning looks from Ria. He'd screwed up one thing after another. First with Dani, then Armond unable to wipe her memories and now with Ria. In his attempt to stay away from Dani, he'd neglected to consider what would happen if Ria connected. Now Ria knew about Dani's psi. *But that's all she knows.* It was clear Dani herself was in the dark, both about the bond and her own psi. She was totally naive. Someone was going to have to train her. *Or kill her.* He ignored an involuntary tightening in his chest at the thought. What a mess. Ian shook his head and settled back into command mode. One crisis at a time.

"Everyone ready?" They nodded. He checked his phone again. The Torog left to guard the portal stood with its back to the concealed door, looking out at the night sky.

"What's that saying? Like taking candy from a baby? Let's get that *crag* out of my villa."

Ian raised his hand, the door disappeared, and they fired.

The Torog fell to the floor with a muffled thud, blue blood seeped into the lush, thick sea grass rug. Within seconds, the smell permeated the room.

Ian scowled. *Time to remodel.* "Marco, scan the villa. Ria, when he calls it clear, get the humans. Armond, let's take a look." The two EPs walked over to the massive fireplace housing the portal. Putting the gateway into an oversized fireplace was a nice touch, started by an enterprising Sandarian.

Wadded up on top of the large metal grate sat a mound of dried out, bloody rags.

Armond picked up a poker rod and prodded the mound. The rags stuck together as one. He flipped the pile over. "Interesting. It appears we have that toy you wanted." Armond reached in and picked up a small rectangular device.

Ian reached out and sensed the reactivated portal. "It's working."

"All clear." Marco's voice echoed out of their phones. Ria went back for the others.

"Care to guess how that thing managed to jam our portal?" Ian said.

Armond stood and turned the device over. The bottom half of one side had four rows of silver buttons. He shook his head. He moved the device into the field of the portal. Nothing happened. He squatted, set the device back on the grate and replaced the rags. Still nothing. "Whatever it was doing, it's stopped."

"What are you thinking?" Ian knew Armond was lost in a world he'd never understand. When his uncle Mordo suggested Armond for the post of EP, he'd mentioned the man had "a relationship" with the Portal Masters. Ian had never heard of such a thing and didn't think it important. He was starting to think otherwise.

"I'm thinking I need to talk with your uncle." Armond stood and handed the device to Ian.

When Ria returned with the humans, Ian went over to seal the tunnel entrance behind them. The Papallo's hurried in first, followed by Ria and Jared. Dani tripped over nothing and dropped one of the backpacks she carried.

"That's sensitive equipment." Ian reached for the bags. He plucked one off the ground and took another slung over Dani's shoulder. "Next time, someone else carry the bags," he called out to the others.

"That was uncalled for," Dani said in a low voice.

A pang of guilt stabbed him. Being an asshole was turning out to be more difficult than he thought.

Ria went over to help but halted when a red beam, about the diameter of a softball, sliced off Marco's hand.

Rage distorted his face as he bellowed. Blood spurted from his severed wrist. He grabbed the stump and squeezed. A final burst of blood spattered his dark hair and face and he roared in pain.

More beams entered the room, moving erratically. Ria jumped to Marco's side and pulled him out of harms way. The Italian couple huddled behind Armond and the group backed up toward the fireplace. Ian and Dani stood separated from the others, and the portal. Marco let out a half groan and half growl.

The images on Ian's phone told the story. "Frack."

Dozens of Torogs streamed in through the front entrance. The leads carried powerful lasers, which they kept trained on the open door as they scuttled toward the library. The angle of the hall prevented them from seeing inside the room. Marco's hand had simply been in the wrong place at the wrong time, but it could have been his body. They only had seconds.

Ian grabbed Dani by the arm and backed up toward the tunnel. He shouted to his team, "Go! Bring help."

Dani struggled to free her arm, but he held his grip and pulled her back into the tunnel.

Ria danced around, looking for a way through the lasers. "No! We're not leaving you." The beams blasted into the side of the fireplace, not yet at the portal but getting closer.

Ian saw the pain and conflict on their faces. "That's an order. Move it."

Jared and Ria steadied Marco, and the trio disappeared into the portal.

Armond took hold of the Papallos. "We'll be back. Stay out of sight."

The Torogs made it to the doorway and Ian waved his hand, closing the tunnel door.

"They saw us," Dani said, yanking her arm free from his grasp and stumbling backward.

"I know. Come on, we need to get back to the bar so we can get to another portal. And try not to fall down."

"Oh you're just hysterical. You know what? You can go shove—" A deafening explosion rang out and echoed from the far end of the tunnel. The sound of crashing boulders followed. "Ian, they sealed the tunnel."

Another explosion hit, this time from the library. He grabbed her again and propelled her toward the store room. They tumbled inside, barely avoiding the boulders now falling from the ceiling. Ian shut the door. The noise reverberated at a painful decibel. Every sound echoed through the tunnel.

"Ian? What are we going to do?" Her voice shook, and she was clearly fighting panic.

"This room is reinforced but it won't withstand what they're throwing at it. Even if the others get help, they won't be able to get to us."

"So, what? We're dead?" She leaned against the back wall and pulled at her hair.

Ian had an idea. A really bad idea. Her psi was nearly as strong as his, maybe stronger. They were deeply compatible, and if they connected on that level, they may end up fully bonded. At very least, it would further the process.

Explosions rocked the ground like a war zone outside the small room. Another blast and the door bulged inward.

Ian had no choice. "There's only one chance and I need your help." He took a deep breath and tried to ignore the noise outside the room. "I need to use your psi. We have to bring the portal to us."

Dani let out a strangled laugh. "Did you hit your head? I'm human remember? I don't have the voodoo."

Ian grabbed her upper arms. She struggled but there was no where to go. He squeezed tighter. "I didn't hit my head, listen to me. When I healed you, in the pool, something happened."

"Yeah? Something happened last night too, as I recall."

"I'm sorry. Dani, you possess massively powerful psi. Armond and Ria have both sensed it. And last night…" Guilt stabbed him when he saw the look in her eyes. "I had to work to keep the connection closed. But you felt it. I know you did. The pleasure, remember?" Her smell intoxicated him. This was the last thing he should be doing. It was also the only thing that could save them.

Another blast. Dani screamed and the door fell in from the top, pushing him toward her. They crouched down, Dani's knees between his.

"Stay with me, Dani. We have to do this."

She cringed when another blast shook the room. Tears rolled down her cheeks. "I remember the feeling. You do that to me. When you're not being a jerk."

He wiped the tears from her face.

Another blast, and she shut her eyes and covered her ears.

"I'm doing what I have to, Dani." He took her face in his hands. "Look at me, please."

She sobbed, anger and fear showing in her eyes.

"I don't expect you to understand. But you have to trust me now. We have one chance of getting out of here alive and I need your help."

She pushed his hands away and rubbed her face. "Tell me what to do."

"You don't have to do anything, just let me in. We know you can because you've already done it, right? The pleasure?"

"I guess. I don't know. Oh God, I'm scared, Ian. I hate being scared. It pisses me off."

"You're beautiful when you're angry, luv." He smiled at her then. She gave him a determined smile back. The door collapsed, bending from the top. He inched forward on his knees, moving away from the door now pressed against his back. Their heads were nearly touching as the space shrank.

"Close your eyes and try to keep your mind clear." He gently caressed her shoulders and reached out to her. Once again the sheer force of her psi astounded him. He grabbed hold this time instead of backing away. The instant they connected, his psi and body erupted in euphoric emotion.

"That's right. You okay?" Ian said telepathically.

"What happened? Are we dead?"

"Not yet. Just stay with me. It's time to work."

He tried not to let her feel his fear as the door forced him closer. Ian reached out with his psi and sensed the walls around them. He pressed farther and found the portal. He tugged. Nothing happened. He tried again. Still nothing. Dani's psi was here but not helping.

"Shit."

"What's wrong?"

"I can't use your psi, I can feel it, but—"

Another blast pushed him against her and Dani screamed, "Here!"

That did it. He had it. He pulled with every ounce of strength.

"It's working, Dani." Dizzy, his arms and legs shook. The door pinned them against the wall, his face now next to hers. Another blast and they'd be dead, their bodies smashed. His strength slipped and he knew they were done when another presence entered his mind.

"Mordo."

"Yes," his uncle responded. *"You can do it Ian. Just a little farther..."* He knew his uncle's confusion when it touched Dani's psi. *"There's two of you? Interesting. Pull Ian. Armond and I are doing all we can from here."*

Ian sensed the portal, so close, but not enough.

"Pull." His uncle's voice exploded in his head. Another blast sent the door slamming into his back and he sunk into darkness.

Chapter 9

Dani couldn't breathe, couldn't move. Something pressed down on her. Raised voices, frightened, all talking at once, but nothing made sense. A male voice boomed nearby, sending a stabbing pain through her head. Just as she slid toward unconsciousness, the weight lifted and her body reflexively inhaled, air filled her lungs to capacity.

"Check for broken bones."

"Get the carrier."

"They will pay for this."

Angry, worried voices swirled around her. She opened her eyes only to find it impossible to focus.

Slowly, her memory filtered back. Cat Island, the attack in Como, Ian, the storeroom... Unable to focus, Dani flexed her fingers. She touched something soft and plush.

We're not in Kansas anymore, Toto. We made it. I'm on Sandaria. The thought swam about her head, increasing her nausea. She opened her eyes again. Better. Something on a flat surface floated out of the room. *Ian. Please let him be alive.* She closed her eyes against the pain throbbing in her head.

"It's unclear...should have killed them...."

The loud voice penetrated the fog. "How could you possibly want her to stay? Get her out of here."

"Rucon." A woman's voice. "She saved his life. Our son would be dead if not for her."

"None of this would have happened were it not for her," the man growled back.

"We don't know that. Without her, Ian could not have moved that portal. Even with Mordo and Armond's help. We must honor that, regardless of the consequences. I am sorry, my love."

Their son? She didn't know who the others were and didn't care as the voices faded to nothing.

* * * *

A quiet conversation drifted into her consciousness.

"I heard he hasn't moved a muscle, but he's breathing." It was a high pitched voice, like a young child.

"Correct." This voice sounded deeper and scratchy. Unlike the other, it held confidence.

An old maid and a mouse. Dani groaned, even the thought hurt.

"At least this one is making noises. Have you ever heard of anyone severing their psi like that?" the mouse asked.

There was a long pause before the elder woman answered. "It's very rare Koora, and it can be deadly. So, mind your tongue and pray to our Mother Goddess for the boy."

Dani wondered if they were talking about Ian. She hardly thought of him as a boy. She opened her eyes and blinked while the room swam into focus. The walls were a soft white with thick blue curtains drawn closed. She lay nestled in a four-poster bed with impossibly soft sheets and a thick comforter.

"Well, well. Look who's awake." The old maid turned out to be a short brunette, dressed all in white, a rough voice belying a more youthful appearance. Next to her stood a slightly taller, much younger woman wearing a blue uniform. Her sand-colored hair needed brushing. *Must be the mouse.*

"Where—" Dani coughed, her throat burned.

"Here, here now. Don't try to talk just yet." The woman in white fluffed her pillows and helped her sit up a little before handing her a drink with a clear straw. "You're weak. A few more days and you'll be good as new."

Dani swallowed gratefully. The liquid tasted like diluted grape juice and soothed the burn as it went down.

"I'm Healer Kane," the woman said. "I've been keeping an eye on you. This is Koora." The brown-eyed mouse smiled at her. "Her Ladyship has assigned her to you while you're here. If there's anything you need, ask her. Are you hungry?"

Dani nodded. "Where's Ian? And the rest? Are they okay?" Her voice came out scratchy and rough.

The two women exchanged a look.

Healer Kane sent Koora off to get some soup before answering. "Ian's alive for now. We're doing all we can for him. Moving a portal all by himself is an unheard-of feat." She fluffed Dani's pillow some more and straightened out the covers. "His uncle tried to help, but still. If you believe in the Goddess, or any other deity, it wouldn't hurt to pray. The others are fine. They've been asking about you."

Dani thought back to Lago Como, being attacked, the sim room. Making love—or had it been only sex? He'd been a real jerk ever since then. Except when he used her to save their lives. Maybe she was just an object to him. "How's Marco? Is he going to be all right?"

"That flirt? He's fine. It'll take a lot more than a missing limb to slow down that boy."

Relieved, Dani closed her eyes as her thoughts drifted back to the store room where they nearly died. *He said I have psi.* And he was right. Somehow, in that closet, she'd thrown it at him. *How can I throw something that has no form?* Dani opened her eyes when Koora returned with soup. The smell made her mouth water. Koora set the tray on the side table and helped her sit up more fully. Unfortunately, this caused the pounding in her head to start up again so she pressed her palm to her forehead and waited for the pain to subside.

Healer Kane reached into a small bag sitting on the side table. "Just relax dear, this will help your head." The woman pressed a small pen-like device to Dani's arm. The pain instantly decreased, but she was woozy.

"That will help you sleep as well after you've eaten something," Kane said. "Sleep is the best thing for you right now."

Koora situated the tray on her lap. Dani took a whiff of the warm soup before tasting it. "Umm, that's good. What is it?" It tasted like chicken soup only different.

"That would be Cook's famous vegetable soup," Koora said. "It's good, yeah? Course, I don't suppose you've ever seen a lot of the vegetables in there, being as you're a human and all." She said the word human with something resembling awe.

Dani paused with the spoon halfway to her lips.

"That's enough Koora," Healer Kane said. "Don't worry dear, nothing in the soup is going to harm you. Quite the opposite."

Dani finished the bite. "Can I see Ian?"

"Gods, no. Nothing personal, but he's gravely ill. And he is the Cavacent heir after all." Healer Kane gave her shoulder a squeeze. "I have received a request, however, for an audience with you. Most unusual." The healer appraised Dani as though trying to figure out a puzzle. "It's his lordship's brother, Ian's uncle, Mordo. He's a very powerful man. Don't know what he'd want with you. Perhaps tomorrow you'll be up for a visit?"

"Yes, of course." Dani hoped so anyway. She finished nearly half the bowl when her arms started to get heavy.

"After you've met with Mordo," Healer Kane said, "we'll let the others see you. The entire Earth crew have been clambering for a visit. It's quite extraordinary having humans here, let alone so many."

Dani took a few more bites and let Koora take the tray away. She wanted to ask how long she'd been there and to see outside, but sleep claimed her first.

* * * *

The room was dark and silent the next time Dani opened her eyes. She propped herself up on her elbows, taking in her surroundings. Koora slept on a couch by the curtains. She listened to the girl's breathing, slow and steady. Something was wrong. A bad feeling tugged at her insides. She sat up, relieved to find her head not pounding for once. Koora was the only other person in the room, but—*Ian*. A ghost of his essence echoed through her but faded fast. If she didn't get to him, he would die.

Okay, now I'm just paranoid. The part she was learning to recognize, her psi, ached. She knew it was the truth. She rubbed her face and watched Koora sleep. An eerie green light seeped through the the curtains behind the woman. Much as she wanted to see the alien landscape, she had to do something for Ian. She slid out of bed. They'd dressed her in white cotton pajama bottoms and matching shirt. Quietly, she plumped up the bedding to make it look like a body underneath and crept toward the door. Like a fish being reeled in, she couldn't resist. The knob was cool in her hand and her heart skipped a beat as Koora mumbled something in her sleep. She pulled the door open a crack, listening for any sound. Nothing. She checked both ways down a long, wide corridor. The place seemed deserted as she stepped out and closed the door behind her. Deserted and very posh. Cream-colored carpet prickled on her bare feet. End tables and flowers dotted the hallway. Portraits of different sizes adorned the walls. To the left was a stair case leading down, to the right an ornate window with hallways going off in both directions.

Ian, where are you? A mental nudge. *Right, it is then.* She navigated carefully between areas of shadow and light, listening. Her muscles ached, like when she had the flu. *What the hell am I doing? I'm probably not even allowed out here.* She stopped, thinking to go back when she sensed him again. She had the distinct impression he needed her, but didn't want her. There was definitely something wrong with him and it scared her. She struggled to understand. The impression was thin, almost ghost-like. *He really is dying.* Fear clenched her heart.

This is seriously messed up. She moved as quickly as she could. She reached the end of the corridor, turned left and there it was. Ian's door. Whatever it was she picked up from him was behind its smooth polished wood. She stood still, closed her eyes, and reached out to him. He was aware of her presence, in some part of his mind, but his body was shutting down. There was something terribly wrong with his body-psi connection. She heard the chime of a clock somewhere in the distance. *Time is running out.* Knowing there wouldn't be another chance, she silently opened his door and slipped inside.

Thank God. On a couch on the far wall, a male figure slept while Ian lay in the center of a bed, much like the one in her room. She closed the door, trembling both from fear of being caught and from her proximity to Ian.

"Stop." His voice in her head, weak and empty. "No closer, Dani."

"Ian, I can help you. I know I can." She sensed his conflict again. For some reason, he both wanted her and resisted her. She took another step.

"You'll die too. You're not strong enough for this."

Is that why he was conflicted? "You're wrong." She didn't listen anymore, she simply climbed under the covers and pressed against him. His body, both familiar and foreign, smelled like the Ian she remembered. His heat permeated her soul and her physical world shifted. She was falling, or more like sliding, down a large, smooth tunnel. It wasn't freefall but it was close. Ian's arousal washed over her again, but this time it wasn't her body that responded. *Like on Lago Como.*

"You shouldn't have done this Dani," Ian whispered in her head. "I can't stop it now."

"Stop what?"

A pleasure so intense it terrified her flowed over them. "Ian?"

Impressions danced across her mind. She had no words to describe what was happening, but there was a terrible problem. Her psi was connected to her on some level, not physical but somehow equally secure. As their psi caressed and folded together, she found only a tenuous link between Ian and his own.

I can fix this. Using her psi, she experimented with different movements and motions. Finally, she imagined dipping their combined psi into Ian's body and back out again. *Yes.* Over and over, she wove through him until she was sure it was working. Like string dipped in wax again and again, each time the connection between his psi and his body grew stronger. Little by little she backed off and simply guided his psi in and out. Time was impossible to measure but slowly her strength waned. *Have to keep going.* Her thoughts became increasingly disjointed and incoherent. Images flashed in her mind. Places she'd never been, people she'd never met. Healer Kane was there, younger. A young couple, the male carrying a woman in his arms and laughing. Then, they were arguing over humans. *That can't be right.* Confusion filled her with fear. The smooth motions of their psi became sporadic and uneven. She couldn't control it anymore, couldn't stop. She wanted to scream, needed to scream. She fell instead, into nothing.

* * * *

A deep rumbling voice penetrated the fog in Dani's brain. A one-way conversation, something about Ian. Phone. *Bed!*

Dani bolted upright in a panic.

"What the hell are you doing here?" A shorter, stockier version of Ian stood near the bed, glaring at her. Words escaped her. She sat and stared at the man, waiting for her thoughts to line up. They weren't cooperating.

Ian sat up next to her, groggy and confused.

"Good God, son, you're awake!"

The man's booming voice worked like a slap in the face to sober her up. She grabbed the covers and looked down, intensely grateful to find she still wore her pajamas. Her head swam with disjointed memories of last night.

Ian rubbed his eyes and glanced at the figure towering over the bed, then back at her.

For a fraction of a second, something akin to sadness glazed his eyes, but anger immediately followed. The look stabbed her like a knife. Why would he react like that?

He flung off the covers and stood. His shirt and briefs, damp with sweat, clung to his muscled body. The man on the couch rushed over, looking thoroughly perplexed. Dani wasn't sure if it was because of her existence in the bed or Ian's being awake. Probably both.

Ian swayed a little, and the man moved to help, but Ian waved him off and told him to fetch his clothes.

"Father," Ian said with a gravelly voice. Avoiding eye contact with anyone, he staggered through a door and slammed it shut.

Ian's father stood bolted to the floor, his face a mask of disbelief.

Join the party. She looked back at the closed door. The servant, or whoever he was, rushed in with a bundle of clothes. Steam billowed out around the sound of running water.

Dani placed her hand over her heart. The pain was real. *Bastard.* She swung her legs off the bed and stood. The room spun a little, but she was better than before. Her brain finally got the message nap time was over. *That was no nap.* Dani shivered. She pulled her shoulders back and lifted her head. "If you will excuse me," she spoke through clenched teeth, "it appears I am no longer needed." *And I'm sure as hell not wanted.* She headed for the door. Her clean exit marred only slightly when the door frame moved four inches to the left and pegged her on the shoulder. "Son of a bitch," she said under her breath. She made her way back to her room, clutching her arm.

* * * *

Ian emerged from the bathroom to find his father waiting. The moment the door opened, Rucon grabbed him in a rare embrace.

"We thought we'd lost you. Your mother's on her way." He grinned broadly and with one last hug, he let Ian go.

"How long—"

His mother burst into the room before he could finish. Her hands flew up to her mouth. Ian opened his arms and held her while she cried.

"Mother, it's all right. I'm fine, really," he said, patting her on the back. Compared to his father's mass, she was a veritable waif with flowing black hair.

Mara Cavacent straightened up, but kept her palm on Ian's heart. She gazed at him and shook her head, fighting more tears.

"How long have I been here?" Ian asked.

"A bit over forty-eight hours," his father said.

"We were terrified when your team arrived without you," Mara said. "They told us what happened."

"We tried to send help, but the villa had collapsed around the portal entrance. We summoned the Portal Masters to move it, but there was no time. Mordo discovered it was already moving." His mother looked at him with awe.

Ian nodded. "I remember. A bit of a surprise, that."

Rucon cleared his throat, stiffening. "He sensed the Standich woman immediately. Just now"—he motioned toward the bed—"what happened?"

Ian took his mother's hand from his chest, kissed it, and turned toward the windows. He flicked a finger and the thick brocade curtains slid open. The city below sparkled in the morning sun. He turned back to his parents. "She healed me." That much was true. His parents didn't need to know he had started bonding with a human.

Mara frowned. "Who?"

"The Standich woman," Rucon said.

"But she's in bed herself. Healer Kane has been taking care of her." Mara glanced between her husband and son.

Ian paced. "She was here. Just now. She arrived some time last night." Ian wasn't going to take this conversation any further than he had to.

"Ian," Mara looked confused. "I realize a human with psi represents certain problems for our family, but clearly healing is one of her abilities. I should think you'd be grateful."

Of course his mother would think that. She didn't know he was fighting to resist the one thing every Sandarian wanted. And he wanted her very much, but not at the price he'd have to pay. The price they would all have to pay.

"That woman…" Ian said, not sure where he was going with this. "Let's just say, we don't get along."

"We had the portal moved," Rucon said, changing the subject. "The villa is destroyed. Crews are setting up now to clear the area and start rebuilding."

"Thank you."

"We've put a near ground cloak up so it will look normal on Earth's satellites. Your team has been back to check the other bases. Your SAs are still here. I didn't want to chance it until we get a handle on the Torogs."

"And?"

"And," Rucon said, "no trace of them. I've added security to the mines, and your team's placed DNA sensors by your bases and random places around the globe. If any of the Torogs are still on Earth, we should know about it. So far, nothing." His father hesitated. "Ria checked in with the mine's supervisors. They have no idea anything is out of the ordinary, so I've not reported this to anyone."

The thought of those *crags* getting away with this made him furious, but he saw the logic. The fewer waves they made, the better chance they stood of not attracting the attention of the council, or worse, the Emperor.

"Are you still convinced they were after the Standich woman?" Rucon asked.

"Her name is Dani." *Shit. Where did that come from?* "If I had any doubts before, they'd be gone now. They tried to abduct her in Bellagio, and they were hell-bent on capturing or killing her on the Island."

"Maybe," Rucon said.

"What are you thinking?"

"I don't know about Bellagio, but as far as Cat Island goes, they may have wanted their device back. They weren't exactly trying to keep you alive there, son."

"You could be right."

"The EPs have been rotating shifts on Earth," Rucon said. "I've agreed to let your support agents stay for a few days. I imagine seeing another planet must be an extraordinary experience. They deserve it."

"That's fine." Ian rubbed his stiff neck.

"Armond has been working with the mystery box. He's made some progress, but I'll let him give you a full report." Rucon crossed his arms. "Your team has been instructed to keep both the device and Miss Standich's abilities quiet."

"Agreed," Ian said.

Chapter 10

Dani burst into her room and slammed the door behind her.

Koora jumped and dropped the blanket she'd been folding. "M'lady! But…" She glanced at the bed, which appeared to be occupied. "I thought you were still sleeping?"

"Yeah, well, I got tired of that so I took a walk. Right now I need a shower. And clothes. And I'd like to see my friends. Can you manage all that?" She'd never been so angry in her life.

Koora sputtered, taken aback. "I—yes—of course, m'lady." She bowed three times and scurried from the room.

Dani peeled off the pajamas and climbed into an oval-shaped shower. The floor was soft and springy. After some fiddling with the controls, she managed to get a strong, hot stream going. She closed her eyes and let the water pummel her skin. Why was he doing this? She resisted the urge to cry. There'd been enough tears already. She figured anger was better and pounded the spongy wall a few times. She was on another planet. Aliens wanted to kill her back on Earth. She had some weird psi connection with a man, strike that, with an alien who hated her. *The jerk didn't even say thank you for saving his life.* She punched the wall a few more times. It helped. *I can handle this.*

Emerging from the shower, she wrapped herself in a towel and found fresh clothes laid out on the made bed. On the floor were new leather boots. *Sweet.* She got dressed quickly and sat on the bed to put the boots on. That done, she glanced at the curtains. *Finally.* She took a step toward the window when there was a knock at the door. *Are you kidding?* The urge to rip the curtains open nearly won. "Come in," she said.

A tall, thin, olive-skinned woman with long, jet black hair entered. Her red silk blouse and black, form-fitting pants made a striking figure. Behind her came Ian's father, dressed all in black and a long cape. Dani's heart pounded, ready for an assault until she took a closer look. It wasn't him. For one, he stood taller, possibly as tall as Ian. For another, his hair was darker and straight, whereas Ian and his father had unruly waves. And unless she was mistaken, this man was older. The face, however, was totally Ian's dad.

"Ms. Standich, I am Lady Mara Cavacent, Ian's mother." The woman held out her hand.

Unlike her husband and son, she didn't appear to be angry. Dani wasn't sure what to do with the Lady's outstretched hand. Kiss it? Shake it? She reached out and shook it firmly. *If you're gonna be wrong, do it like you mean it.* "Nice to meet you, Mrs. Cavacent."

"Please, call me Mara."

"Only if you'll call me Dani."

Mara smiled and Dani's heart constricted. Clearly Ian got his smile and olive skin from her.

"All right, Dani."

An image of herself and Ian in bed with Rucon towering over them flashed across her mind. *Doesn't matter, nothing happened.* Well, something happened. Either way, the whole thing was embarrassing.

Mara smiled and stepped forward. "My husband and son have neglected to thank you. You saved Ian's life. More than once, from what I'm told. I will not forget that."

He has her eyes too. "Thank you. I don't... I don't know why I..." Dani looked away, feeling her face heat. "I just somehow knew I had to go to him."

Mara surprised her by embracing her in a firm hug. "It was your psi, darling. If you hadn't listened... Well, enough of that." She turned to the man behind her. "This is Mordo, Ian's uncle, and my husband's brother," Mara said.

A twinge of recognition flicked over her.

"I believe we've already met. In a manner of speaking." The man smiled and approached, hand extended.

"I'm sorry, I feel I know you but..." Dani shook his hand.

"I helped you and Ian escape." His familiar voice whispered in her head and a wispy blue light seemed to flicker and was gone. Dani tried to stay focused. "When Ian moved the portal. You're the one who helped us."

Mordo's smile broadened.

"Can you all do this?" Dani asked. "Talk in my head?"

"No dear," Mara said. "Only a few exceptionally powerful psi can. Unless, of course, you're bonded. Psi-mates can do it too. You have a lot to learn, don't you?" Mara motioned to the couch. "Please, come sit down."

Dani took a seat next to Mara on the settee. Mordo pulled up a chair to face Dani. Mara and Mordo exchanged a glance before Mara patted her hand. "Mordo would like to take a look at you, dear."

"Or more precisely, at your psi," Mordo said. "With your permission, of course."

Dani flashed back to when Armond had done the same thing. She hadn't known it then, but that's what he was doing. Afterward, Ian had changed. Dani struggled to make sense of it all. "All right, but you should know, this doesn't seem to go over too well with you guys."

Mara gave her hand a squeeze and sat back. "I'm sure it will be all right."

Mordo leaned forward and placed his hands on her knees. He closed his eyes and relaxed visibly, taking slow, deep breaths.

"Should I be doing something?" She whispered to Mara.

"No dear, you're fine," Mara replied.

Dani shivered. Mordo's psi was completely different than Ian's. A bizarre array of emotions flitted through her with an accompanying counterpart, affecting her psi. Joy followed by anger, a wave of wonderment followed by a devastating sensation of loss. Dani held back tears as the memory of her parents death flooded through her.

Mordo opened his eyes, a quizzical look on his face. "My apologies. The triggering of memories is…unusual. I'll try a different approach. Can you bear with me a moment longer?"

Dani chewed her lower lip and nodded. Mordo resumed his closed-eye examination. This was better. She sensed the probing of her psi, but no random memories assaulted her. Slowly, images started flooding through her mind. People she didn't know. A regal-looking man in ornate robes and a flash of hatred. A young man laughing accompanied by a flood of love, desire and longing. Mordo cleared his throat and the images stopped. Next came rage—fury at the loss of her parents and something not entirely her own. Intense anger at herself and Ian alike stabbed through her. *This isn't my anger. It's Ian's.* A force inside exploded and the couch she and Mara sat on flew back and slammed against the curtained wall behind. Mordo, in his chair, flew in the opposite direction. The chair started to flip over when he raised his arms and froze. He sat suspended a few inches off the ground.

Dani gripped the cushions of the couch. "Did I do that?"

Mordo lowered his arms and the chair righted itself and settled to the floor. With a slight waive, the couch and chair returned to their original positions. "I'm afraid so," Mordo said, straightening his cape.

Mara let out a little huff and adjusted her collar. "Well, that was interesting."

Mordo gazed at Dani, then at Mara next. *"This could get complicated..."* Mordo's voice, but it was directed at Mara and was accompanied by another blue flash. Returning to her, he spoke up. "You, my child, have extraordinary power. And because of this, you are extraordinarily dangerous. We must begin your training immediately."

Dani had been given a reprieve, but from what, she wasn't sure. The fact that she was on an alien planet with her life at the mercy of these people, struck home. "Thank you. What do you mean by train?"

"Let me ask you something first," Mordo said.

"Of course."

"Have you ever used, or even noticed, your psi before?"

"No, I don't think so." Dani thought back. "Although, maybe, in a way."

"Explain, please," Mordo said.

"I do mixed fights. For a hobby, and exercise. I'm really good. Too good. I don't train like the others, and to be honest I'm kind of a klutz. I've won more than one because I tripped and ended up doing something totally unexpected, even to me. Somehow, it almost always works out. Do you think psi has anything to do with that?"

"Most certainly." Mordo looked her up and down. "By train, we mean to teach you how to harness and control your psi." Mordo smiled at her then. "Your ability to heal is remarkable. I'd like to find out what else you can do."

"I'd like that. I'm feeling very restless right now."

"I'm sure you are," Mordo said, standing. "Like any other form of energy, psi needs an outlet or it will erupt in unpredictable ways." Mordo glanced at a timepiece around his neck. "I have a number of appointments I must attend. Shall we say nine o'clock tomorrow morning to begin your training?"

"Sure," Dani said.

"And now," Mordo said, standing and moving the chair aside. "I believe you have some guests." The door flew open and the entire Earth crew piled in. Jared led the way followed by Marco, Gina, Battista and Ria. Armond strolled in a moment later.

Dani flew to her feet.

"Dani, my girl!" Jared hugged her and squeezed so hard, she could barely breathe.

Ria pushed him out of the way and gave her own crushing hug. "Girlfriend, I thought I lost you. Don't *do* that ever again, you hear?"

Dani laughed. "You have my word."

"*Si, Si.* Dani, you scare us most to death." Gina dabbed at tears in her eyes.

Battista gave her a kiss on both cheeks.

The group surrounded her, and everyone spoke at once.

"How are you?" Marco asked.

"I'm fine. I promise."

Marco swooped in when Ria let go, and scooped her up into a bear hug and swung her around.

"Marco! Your hand. How is it?" She squirmed until he let her down, and pulled his wrist from behind her back.

"What, is that?" Dani asked.

A bulbous plastic sphere protruded from the wrist where his hand should be. "I'm growing it back, baby! You didn't think a little Torog laser treatment would stop me, did you?" He held the bulb up to her face.

Inside she could just make out appendages within some kind of liquid. They were far too short for Marco, but had plenty of room to grow. "Gotta get the bone and cartilage done first, then we start on the skin. Should be good as new in a few weeks or so," Marco said, grinning from ear to ear.

"Un-be-lievable," Dani said. "And kinda creepy too." She leaned closer, and the bony sticks waved at her, making her laugh. "This would be killer at Halloween."

Ria sidled next to her. "Did you hear, Ian's up and okay?"

"Yeah, I heard. Great news huh?" She could only hope she wasn't blushing. "Hey, what are you guys still doing here?" she asked Jared.

His face lit up. "I asked Rucon if we could stay awhile. Seemed kinda harsh to get us to an alien world then send us back without so much as a look around."

"He say yes." Gina clapped her hands. "Is so amazing here."

"Rucon is Ian's dad, right?" Dani asked.

"Yes," Jared said. "Haven't you met him yet?"

"Not exactly, no." She was pretty sure she was blushing now.

"So, Dani," Marco leaned in with mock intimacy. "We gotta know, just how strong a psi are you?"

Silence reigned. Ria punched Marco in the arm.

"Why," Mara said, rising to her feet, "would you ask such an absurd question, may I ask?"

Marco spun around. He'd clearly forgotten Mara's presence. "Your ladyship." Marco bowed low.

Mara let out a great sigh. "Marco, you know I do not like that level of formality. You EPs are like family. Now, answer the question before I have you shot."

Marco scanned the faces of the others before replying. "I sort of figured it out. Ian is strong, no question, but not that strong. Even with Mordo's help, there's no way he could have pulled that off. Dani was the only other one there."

"Armond helped too," Mordo said.

"Yeah?" Marco asked, giving Armond a sideways glance. "He didn't mention it."

"You neglected to ask," Armond said.

Ria spoke up next. "I found out when Ian asked me to help with her claustrophobia. From what I could tell she's seriously powerful."

Jared and the Papallos stared at her wide-eyed.

Mara rubbed her temples and gazed at each person in the room, in turn. "You are not to say anything of Dani's abilities to anyone. Do you understand?"

"Of course, your ladyship," Ria said. "We would never jeopardize the Cavacent family."

More was being said here than Dani understood, but before she could dig deeper Ria suggested Dani join the team for lunch. Her stomach growled a response.

"Great idea," Marco said. "You can come and watch us train afterward."

"You're gonna train on a full stomach?" Dani asked.

"Enemies don't wait for one's food to digest," Armond said as though she were a child.

Dani ignored his tone. "Good point." She looked to Mara. "Is that all right? Am I allowed to wander about?"

"Of course, dear."

"Please don't leave the Cavacent grounds," Mordo said, turning to leave. "And I'd suggest you not interact with anyone outside our little group here."

Dani nodded, knowing full well it was no suggestion.

"Come on," Ria said. "We'll show you around. Are you ready?"

"Yeah, but first," Dani said, "I really need to see what's behind the curtains."

"You haven't seen it yet?" Ria asked.

"Didn't really have time, did I? Do you mind?"

Mara turned, waved her palm, and the curtains slid away from the large window.

Dani walked over to the glass. The others gathered around. The room was elevated with a tremendous view of a city below. Nestled amongst mountains, it sparkled in beautiful yet bizarre light. "Your sky is...green. With green and purple clouds. Wow."

"Well, duh," Marco said.

Dani responded by punching his arm this time.

"Wait'll you see a storm," Ria said, stepping up next to her. "The clouds are spectacular." She leaned in closer and gave her arm a squeeze. "Your dad was right."

Dani closed her eyes and nodded. *Oh dad, if only you were here to see this.*

"Welcome to Sandaria, dear," Mara said. "The city below us is Ardos, our Capital, and home"—she pointed to a massive castle-like building in the center—"to the Emperor and Empress Sandar."

The city was traversed by an oddly reflective winding river, like liquid silver. Boats were just discernible on the surface, and she let out a small gasp when flying vehicles zipped by outside. Parks sat scattered throughout the city, all connected by trails and roads, which lead to the center.

Mara came and stood at her other side. "Beautiful isn't it?"

"Amazing."

"I remember the first time I saw it," Mara said. "I was speechless too."

"You're not from here?" Dani asked.

"Oh no, I'm from Mitah. Relatively far, even by our standards."

"But you're Sandarian, right?"

"Of course, dear."

"Do you miss your home?" Dani asked.

Mara looked out over the city. "Very much at times, but this is my home now, with Rucon. I wouldn't want to be anyplace else."

There was an odd resonance to her voice that made Dani wonder what she wasn't saying.

* * * *

As soon as they got outside the questions started. Jared and the Papallos relentlessly drilled her about psi, what it was like, and how she got it.

"I have no idea," Dani said. "But, I think maybe I've always had it. It's why I win the mixed fights and always manage to get the perfect shot with the camera. Still, something happened when Ian healed my wrist." *And when we were together.* Angry as she was at Ian's behavior, it was impossible to deny the effect he had on her.

Nearly forty minutes later they were finishing up the tour of the compound. "Mara wasn't kidding. The grounds are huge," Dani said. They traversed an outside courtyard full of flowers and manicured lawns, their boots crunching on white gravel. "Wow." Dani bent down and plucked a few blades of grass. The base, like grass on Earth was green, but halfway to the tips, they turned purple. Not a glaring purple, more a violet. On Earth, the main plant color was green, here it was purple. "Does it have anything to do with the purple and green clouds?" She asked Ria.

Ria shrugged. "I think so, but it's been a long time since I studied biology."

Armond cleared his throat. "An element exists in our atmosphere which accounts for the dominance of purple flora."

"Thank you, Armond. It's crazy beautiful," Dani said standing.

"*Si*," said Gina. "And the colors, they are so bright."

Ria bent down and picked a small, red flower off a shrub. "Wait till you see a partially cloudy day. The purple and green colors of the clouds are splashed everywhere like paint."

"Literally?" Dani asked.

Ria flicked the flower at her. "No silly. The light filters through the clouds."

Armond scoffed at her.

"Hey," she said. "I'm on an alien planet, for crying out loud. How am I supposed to know?"

Ria threw a scolding look at Armond. "You couldn't possibly know. Ask anything you want."

Jared, who had been conversing with Battista, spoke up. "We have a question. Why all the old fashioned weapons? You guys created portals and laser guns. Why spears, shields, and knives?"

Marco turned to Jared. "Before all our high tech, Sandaria had a rich tradition in all kinds of hand combat. We've kept it alive with our games and comes in handy in the field. Nothing beats a good fight with swords and shields." He danced around, pretending to ward off blow after blow.

"What are the games?" Dani asked.

Marco feigned another attack. "Like your Olympics. Only better of course. It's a mix of high and low tech. Best time ever."

"You're right," Dani said. "This place feels like a high-tech, medieval castle." *Awesome.* Clusters of buildings formed a compound joined together by courtyards and park-like areas. The sun's rays warmed her skin. *It may be an odd color, but it feels the same.* People came and went, attending to their own business. Some wore almost Victorian-era finery, while others contemporary Any-town, USA clothes. A young couple sat beneath a tree. The male laughed as he fed the woman something small and round. Dani wondered if they had grapes on Sandaria.

"How many people live here?" she asked.

"Do you mean the Cavacent grounds?" Ria said.

"Yes," Dani said.

"The population varies," Armond said in his deep, quiet voice. "Close to forty Cavacents and their direct relations live here. Their private residences are spread throughout this complex," he said, motioning with his hand. "A significant number of the staff live here as well, although plenty commute from nearby towns. Like Ian, many are away for weeks or months at a time, so the population varies. I'd say between two and three hundred."

"The compound can accommodate hundreds more, however," Ria said. "During the Games, this place is a mad house."

"I bet." Dani's stomach rumbled. "So, I've had some of your vegetable soup, what else you got to eat here?"

"Given our biological similarities, you'll find our food to be similar as well," Armond said.

Ria nodded. "Plus, as long as you're in the Cavacent's domain, you can get pretty much any Earth food you want. Mara's always been a big fan of the stuff. Come on, we'll show you where we eat."

* * * *

The main dining hall of the Cavacent compound offered both cafeteria style and sit-down dining options. Rather than one large space, the facility was divided into six separate dining rooms. The EPs led Dani through the main entrance, past the cafeteria line, and into a smaller room. Once seated, waiters descended with the day's drink and food options. Dani opted for the Sandarian equivalent of a veggie wrap. Aside from the fact the vegetables were more on the neon side of the color spectrum, and the hummus stuff was kinda purple, the wrap tasted very much like the ones from home. After lunch, the EPs led her to the training arena. A one-story building, it seemed to go on for blocks.

Dani recognized Mordo standing just outside the entrance. His dark hair brushed the collar of his calf-length cape.

"Enjoy your tour?" he asked when they approached.

"The compound is amazing. I've no doubt I'll be getting lost on a regular basis," Dani replied.

"You'll meet me here tomorrow morning," Mordo said.

"Sounds good."

Ria held the door and they filed in.

Dani caught her breath as she took in the surroundings.

"What is this?" Gina's hands came to her face as she took in the sight. The arena could easily hold three or four football fields. They walked down a short, gray hall to a railing that ran the length of the place. The field was a good twenty feet below ground level, and the ceiling four or five stories tall.

"Ha, it's a Tardis right? Bigger on the inside?" Dani said, looking at the ceiling.

"A what?" Ria asked.

"Dr. Who?"

Ria shook her head.

"I'll introduce you when we get back to Earth," Dani said. "How is this not visible outside?"

"A simple bending of light," Mordo said. "I believe your scientists on Earth are getting close to having the same technology."

"The effect is cosmetic," Ria added. "It's hard to make such a behemoth building look good, so we just make them go away."

Gina turned to Mordo. "How do you keep birds and your flying cars from crashing into it?"

Mordo nodded. "Good question. It emits a sound that's audible to avian creatures. Our cruisers, of course, can detect its presence. Anything that flies is equipped to detect cloaked structures."

"Assuming they're transmitting," Marco said.

"Yeah," Ria winced. "There've been a few spectacular accidents caused by the transmitters not functioning. Entire flocks and a few cruisers. Pretty ugly. Hasn't happened in a long time."

Dani pictured a flock of geese smashing into the dome above. To the left and right of where they stood were stairways. The right led down to the arena floor, and the left up to what appeared to be a large viewing area. The rooms were spread out in intervals all the way around the arena.

"We'll see ya in an hour or so," Ria said, as she and the other EPs headed for the stairs. "Depends on how Ian is feeling today."

Mordo led the humans up the other flight of stairs to a glass enclosed room, large enough to seat a hundred or more. Comfortable looking chairs sat configured like a movie theater. They sat closest to the window and waited.

Ian entered from the far side and the EPs gathered around him.

"Shouldn't he be resting or something?" Dani asked.

"Do *you* feel like resting?" Mordo responded.

Dani thought about it. "Not even close. I'm almost fidgety."

"It's the psi. It generates a great deal of energy. We'll put you to work tomorrow."

The lights dimmed throughout the arena and the empty space morphed into a lush terrain with massive trees and grassy hills. Clusters of foliage provided ample opportunity for cover and ambush. The sim arena was like Ria's practice room, only on a massive scale. The sound of a waterfall in the distance and multitudes of birds created a constant background noise. The arena was alive with creatures of all shapes and sizes, none of which Dani had ever seen before. The trees were full of three-legged spider-like creatures that gave her the creeps.

"Not wasting any time today," Mordo said.

Ian moved with a natural grace, but his fists clenched and unclenched as he made his way to the center. She leaned toward Mordo. "How do you fight with all those distractions?"

"How indeed," Mordo said.

"Oh, right. That's the whole point." Dani leaned forward with elbows on knees, and waited. She couldn't help but follow Ian's movements. A knot tightened in her stomach as she recalled what it was like to run her hands over his lean muscles. She pulled her gaze away and tried to focus on what was going on below.

Ian's voice came through speakers into the room. "I hope everyone is ready for a workout."

The EPs maneuvered.

"What's the game?" Armond shouted out.

"Everyone for themselves," Ian replied, as he fired at the tree shielding Marco.

Half the trunk exploded. Marco rolled and dove under some foliage. Silence reigned as Ian kept them all on the defensive.

Damn, that man is a machine. Dani couldn't take her eyes off the action below. Ian cycled through the team members, alternating between his sim weapons and his psi. At one point he had both Marco and Ria pinned against a small cliff while simultaneously pursuing Armond. Ian had to focus on the two at the cliff, which gave Armond an advantage he wasn't going to waste. Ian grunted as Armond's laser made a direct hit to his head. Marco and Ria dropped the ten feet or so to the ground and took off in different directions. The pace was relentless, and Ian showed no sign of slowing.

Mordo leaned forward with his brows furrowed. Dani jumped as a translucent blue beam shot out in front of Mordo's face, straight into Ian's head. Direct hit.

"What are you doing?" Dani whispered.

Mordo held up a finger for her to wait. His voice rang in her head quite clearly. *"Ian, you need to pull back. Your anger is affecting your judgment."*

"Don't care, Uncle." Ian fired another shot, this time slicing into Ria's forearm.

Dani grabbed Mordo's arm.

"It's all right," he said. "The arena simulates injuries. She can feel it, but not too much. If it were a 'mortal' wound, there would be a great deal more pain, but only temporarily." Mordo turned back to Ian.

"Stop now. Go to single sim, Ian. Your team doesn't deserve this treatment," Mordo projected.

The beam or light, Dani wasn't sure how to describe it, pulsed at this command, then disappeared.

"Halt," Ian called out, breathing hard.

Marco stood up from a crouched position on the floor. "What's wrong?" His chest heaved, and sweat dripped from his face.

Ria cradled her arm. "You're in rare form today."

"So I've been told. I'm going to single mode. You three join Mordo in the box."

The EPs protested all at once.

"Now," Ian said.

Ian paced, waiting for them to clear the floor.

Dani leaned into Mordo. "Does his anger always cloud his judgment?"

"Interesting choice of words."

"They're your words. You said it to Ian just now."

Mordo's face paled. "How did you know that?"

"I saw it. A light or something. It's beautiful. Started about here." Dani pointed to the spot in the air in front of his face. "It shot out, and nailed Ian right in the head. I thought you were shooting him at first. Then I heard you talking, and his response. Not with my ears though, in my head, with my psi, I guess. Sorry, I didn't mean to eavesdrop. I don't know how to stop it."

Mordo shook his head. "Extraordinary." He spoke low so that Gina and Battista couldn't hear. "You must not speak of this, child. I will help you make the most of these abilities, but there are perhaps some which you should keep between us. If the council knew that you could overhear a psi conversation…" He paused. "It could be very dangerous for you. Don't mention it to anyone else."

The concern in his voice made her nervous. "Okay. Problem is, I don't know what's normal and what's not. I'll let you know what else turns up."

"Please do. If you're uncertain, keep it to yourself and contact me."

Dani wondered about the light. She was pretty sure it didn't happen when Ian talked to her with psi. Maybe it was part of the strange connection they had.

The EPs filed in and sat behind the rest in the second row.

Marco plopped down behind Dani. "What's up with him?"

"No kidding," Ria said, sitting next to Marco.

Ian's voice came over the speaker in a low rumble. "Sim level nine. Activate."

"Did he say nine?" Armond sat down, and placed his arms on the back of the chair in front of him.

"Well this should be entertaining," Marco said.

"And short," Ria added. "The record for level nine is twenty-two minutes. And everyone knows Ian does better with live opponents."

Forty-five minutes and six seconds later, Ian was "killed" and the lights came on. Trees, boulders, everything melted into the floor, returning the arena to bare gray walls. Everyone in the room started talking at once, and someone opened the windows, which slid up into the ceiling leaving the room open. A wave of hot, humid air blew in, then quickly dissipated. The lingering smell of damp forest presented a strange contrast to the now bare space below. Ian's team gathered around the windowsill and called down to him.

"Over forty-five minutes, Ian. You rock, boss man." Marco punched the air with his bulb-encased bony hand, and danced around. "Wait'll the academy get's a load of this."

Ria nudged Dani and explained. "The academy is where all military personnel are trained. The old record was set five or six years ago."

Ian held his weapon with one hand and pulled up his shirt to wipe sweat from his face with the other. Dani cursed his near perfect abs as he started for the stairs.

"I needed that," he called up, smiling. The smile disappeared when he saw her. "What the hell is she doing here?"

Everyone turned to Dani, confused.

"Don't look at me," she said. "He's the one that went psycho after I healed him."

"You healed him?" Armond and Ria asked at the same time.

Open mouth, insert foot. "Yeah, but I don't really know how. It just, sort of, happened."

Mordo leaned out the window. "She's watching a training session, Ian. She has much to learn."

Ian slammed his weapon into the thigh holster and stomped off toward the stairs. "My team in the conference room, one hour," he called out as he headed for the exit.

"What was that all about?" Marco asked. "Why's he so pissed at Dani? Sounds like he'd be dead without her."

Dani cleared her throat, not wanting the conversation to continue along this path. She could still see Rucon and Ian's expressions as she sat in his bed. The embarrassment still burned. Armond looked at her intently before turning to face Marco. "Perhaps we will find out what bothers him in the meeting."

Yeah, not likely. Whatever happened between us, that man doesn't want to admit, let alone talk about it.

Chapter 11

The following day, Dani made her way to breakfast alone. Mara insisted she use the Cavacent's personal dining room which was located near their living quarters. Her training with Mordo didn't start for another two hours, and at the moment she was out of sorts. *I just need food. And coffee. Please let them have coffee.* Although smaller than the main dining area, the Cavacent's private dining room was still quite large. To the right, was a wall of French doors that overlooked a patio outside. Along the back wall, to the left of a massive fireplace, a buffet beckoned. The enticing smells made her stomach growl. Along the interior wall were four smaller fireplaces, surrounded by more intimate seating areas. Lord Rucon and Lady Mara occupied one of these tables. Aside from them, the room was empty except for a single male server near the buffet.

"Dani dear, please come and join us," Mara said, wiping her lips with a white linen napkin.

Rucon ignored the two women.

Mara said something to Rucon under her breath.

He didn't appear impressed. Instead he nodded toward the chair next to Mara. "You may sit there if you must."

Like father like son. Dani bit back a smart-ass remark.

Mara scowled at her husband, then got up and showed Dani the buffet. There were eggs, bacon, smoked salmon, pancakes, and an assortment of fruits, some recognizable and some not. Crusty bread and different kinds of cheese adorned a side table. Dani resisted the urge to start shoving food into her mouth. "Is this from Earth?"

"Much of it is, yes, but we grow it here now. I have a fair-sized farm where we produce fruits and vegetables. We also raise cattle and poultry. Ian brings me the salmon. I just love the food on Earth, don't you?"

Dani laughed. "I guess. I never had anything to compare it to."

"Help yourself, then please come and join us. I'd like to get to know you better. It's not often we have humans here."

Dani glanced over to the table where Rucon sat reading a tablet of some kind, suspended in the air in front of him. "I don't want to impose."

"Nonsense." Mara addressed the server next to the table. "Dax, see that Ms. Standich gets what she needs."

"Yes m'lady."

Dani opted for the salmon with tomatoes and capers with toast. Next she pointed to some purple cubes. "What are those?" she asked Dax.

"Those are reechy. Rather like your melon on Earth."

She asked the names of a few more items, then selected one of each. "Can you make a latte?"

"Yes, madam," Dax replied and scurried off through double doors behind the buffet.

Dani returned to the table with Mara and Rucon. She didn't relish eating at the same table with Ian's father but didn't want to offend his mother. As she put her plate down, the knife slid off the side and clattered onto the wooden table top. "Sorry," she said to Rucon's glare.

Mara placed the knife next to Dani's plate. "It's all right, dear. Rucon, please be nice to our guest."

Rucon gave a curt wave through the air and the display he'd been reading, disappeared, leaving a small square lying on the table. He scooped up the device and dropped it into his chest pocket. "It's time I got to work." He stood and left the room.

Mortified, Dani watched him leave.

Mara let out a sigh. "Don't let him bother you, dear. He has a great deal on his mind right now."

"There's something about me and Cavacent men. They don't like me much."

Mara gave a sympathetic grin. "Mordo likes you."

Dani looked up from toying with her food. "One out of three isn't exactly a winning record."

Mara placed a hand over hers. "I'm afraid our lives are a bit complicated at the moment. Rucon is under a great deal of stress. Try not to take it personally." She paused, as though uncertain whether to go on. "I wanted to talk to you about yesterday morning."

Dani's cheeks burned. "Nothing happened, I swear. I curled up with him. That's all."

"You saved his life. Again. How are you feeling now?"

Dani poked at the strange fruit on her plate. "Physically, I feel amazing, like nothing ever happened. Mentally, I'm kind of a mess. Hard to concentrate. I'm sure coffee will help."

"Can you tell me how you healed him exactly? You see, healers tend to be quite unique in their methods. Healer Kane, for example, simply needs an image in her head and she can affect a person. None of the healers were able to do anything for Ian. Except you."

Gee Mara, I just had the most mind blowing psi-body orgasm imaginable. "I really don't know. When I laid down next to him, I just fell asleep." Dani was compelled to keep the bit about a psi orgasm a secret, and the relieved look on Mara's face told her it was the right thing to do.

* * * *

Dani arrived for her training a few minutes early and entered the arena to find a group practicing. A quick head count showed at least thirty people, approximately her age, both men and women. They worked in teams, using a variety of weapons as well as psi. The use of psi was obvious as bodies flew or lurched in unnatural ways. Three-dimensional spheres, squares, and triangles filled the landscape. They were all different colors and sizes and the balls moved continuously. Some of the obstacles stood over ten feet tall, while others were barely knee-high. The effect was bizarre.

Mordo came up beside her, sporting his usual black cape. "Impressive isn't it?"

"Good morning," Dani said. "Yes, impressive and a little surreal. Can I ask…why do you guys use weapons at all when you have psi?"

"Because psi has a limited range and uses up energy. A couple of hours of constant battle, and you're going to be drained. The combination of weapons and psi is most efficient."

"Makes sense," Dani said. The group finished up and left the arena.

"You ready to begin?" Mordo asked.

"Sure," Dani said.

Mordo turned and led the way to the exit.

"I thought we were training?" she asked, glancing back.

"We are, but you need to learn to walk before you can run. You see, our children are trained in psi from the day they are born. Along with eating, walking, talking, and everything else, controlling one's psi is just another aspect of growing up. With you, it's different. We're going to have to experiment a bit to see how best to proceed. We'll start in the sparring room."

Dani smirked. "Don't I feel special."

"You are dear, you are."

She followed Mordo to a small, wood-floored round room with an impressive assortment of knives, daggers, spears, and other hand-to-hand combat weapons hanging around the walls. "Nice," she said as they entered.

"Indeed," Mordo said, closing the door with the wave of a hand. "Now, take a good look around, and pay attention to the weapons and their placement."

Dani did as asked, turning three-hundred and sixty degrees as she scanned the walls. "Okay."

"Did you see any that you particularly liked?" Mordo asked.

"I like the look of the long spears over there."

"Good. I want you to try to focus your psi and remove one from the wall."

Dani frowned. "I don't know how to do that."

Mordo rubbed his chin. "You know what your psi feels like, correct?"

Dani hoped she wasn't blushing. "I guess. I've experienced it a couple of times."

"You need to find it."

After fifteen minutes of trying to "find" her psi, Dani sat frustrated in the center of the room. "I'm sorry, I don't know how to do this. Maybe I'm too old to control it."

"Nonsense. You helped move a portal and saved Ian's life. You sent furniture flying yesterday. Occupied furniture, I might add. You are far too powerful to run around without proper constraint."

Saved Ian's life. *Pfft.* Should've skipped that one. Dani's anger grew as she thought of Ian. If he'd just stayed out of the pool that day, none of this would have happened. She'd be home, going about her business in ignorant bliss. No aliens, no psi. Something tugged at her emotions, but she chose to ignore it. Her mind flashed to the morning she'd healed Ian, and the way he'd treated her. The way Rucon glared at her like so much garbage. Little human not good enough for your precious son? Her teeth clenched.

Mordo stood near and tapped his foot on the floorboards, adding to her anger.

She stood and was about to tell him to piss off when she felt it. Like a ball of water gathered in front of her in zero-g. She'd watched the others, how they moved their arms and channeled the energy.

Tap, tap, tap. The tempo of Mordo's foot increased.

Dani whipped around, lifted her hand and "grabbed" the spear with her psi. *Holy shit.* She ducked as the contents of the entire wall exploded. Daggers, knives, spears—everything flew in all directions, including theirs.

Mordo stood calm and shielded them from the oncoming barrage. Within seconds, weapons covered the floor, a few stuck in the walls.

Dani straightened up. "Oh, man. Sorry. I was only going for the spear in the middle."

"No, no, don't apologize," Mordo said, with a gleam in his eyes. "This is excellent. Precisely what we wanted. Now, tell me, what did your psi feel like?"

"Like a big ball of water, floating in front of me. I couldn't see it but I felt it somehow."

"Interesting." Mordo rubbed his chin and paced. "You see our psi is energy. It permeates our bodies, but is independent of them as well. It takes some children months to manifest that external form of psi and even longer to control it. For others, it comes naturally. Now, what did you do to find it?"

"No idea."

"Yes, you do. Think."

"Look Mordo," Dani's anger rose and the ball was back again. "Oh. I got mad," she said, feeling relieved.

"Mad at what, or who?"

"At Ian if you must know. He's a world-class jerk." Her psi swirled around her. "No offense."

"None taken. So," Mordo said, clapping his hands together, "now you know where to begin. Excellent." With that, Mordo turned to leave.

"Are we done?" Dani asked.

"I'm done. You have a mess to clean up. No cheating. Use your psi and put everything back."

"What? You saw what happened. I can't put everything back. I'll probably kill myself."

"That would be most unfortunate. Do try not to. I'll be back in an hour to see how you're doing." "Ugh." Dani turned around, surveying the damage. *Fine. I can do this. I'm certainly angry now.* She lifted her hands and reached out for one of the smaller daggers on the left. She could feel her psi, and gave it a little nudge. She had to duck as a hand full of weapons hit the wall and rebounded.

Holy crap. I really could kill myself doing this. She found the dagger a few feet away. She needed to try it with less distance, so she sat down about a foot from the dagger and took a few deep breaths. *Clearly I have to figure out how to limit the amount of psi I use. I must be using a hammer when I need tweezers.* Dani crossed her legs and placed her elbows on her knees, staring at the shining metal of the blade. *When I reached for the spear and dagger, it felt like a big ball coming out of me. So, that's my psi, and it's serious overkill.* Dani remembered Mordo speaking to Ian with his mind. She saw a field then too, about the size of a baseball. *I need a straw-sized field.* She squinted her eyes and thought of a metal straw to channel the energy through. She mentally nudged the tip of the blade.

The dagger spun in a circle a few times then stopped. *That's better.* Dani concentrated on holding the dagger's handle. She saw it move a bit, and somehow experienced the connection with the cool leather of the handle. She moved the dagger left then right, then lifted the weapon into the air and smiled.

An hour later Dani placed the last weapon on the only available hook. *Ha. Not precisely where they started, but I didn't use my hands.* Fatigue pulled at her and she wished she'd eaten more of her breakfast. She turned for the door and Mordo walked in. He surveyed the wall and his eyes brightened. "Not bad. Well done, in fact. However, the order is a tad off, wouldn't you say?"

"Well yeah, but I didn't exactly memorize where everything went," Dani said.

"You should have." Mordo raised his hand, and weapons started rearranging themselves. Within a few seconds, everything hung in its designated location.

Feeling a little less proud, she asked, "How did you do that?"

"Something akin to your photographic memory. I can access my memories like a book. I simply flip the page to where I need to be. You may not be that proficient, but I feel certain we can greatly improve your recall."

"Cool," Dani said, blinking as her head swam slightly.

"Are you all right?"

"I'm feeling a little drained, probably hungry."

"As you should be. Go get lunch. Practice whenever you can." Mordo raised his eyebrows with a knowing look. "Carefully. I'll meet you back here tomorrow."

"Sounds good, and Mordo?"

"Yes?"

"Thanks."

He nodded and left her to her thoughts.

* * * *

She closed the door to the sparring room behind her and took a moment to get her bearings. Her stomach rumbled. Not wanting to risk another run-in with Rucon, she headed for the main dining hall. Crossing an outdoor courtyard, she inhaled deeply. The increasingly familiar spicy aroma added to her sense of well being. A few minutes later, she entered the great hall. Delicious smells greeted her. Definitely some kind of meat, and something foreign and sweet. She spotted Ian and his team, sitting with the SAs, at the table they'd occupied yesterday. Her stomach tensed as their night on Como came back to her. Part of her was glad he was acting the way he was. The intensity of emotion where he was concerned made her uncomfortable. Her stomach grumbled and she prepared herself for more drama. Ria saw her first and waived her over. The look Ian gave her almost caused her to leave, but she resisted the urge. She wanted to see her friends. She put her shoulders back and strode over to the table.

Ria jumped up and gave her a hug. "How'd training go?"

"Amazing. I'm actually getting the hang of this. Of course, I did send an entire wall of weapons flying at first, but hey, gotta start somewhere, right?"

"Absolutely," Ria said. "Here, have a seat and join us."

Ian stood, placed his palms on the table and glared at Dani. "I thought you were to be dining in the Cavacent hall?" His voice sounded low and strained.

Dani crossed her arms. "I found the company this morning to be somewhat hostile. I'll be eating here from now on." She caught her breath when, for a split second, their psi touched. Desire, anger, and something else whipped through her. *He wants me as much as I do him. Why is he acting this way?*

A look of pain flashed across his face, only to be replaced by his usual, emotionless mask. He straightened up. "Good to know," he said. "I'll eat elsewhere."

Armond stood, mumbled something about needing to go, and left after Ian.

Dani let the tension in her relax. "Sorry guys. I didn't mean to ruin your lunch."

"Are you kidding?" Jared asked. "Ian isn't exactly fun to be around these days. You're much better company."

Gina handed Dani a menu and flagged down a waiter. "Here dear, you must be exhausted. You need food and something to drink."

Twenty minutes later, Dani wiped her chin with a napkin. "I can't believe I ate all that." She'd consumed a massive cheeseburger and two different Sandarian side dishes.

"I can't either," Jared said, eyeing her empty plate suspiciously.

Battista leaned toward Gina and gave her a nudge. "You're going to have to cook enough for an army with this one."

"Welcome to the world of psi." Marco gave Dani his signature wink.

"I bet you feel pretty good too, huh?" Ria said.

Dani thought about it. "I do. I was really tired when I got here, but now I feel like I could run a marathon."

"Psi does that," Ria continued. "It takes what we eat and turns it into a source of energy. That's why our armed forces carry as much food as weaponry."

"Armed forces?" Dani asked. It struck her there was a great deal she didn't know about this world.

"Yep," Ria said.

"Is that what you Earth Protectors are? Military?"

"No," Ria explained. "We were trained at the academy—"

"Except for Armond, a.k.a Mr. Ego. We don't know where he was trained," Marco said.

Ria picked at the crust of a muffin-like bread. "Yeah, well, we chose to work for the Cavacent family. If not for them, I'd still be part of the fleet."

"You mean cruising around the galaxy like interstellar cops?" Dani said.

"Yeah, pretty much." Ria laughed. "The empire has to keep the peace and maintain order."

"That's one way of putting it," Marco said, giving Ria an odd look.

"It is what it is." Ria turned to Dani. "I love that saying. I'm going to spread it all over Sandaria. And don't mind Marco. Our politics are complicated."

"*Cragshit* is what they are. Crumbling *cragshit.*" Marco's dark eyes flashed with anger. "You'd think Gordat was the bloody Emperor the way he lords it around this place."

Dani had never seen Marco this serious, but before she could dig deeper, his phone beeped. When he disconnected, he was once again his smiling self. "Time for my checkup with Healer Kane." Marco waved his bulbous hand and stood to go. "I'll check you guys later."

"Remember," Ria called after him, "Ian wants us in the conference room at four."

"Got it," he called, halfway to the door.

Jared tossed his napkin onto the table and leaned back. "I talked to Ian this morning. The Papallos and I are heading home tomorrow. He said you're staying here for more training. You good with that?"

Dani nodded. "I'm good. I have a lot to learn still. This stuff is pretty amazing. Oh, and I'm on an alien planet that I've yet to see much of, so yeah, I'm good."

They spent another ten minutes discussing Sandaria before Jared and the Papallo's excused themselves to do some exploring. Jared asked if Dani wanted to join them, but Ria had other plans.

"Sorry, but she's coming with me." Ria gave her an apologetic shrug. "I promised Mordo I'd help with your training."

"Ah. All right guys, rain check."

Chapter 12

Dani walked with Ria out into the bright sunny day. Marveling at the clear green sky, she nearly knocked over an elderly lady. Catching the woman's arm before she toppled over, she apologized profusely while Ria watched and tried not to laugh.

"Thanks for the help," Dani said, once free of the older woman.

"What? I wasn't gonna let her fall. Good catch, by the way."

Back at the arena, Ria set up a corner of the massive space for their practice. Like she'd seen the day before, large and small shapes surrounded them. Some sat stationary on the ground and others hovered in mid-air. Unlike the previous day, one- and two-story obstacles dotted the landscape. The tops of the structures were connected together with various types of bridges. Some appeared solid, but others were nothing more than ropes. Zip-lining, without the zip. Red spheres the size of basketballs floated steadily around the arena as well.

"Okay." Ria punched the side of a tall rectangle positioned beside her. Its cushy surface gave way. "This is a good way to start. These obstacles will block an opponent's psi, but they're soft if you crash into them. These guys"—she pointed to the multi-storied structures—"we get to climb on. They're all connected, but some are easier to get across than others. We'll get a great workout here while you hone your skills."

"Ria, I don't know if I'm ready for this. I have to concentrate on what I'm doing. I could hurt us both."

"Don't worry. This is a protective sim-mode. You can't get hurt in here. Watch." Ria took off and climbed up the small one-story structure. She walked over to the edge and belted out a horrid rendition of Mick Jagger's "Dancing in the Street." She pranced about, flailing her arms up and down.

Dani laughed until Ria misstepped and went sideways over the edge. A piercing buzz sounded and Ria's body stopped falling, righted itself and lowered to the ground. "See? This'll be good for you. Don't worry about control, just let it flow and have some fun. Oh, and don't let the red spheres touch you."

"What happens if they touch you?"

"It hurts. Now move." Ria flicked her hand and sent the nearest ball smashing into Dani's shoulder. An electric shock zapped her arm.

"Ow," Dani laughed. "Game on." She took off after Ria, who was already halfway up the smallest structure. Without the need to concentrate and make precise movements, Dani let go. A sense of joy and power flowed through her as she recklessly blasted objects. She couldn't help but laugh when her imprecise attempts at control had unexpected results. The arena's safety functions were working overtime today. Twice, Ria was laid horizontal in the air and sent spinning like a frisbee. The second time, Dani laughed so hard she cried. The tears blurred her vision and she tripped over an orange square, tumbling head first over the edge of a two-story building.

"Stop," she cried as she came to a gentle landing on the floor. "I have to stop laughing." She wiped her face and tried to clear her eyes.

Ria peered over the edge above her, wiping her own tears. "I haven't laughed this hard or had this much fun in years. What is up with that flying disc move?" Ria stepped off the ledge and made a graceful landing next to Dani. She reached out and gave her a hand up.

Dani shook her head. "No idea. I'm trying to push you but something happens. I can feel my psi splitting. The top half pushes your torso and the bottom kind of sucks at your feet." She lifted her hands up. "Not trying to do it, I swear."

Ria nodded. "No, it's good. You'll get different results depending upon what your opponent is doing. I was using a small, targeted beam. You must be broadcasting a larger area that my psi basically sliced in half." Ria crossed her arms. "Still, I've never seen that result before. Try narrowing your psi. Should give you more control and use less energy."

Dani nodded agreement and grinned. "Probably won't be as entertaining."

Ria's suggestion helped a great deal. Forty minutes later, she spun around and dealt a psi blow to Ria's back.

"Damn girl, you are amazing. Seriously, I can't believe how much better you've gotten." Ria dodged, then blocked the next of Dani's attacks.

"Thanks. It's weird. When I started this morning, I had to focus on everything, but not now. Like when you first learn to drive. In the beginning, everything scares you, and you have to think about every move, but after a few months, you don't even realize what you're doing half the time."

"You are going to be a force." Ria signaled for a stop and they both used the time to catch their breath. Ria performed some stretches and Dani followed suit.

"Do you mind if I ask you something?" Ria said.

"Of course not. What's up?"

Ria rubbed her neck. "If I'm out of line say so, but I can't help but wonder what's up with you and Ian. You saved the man's life. What exactly, is going on?"

"I wish I knew." Dani sighed and kicked a nearby circle, sending mild shock thru her boot as it careened over a large purple square. "Stuff happened, Ria. Stuff I don't understand."

"Maybe I can help," Ria said.

"I'd like to tell you, but it would put you in an awkward position."

"What do you mean, awkward?" Ria frowned.

"He's your boss. You know, awkward." Dani stressed the last word.

"Mother Goddess. You slept with Ian?"

"Shh. Keep it down." Dani looked around frantically. "Yes, okay? Twice. Kind of."

"Twice? Mother Goddess." Ria leaned against a yellow prism.

"Please stop saying that."

"Okay, tell me what happened. I don't mean the details of course, but what do you mean, 'Twice, kind of'?"

"Well, the first time was the night in Como."

"You did it at my house?" Ria put her hands on her hips.

"Yeah. It was incredible."

"I bet it was. So, what next?"

"I don't know. The next morning Armond checked something in me. He didn't seem happy with the result. After that, Ian changed. Remember the cave? He was being a real jerk by that time."

"What did Armond do?" Ria asked.

"Nothing as far as I could tell. He took my hand and closed his eyes a few seconds, then sent me on my way."

"He tried to erase your memory."

"Of what?" Dani said. "Oh. That. Well, it didn't work. Then, something happened when we moved the portal. That was intense, because he talked to me in my head."

Ria started pacing and shook her head. "Okay, that was an extraordinary circumstance. You guys were going to die if it didn't work. Ian's strong enough to be able to communicate telepathically. Nothing unusual so far. Aside from the fact he slept with you, which seems way out of character for him. And what about the 'kind of' part? What do you mean by that?"

"The night before last, when I healed him. I went to his room. I had this overwhelming feeling that if I didn't, he'd die. Mara said it's because I have healing abilities, and knew, somehow, that I'd be able to help him. Anyway"—Dani glanced around, and lowered her voice—"I got into bed with him and basically wrapped myself around his body." The memory rippled through her psi. She had to turn away from Ria, so she studied the far wall instead. "Nothing physical happened, Ria, but something else did—with our psi. It was the most amazing pleasure I've ever had, but again, it didn't involve our bodies. Which for a human is pretty weird."

Ria stopped pacing and stared at her.

Dani decided someone needed to pace so she took up the task. "When it started, his psi was only barely attached to his body. I figured out a way to re-anchor him. It was unbelievable. Our psi wove in and out together. And then the pleasure, oh man. It just took over." Dani wrapped her arms around herself. "That's the last thing I remember. The next morning, Rucon came in and—he was so mad when he saw me. But then Ian woke up, and you should have seen him. He was enraged. You know the old saying, 'If looks could kill'?"

Ria shook her head.

Dani dropped her arms to her sides. "It's an Earth thing. 'If looks could kill, I'd be dead.' I mean, what the hell? I'd just saved his life and the sensation was so good it was scary. You'd think at least a thank you would be in order, but no. Both those guys treat me like dirt. Does any of this make sense to you?"

Ria's eyes were wide and her mouth partially open.

"What?"

"I might be wrong. I mean, what with you being human and having psi and all. That's huge enough, but now..." Ria exhaled.

"Ria, please. Now what?"

"I... It...um.... How do I explain this to a human? You have nothing like it. Okay so, you kind of know how the psi thing works right?"

"I'm learning."

"Well, there are other aspects of psi. One of the most amazing is called a psi-bond, or just bonding. It doesn't happen to everyone Dani, but everyone wants it. Probably less than fifty-percent ever find a psi-mate. You just described bonding, or at least partial bonding. With Ian. Oh, Mother Goddess."

Dani threw her an annoyed look.

Ria took up pacing again. "No wonder he's a mess. Bonding with a human. That's just not, I don't know— I mean it shouldn't be possible. Oh Mo—"

"Please, stop saying that."

"Right. Sorry. This is so unbelievable. And you're human, so there's no way this can happen, not in our society. This is bad on so many levels. And he knew it, which is why he tried to make you stop."

"Hey, he's the one that got me in bed on Como. I experienced this bond thing then, but it didn't last."

Ria shook her head. "You said he healed you in a pool, right?"

"Yeah, on Cat Island. That must have been when he figured out I had psi. The first time it happened to me."

"I'd be willing to bet you guys started bonding in the pool. Ian's been fighting it ever since. Which is crazy, but it makes sense. He'd have to fight it. But how can you?" Ria stopped pacing. "So the question is, are you or are you not fully bonded? If you were, surely you'd be together. Human or not. I think you guys are, somehow, only partially bonded. I've never heard of anyone resisting a bond before. I mean, who would want to, right? It feels incredible, doesn't it?"

"There are no words to describe how it feels. Humans don't have that level of pleasure. It's not only in your body but outside as well." Under the circumstances, the look of envy on her friend's face was comical. "You can't possibly be jealous of this bond?"

"Let's just say, I'd like to know what it feels like."

"Fair enough. Okay. So what's the big deal? I finish my training and go home. It's not like I saw much of Ian before."

Ria knitted her brows. "Can you simply walk away? Do you really want to?"

No. I don't want to. Fear shot through her. She knew what it was like to lose the people you love most in the world. She'd spent her adulthood avoiding any deep emotional connection with men. Now, here she was, bonding on some level she couldn't even understand.

"He's so angry with me. With this situation. How can I want this?"

Ria sighed. "No idea. This sucks. At least we know why he's acting the way he is. He's being a jerk to keep you away."

"Because I'm human," Dani said.

Ria chewed a thumb nail, thinking. "Try to understand. Sandaria's upper class is based on pure bloodlines. Ian marries you and it's a downward spiral for the family. Maybe even a crash and burn. He's an only child. Gordat Prayda would use this to take down Rucon. Those two hate each other. Rucon has stayed out of politics as much as anyone can, but Ian marrying a human would be devastating to the Cavacent power base." Ria lowered her voice. "A lot of people think the empire is ready to fall. And a lot of us don't want to be involved with it when it does. Until then, you play by the rules or you lose. Rucon and Ian know this better than most."

"Okay, so we don't have a problem. Ian couldn't have me if he wanted me. I'm not in the market for a relationship, and this whole bond thing can just go away."

"Bonds don't just go away, Dani. It's for life."

"What?" Ria's words echoed around her head. *Like hell. Not my life.*

* * * *

The next day Ria showed up just as Dani finished dressing. Her red hair was a welcome sight as she slid into the room and perched herself on the arm of the chair facing Dani. "How are you doing today?"

"Edgy. I need to move. I feel like a kid that's had too much sugar." Dani pulled the zipper up her boot. "This is normal right? Mordo said psi produces energy that needs to be burned off."

"It does, but not that bad. I can go a week before I start getting edgy. You've been working hard. Between training with Mordo and our practice sessions, you should be fine." Ria crossed her arms. "Maybe it has something to do with your psi being newly…newly what? I don't even know how to talk about it. Newly released? Newly discovered?"

"Newly annoying?" Dani grinned.

"Yeah, that," Ria said. "Listen, I can stay till after lunch, but then we're heading back to Earth with the SAs. There's been some Torog activity and Ian's worried about the mines. The gang is going to meet us at the dining hall. They all want to say goodbye before heading back."

The reality of being left on Sandaria while the others returned to Earth sank in. It must have showed on her face because Ria gave her a gentle punch in the arm. "Don't worry. You can reach us with this." Ria handed her a phone like the other's had. "It's called a com. I asked Ian, and he agreed you should have one. As long as the portal is active you can call. I'll come back every few days and practice with you, too."

Dani inspected the small device. "I can call Earth. How is that possible?"

Ria shook her head. "You need to ask a Portal Master."

"Guess it doesn't matter as long as I can reach you. I need to make some other calls as well. Check in with my aunt. That okay?"

"Sure."

Ria showed Dani how to use the device.

An hour and half later, Dani and Ria battled it out in their favorite rain forest sim. They were soaked to the bone, but as soon as the sim stopped, they'd be dry in minutes. Dani climbed a massive forty-foot tree and scanned for Ria. A sim-blast grazed her shoulder and she laughed as she spun around to find her on a tree opposite. "Great minds, huh?" Dani said.

"You know it, girl. Come on. I'm hungry and tired. And wet. Let's get lunch."

Dani holstered her laser. "Sounds good." She tapped into the arena's interface with her psi the way Ria taught her and waved her hand. The world morphed around them. The trees lowered the women to the ground and merged with the floor. Ten seconds later they stood near the entrance to the arena, a bit disheveled but drying fast.

"Outstanding!" An unfamiliar voice startled them.

A chill rippled down Dani's spine. Above, at the entrance level, a tall muscular man with light brown hair stood next to Rucon. His smile radiated from a face with azure blue eyes, amazingly like her own.

"Who's the hunk?" Dani whispered to Ria.

"Careful," Ria said, under her breath. "He's the youngest member of the council."

Rucon motioned for them to come up. They climbed the stairs and approached the men. *Oh my, this one easily gives Ian a run for his money.* Slightly shorter and leaner than Ian, the man had days worth of stubble on his face that gave him a decidedly ruffian look. Their eyes locked and a thrill ran through her.

The stranger took a step forward with outstretched hand. "You are have extraordinary skill," he said, as the warmth of his skin enveloped her hand. "With rather amazing eyes." His smile was genuine.

A blue cloud puffed out of Rucon and covered herself and Ria. His intent was instantly clear. They were to go along with his next words. She made a mental note about the different way he communicated.

"Council Member Balastar Alder, I would like to introduce Dani Standich and Ria Montori," Rucon said.

Balastar turned. "Ria, you are equally extraordinary." He took her hand and gave a slight bow. "But you"—he turned back to Dani—"fascinate me. Maybe it's your eyes, so much like my own." He waved his hand toward the arena. "I would match either of you against any soldier I know."

Rucon stepped forward. "That was good work, you two. I explained to Balastar that you are both new to Ian's Earth Protectorate team. Balastar heard rumors of troubles on our little blue planet and came to see how things were going. I've assured him everything is under control."

"We wouldn't want our supply of carnium to be interrupted now, would we?" Balastar asked.

"No, sir," Ria said. "I'm not sure what you heard, but everything is fine on Earth."

"Good. I'm glad to hear it. Unfortunately, I must be going. Rucon, may I have a few more minutes of your time?"

"Of course, councilman."

Balastar nodded to Ria, then Dani. He held her gaze slightly longer than comfortable, and her heart skipped a beat.

"I do hope we meet again," he said.

"Yes, sir. Um, councilman." Dani knew she'd somehow screwed up the formality.

"You may call me Balastar. The Cavacents are infamous for being informal. I wouldn't want to cause any trouble."

"Okay, Balastar. I'm sure we'll meet again."

"As am I Dani. As am I."

A delicious warmth flooded her core when he smiled at her before turning to leave.

* * * *

"What was that all about?" Dani asked Ria in a low voice as they made their way to the dining hall.

Ria walked fast, arms swinging. "We should have thought of this. That, my friend, was a near disaster. Balastar is on the council. He can't find out you're human."

"Gordat's council?"

"It's not Gordat's, but yes, one and the same." Ria pulled them to a stop and scanned their surroundings. "Dani, you need to be careful. Balastar wants you big time and although he's no fan of Gordat, he's still on the council. They can make life for the Cavacent's very difficult."

"I promise, I'll be careful with Mr. Yummy."

Ria fought a smile and lost. "Oh, girl, we are in so much trouble. I'm sure Rucon will contact us when he's done. He had no choice but to say you were an EP. It makes sense. It lets us keep you close and explains your talent to some degree. Now you have to learn to act like a native. You've got to know about Sandaria and our customs. It means"—Ria nudged her with an elbow—"you act duly impressed by a council member. And, you need to be from somewhere, complete with a history. Oh, boy. You need to avoid him at all costs, till we can get you up to speed enough to fake it."

Dani grinned. "I seriously doubt I'd have to fake anything where he's concerned." A twinge of guilt poked her in the side when she thought of Ian, but that just pissed her off. He'd made his position loud and clear.

Chapter 13

Later that day, Dani sat perched on the arm of a large couch in Rucon's library. The Cavacents and the EPs were scattered around the room. Vague memories of the day she and Ian arrived, half dead via the portal in the corner, made her uneasy. So did the fact she was now the only human on the planet.

It was impossible to be near Ian and not notice him on some level. He looked hot as ever in his usual Earth Protector attire.

She hadn't sensed anything from him. He kept his psi closed to her.

Rucon told the group about Balastar's visit and his interest in Dani.

"You said what?" Ian didn't hide his distaste for Rucon's solution.

"There was no other option," Rucon said. "I could hardly say she's human, and if she wasn't one of ours, then who was she? Unfortunately, that's not all." Rucon leaned back in his chair. "Balastar has requested a formal gathering to get to know the Earth crew better. Says he's fascinated by humans and where they are technologically."

"*Cragshit*," Ian said. "He doesn't care about Earth or its technology."

"Most likely not. I suspect he wants to get to know Dani," Ria said.

"Tell him she's not available," Marco said.

"At ease, everyone." Rucon toyed with his com. "Balastar didn't come here because of Dani. The arena was clearly the first time he'd seen her."

That got everyone's attention.

"I believe he wants to talk, but doesn't know if he can trust me. His father was a good man, but since he died, Balastar has kept to himself. If he's reaching out now, the fall of the empire may be farther along than I thought. Which may be a blessing." Rucon eyed his son, then Dani.

Rucon penetrated her with a look. In his eyes and from the brief touch of his psi, Dani sensed part of his animosity slip away. He had a complicated mix of emotions where she was concerned, none of which she understood.

Rucon took a slow, deep breath before continuing. "Ian, what's the status on the additional Earth properties?"

"Nine purchased and three under contract. All close to existing portals," Ian said.

The other EPs exchanged glances.

"What do you mean?" Dani asked.

For the second time, Rucon truly looked at her. "It means we've been quietly preparing to evacuate our families at a moment's notice."

"To Earth? Why?"

"When the empire falls—when, not if—Sandaria has the potential to be a very dangerous place. Rucon turned. "Armond, I understand you have no family on Sandaria."

"Correct, sir." The albino spoke with no emotion.

Rucon nodded and addressed Ria and Marco. "There is no guarantee, at this moment, Earth will be safe, but I'm offering my protection, as best I can provide it, to you and your families. If all goes according to plan, I will have the support of the GTO and the military to make Earth our home. If not…"

Rucon glanced to Marco then Ria. "I ask for your complete discretion, of course. We'll discuss the details later. In the meantime, everything must appear normal, so we entertain Balastar's whims. He's asked for the entire Earth Protectorate team to be present. We'll bring the SAs back on Saturday. Mara is arranging a mid-sized gathering. Enough to appease Balastar without causing friction from those not invited. Dani, we've decided our best bet is for you to be from Mitah."

Mara stood next to her husband behind the large desk. "Yes, I have a large amount of materials covering my home planet. Mitah is not significant politically and we doubt Balastar will know much about it other than perhaps the Summer's Ball in Watersedge. We've also compiled information on Sandaria and the empire."

"What about my training? Don't all your EPs have military training from some academy?"

"We considered that," Rucon said. "We decided it would be best to say we broke with tradition and took on the daughter of an old family friend. A daughter that was trained on Mitah."

Mara continued. "I'll also get you the course used by foreign dignitaries coming to Sandaria for the first time. We'll all take turns drilling you on our government and other aspects of life in the empire. I do hope you're a fast reader, dear."

"I am, thankfully."

"All right," Rucon said. "With any luck, Balastar will keep his mouth shut and we won't have to invite any other council members. If anyone asks, it's a small affair regarding Earth. Keep Dani out of sight as much as possible. And for the sake of the Goddess, Dani, do not encourage Balastar."

"I assure you I have no intention of encouraging anyone," Dani said. Okay, that wasn't entirely true. She wasn't sure what annoyed her most. That fact that he'd say such a thing or that he might be right. She resisted the urge to stick her tongue out at him.

* * * *

Dani had never studied so hard in her life, but it wasn't difficult because the material was intensely interesting. She'd focused on Mitah first: history, geography, politics, economics, social structure. She hadn't finish until well after midnight, leaving only a few hours sleep. Today, Ria was giving her a lesson on the Sandarian Empire, the council and the Galactic Trade Organization.

"Thanks for doing this Ria," Dani said, turning to sit on the couch. "I'm trying to figure out how the GTO, the council, and the Sandarian Empire all fit together. It's pretty fuzzy."

"I'm not surprised. The lines are blurred in ways they were never meant to be, and worse, the whole thing is a sham," Ria said.

"How so?"

"The book you read? About the council being formed to take a step toward what you would consider a more democratic system? That's the way it's supposed to work. The council is made up of representatives across the galaxy, providing guidance to the benevolent Emperor, working with the GTO to establish fair trade policies and guiding the military to keep the peace. But everyone knows it's *cragshit*. There's nothing benevolent about the Emperor and the council has little power."

"So, the uprising—what, ten years ago? When they formed the council, it didn't really work like the book says?"

"Not even close. The whole thing started when the previous Emperor, Korzan's father, died. Korzan came to power amidst tremendous social upheaval. The empire almost ended then. There were many who thought it was time for the monarchy to be over. It almost worked. In the end, the council was formed to govern the GTO and the deployment of the military, but the power never left the Emperor. He made sure of that. Those who opposed had a nasty habit of dying. Balastar's father is one. He was a good man but didn't know when to shut up. He openly fought against the Emperor. In a way, his death was the tipping point. No one has spoken of dissolving the empire since. At least not out loud. There are rumors of a coup. We have no way of knowing how, when, or where, but I'd be willing to bet Balastar knows something."

Great time to be finding out about aliens, just when their world is falling apart. "Your emperor sounds like a real piece of work. Are we safe here?"

"Clearly Rucon has started to doubt it. We talked to him after you left yesterday. Rucon is a merchant. He has ships. Heavily armed ships. I don't know how many, but he plans to both retain the rights to Earth and protect the planet." Ria leaned forward with a somber look. "I'll be honest, I don't know if he'd go to such extremes to protect Earth if it didn't have carnium, but it's a good thing for the people of your planet that it does."

Ria's eyes narrowed and she tilted her head to the side. "You know," she said slowly, "if it weren't for the emperor and his pureblood crap, you and Ian could be together."

"What?" Dani stood, her blood boiling. "I told you I like my relationships uncomplicated."

"I know, I'm sorry. It's just that you two are in a tough spot."

"So? It doesn't give him the right to treat me like shit." Dani held tight to her anger. It kept her balanced where Ian was concerned. She didn't want to feel sorry for him or his position.

"You're right. Change of subject."

"Fine." Dani sat back down. "What if the empire was dissolved? What happens to the armed forces?"

"No one knows for sure. The original plan was for the GTO to oversee them. They would be used solely for the protection of GTO member planets and law enforcement. These days their primary function is keeping those planets from any further rebellion. The situation is ugly. One thing is for sure. The military will have the advantage."

"So there's no other army that can face yours?"

"Our psi gives us multiple advantages. The most important is our ability to directly interface with machines. And, as you know we're physically powerful, faster than non-psi abled, and, of course, psi-mates and the more powerful individuals can communicate telepathically. It all adds up."

"Damn. Dictatorship on a galactic scale," Dani said. "So, this coup. Any idea who or how?"

Ria shrugged. "It's anyone's guess. The empire's force is enormous but there are only so many planets it can contain at once. A multi-planet rebellion could work. The loss of life would be staggering. A more likely scenario would be from within. The military, the GTO, members of the council. Any combination of these could take over, but then the question is what happens to Sandaria? Not just the emperor but the entire planet? It's a mind-blowing concept."

Ria was visibly shaken.

"The fall of an empire," Dani mused. "It all seems so...I don't know, primitive for an alien race."

"Advanced technology doesn't have much to do with how a civilization is ruled. In the end, as with any society, it comes down to power. And without the emperor, Sandaria wouldn't have much. It doesn't have anything truly outstanding from a trade perspective. Not like Earth and its carnium." Ria gave Dani a concerned look. "Everyone would want a piece of that."

A shiver ran down Dani's spine when she realized just how precarious Earth's safety was.

Chapter 14

The following Saturday night, Dani glanced at her reflection in the full length mirror. All the hours of training had transformed her from simply lean, to lean and toned. *Now, I look like a mixed fight champion.* Mara procured a stunning, floor-length gown that matched Dani's blue eyes. The left side was gathered from under her arm to the floor causing the fabric to drape in folds across her body. Long sleeves were open on top, held together with crystal buttons every four inches. The neck line plunged with the perfect amount of cleavage, enticing, not vulgar. She couldn't figure out the material, soft and flowing like silk, but more weighty, like heavy cotton.

Now this, is a party dress. Dani spun around and admired the way the material flowed.

A knock at the door in the sitting room stopped her twirling. "Come in," she called, making her way from the bedroom.

"Wow." The word echoed as both Dani and Ria spoke.

"Ria, you are stunning. The cream color makes your red hair pop. It's beautiful." Ria wore a floor length, sleeveless, silky dress. No bunching there, just a straight line that flared slightly at the floor. The design showed off her figure perfectly.

Ria smiled. "Thank you. I'm going to assume my hair popping is a good thing?"

Dani laughed. "Yes, a very good thing."

"You're stunning as well. That dress is incredible. Turn around, let me see."

"Isn't it great? Mara got it for me. I wonder if I'll be able to keep it. I just love this material. What is it? Do you know?"

Ria fingered one of the folds. "If I had to guess, I'd say it's Morvian. The planet is known for its food and fabrics. Very expensive."

"I hope she'll let me pay her for it."

Ria touched up her lipstick in the mirror. "Oh, you ready for a laugh?"

"Always."

"Ian told me to tell you to try and stay away from Balastar as much as possible."

"You're kidding, right?"

Ria shook her head. "He actually said that to me. As if you'd have a choice."

"Yeah well, if you see him, remind him there's only so much I can do without pissing him off, and I'm not supposed to do that either."

"I know, I know. I told him pretty much the same thing. I did, however, leave out the bit about how hot we think Balastar is."

"Thanks. He called twice this week trying to get together for lunch. I told him we were busy with Earth. I have to be honest Ria, I like him. He's not only hot, but I think he's okay. As in, not evil. I don't get any bad vibes or anything when we talk."

"He obviously likes you," Ria said.

"He does and he's willing to show it."

"Just be careful."

"I will."

* * * *

Dani gasped as she and Ria entered the Cavacent's private dining hall. They stopped a moment to take it all in. The space exuded plush elegance. A massive chandelier radiated soft sparkling light. Red velvet drapes covered the walls, and the dining table stood bathed in a purple table cloth. The French doors stood open to the balcony, and music played from a quartet nestled in the back corner.

True to his word, Rucon kept it small. Jared, Gina and Battista, supposedly the only humans present, were the center of attention. A small group of Sandarians pelted them with questions. Dani wanted to swap some hugs but according to their story she'd just returned from Earth so she'd have to wait. "Wow, they sure clean up well, don't they?" she said to Ria.

"Aw, Jared's got a bow tie," Ria said. "Bow ties are cool."

"Someone's been watching Dr. Who." Dani smiled at her friend.

"You were right." Ria nodded. "That is a great show. I'm almost done with the list you gave me. You're gonna have to give me some more movies and shows to watch."

"No problem." Dani waved to Jared, who raised his glass to her and Ria. It was obvious the three humans enjoyed the attention. Waiters appeared, offering delicacies and drinks. Dani opted for some bubbly stuff, and Ria, wine. Dani took a small sip and was glad to see she'd guessed right☐champagne, or at least something like it.

Dani sensed Ian before he spoke.

"Ladies." He came in behind them and stood next to Ria. "You two are stunning." He raised his glass to them. He wore a tux that fit like a glove. His psi was held in check but her stomach still did flip flops. "I hope you enjoy your evening."

Before she thought it through, Dani blurted out, "So our cover means you're going to be civil to me tonight?"

Her words hit home. He met and held her gaze for the first time since the portal move. "It does." His psi brushed over hers. It had the feel of an apology which totally confused her. "I'll see if I can work on my manners moving forward."

Dani ignored the tug on her heart. She could fall for him, she knew. *More like drown.*

Ian raised his glass again and joined the Earth support team.

Dani couldn't help but watch him go.

"What, was that?" Ria said.

"I don't know." Dani took a rather large sip of bubbly. "And I don't care."

"Uh, oh. Incoming," Ria said, under her breath.

Balastar sauntered in from the balcony with what looked like a very dry martini.

Shaken, not stirred. The photographer's eye in Dani drooled. The black suit he wore was definitely bespoke, and the subtle grin on his face could melt an ice queen.

He was safe. The attraction physical. Neat and clean.

Ria let out a slight whimper. "Why couldn't he have the hots for me?"

"Good evening, ladies."

"Councilman Alder," Ria said with a slight bow.

Dani did the same.

"Balastar, remember?" He held out his arm to Dani. "Do you mind if I steal her away awhile before dinner?"

Ria gave a shrug. "How could I possibly refuse?"

Balastar flashed his killer grin. "I suppose you couldn't."

"Indeed." Ria returned Balastar's smile. "I'll just go check on our Support Agents. See you two at dinner."

Dani took Balastar's arm, and he led her out to the balcony.

Outside a warm breeze caressed her skin. The spicy aroma Sandaria exuded wafted around her. Something was different out here, but she couldn't put her finger on it. "It's lovely tonight but…" She tilted her head and looked around.

"There's a storm coming. Another two or three hours." They reached a semi-private corner and set their drinks down on the balustrade.

Dani turned to him. Soft music spilled from the double doors, and the sound of laughter and conversation filled the evening air.

Balastar brushed her fingers. "Your eyes are extraordinary."

"Which means your eyes are extraordinary," Dani said playfully.

"And so they are. I've never met another with eyes the same color as mine."

"I haven't either. We must share some distant relative," Dani said.

"Exactly what I was thinking. Not too close, I hope." He winked at her, which stirred the butterflies in her stomach. "I think we should research that. Compare our family trees. What do you say?"

Dani kept her face neutral as she tried to find a way out of this. *Crap. Comparing family trees? Not happening.*

"There you are, I've been looking everywhere for you." Jared's voice boomed across the balcony. Dani suspected he'd been sent by Ian.

"Jared! Don't you look dapper," Dani said. Truth was, he looked a bit frumpy next to Balastar, but then who wouldn't?

"Thank you, Dani. 'Course, I know you're just being nice and all. You however, belong in one of them magazines you like so much."

Dani's heart pounded. She thought he was going to say something about her being a photographer. She smiled and squeezed his arm. Hard.

Jared reached out a hand to Balastar. "I hear you're the one responsible for this shindig. That's real nice of you. I'm Jared O'Conner, Ian's Support Agent."

The two shook hands. "Balastar Alder. A pleasure to meet you, Jared. May I call you Jared?'

"Be kinda weird if you called me Bob now, wouldn't it?"

Dani groaned, but to her surprise, Balastar laughed.

"That would be weird indeed. Dani and I were just remarking on—"

Jared leaned forward as he interrupted. "Your eyes." He looked from Dani to Balastar and back. "That's amazing, given Dani's—"

"Background? Being from Mitah and all?" Dani finished. She was getting frazzled. First Jared saves her, then seems determined to give her away.

"Exactly. Just what I was gonna say. You're from different planets," Jared said, clearing his throat. "Speaking of different planets, Balastar, how long you guys been flyin' all faster than light? I find it fascinating, you know. Do you time travel when you do that?" Jared asked.

"Only a short period of time is actually faster than light," Balastar said. "The bigger piece is bending space."

"Bending space?" Jared asked, placing his drink down and crossing his arms.

Balastar settled against the rail. "Yes, it's all very complicated and fascinating. Think of a round ball made out of sponge. You're on one side and want to travel to the other, say from Sandaria to Earth." Balastar raised his eyebrows a hint when he looked at her.

He continued, "First, you jump to FTL speed, then you squeeze the ball."

"Beg pardon?" Jared said.

Balastar pinched his finger and thumb together. "The points on opposite ends of the ball come together momentarily. You move to the other side, release the ball, and decelerate. The mechanics involved are exceedingly complicated, but that's basically what happens. I share your fascination with the subject. When I was younger, I flirted with the idea of becoming an engineer so I could more fully understand. However, by my calculations, I would still be in school right now, so I decided against it."

"I can see why. How about those portals? Now that'll blow your mind, huh?" Jared said.

Balastar smiled, enjoying himself. "Yes, another interesting topic. From what I understand, it uses a similar principal of bending space; however, it's completely powered by psi. That's why there are limits to their use. The Portal Masters that created the portal are drained a little each time the gateway is used. You get four uses per hour and no more."

"What happens if you go more than four times?" Jared asked.

"They have safeguards built in and will shut down automatically. Same thing happens if you try and exceed the weight limits. It just won't work."

Dani got sucked into the conversation as Jared picked Balastar's brain on everything alien. She was surprised when a server came to announce that dinner was ready in the main hall.

Jared rubbed his stomach. "Ah, food! It was real nice talking to you, Balastar. Hope we can chat again someday."

"As do I. Would you mind giving Dani and I a moment before dinner?"

"What? Oh, yeah sure. Sorry if I interrupted. Great talk, though. See you inside, Dani?" Jared asked.

"Be right there," she said.

"I was hoping for more time alone, but I like Jared. He reminds me of my uncle."

Dani laughed. "A bit rougher around the edges I'd bet."

"Perhaps." Balastar caressed the back of her hand.

"He's a good guy," Dani said, feeling the butterflies in her stomach. "I mean, I've only just met him, but he seems really nice."

Balastar paused, then said, "Did you enjoy the topic of conversation? The workings of FTL and portals?"

"Of course, it's fascinating stuff."

"Indeed. I thought the information would be good to have."

"Why do you say that?" Dani asked.

Balastar held out his arm to walk her inside. "Because it's something every child in the empire learns from an early age."

Oh shit, Dani thought as she looped her hand over his arm.

* * * *

Dani set aside Balastar's apparent knowledge of her secrets and tried to enjoy herself. There wasn't anything she could do about it, and truth be told, she liked the man. When they were outside earlier with Jared, she completely forgot about him being a councilman. He was just Balastar. A drop dead gorgeous man who was nice. And not just to her. He clearly liked Jared as well.

As they entered the lavishly draped dining hall, her psi constricted in an unfamiliar way. The tension in the room was palpable and Balastar's arm tightened. At the far end of the table, Rucon and Mara stood talking to a fleshy, older man, dressed in black floor-length robes. Rucon stood stiff and perfectly still. Mara spoke calmly, placing herself between the two.

"Oh *fragit*," Balastar said, pulling her to a stop.

"Fragit?" Dani whispered.

Balastar shook his head. "Have Marco give you a lesson in Sandarian swearing. He's quite good at it. 'Fragit' is like Earth's 'Damn it,' although a bit stronger."

"How do you know that?"

"Let's just say I've been studying up on it. I find your Earth movies highly entertaining."

"My Earth?"

Balastar reached up and placed a warm finger on her lips. She smelled the exotic scent of his cologne and thrilled at his touch. The butterflies in her stomach fluttered about.

"Shhh. Your secret is safe with me. Perhaps I can help with your education?" He removed his finger from her lips and drew it across his own.

The butterflies did a little happy dance.

Balastar nodded toward the stranger. "That's Councilman Gordat Prayda."

"I've heard of him," Dani said. "Ria calls him Prayda the Predator."

"I guarantee he wasn't invited," Balastar said.

A familiar pull turned Dani to find Ian staring at them. His face was a mask of stone and his psi completely blocked. She turned back to Balastar, determined not to let Ian ruin the night.

Balastar whispered into her ear. "Gordat likes pretty women. If he comes over, address him as Councilman Prayda and bow your head. Not too deeply."

"I know that," she answered. "Now."

"Good girl. He's dangerous."

Every time Balastar looked at her, she got all squishy inside. Normal attraction between two people. Nothing threatening to overwhelm her. She cleared her throat. "Some fear you may be dangerous too."

He sighed. "I know. I'll take care of it. I want you to know, you can trust me. All the Cavacents can trust me. I'm on your side."

She nodded. She did trust him. She feared the situation around them with the empire, and now Prayda, was starting to unravel, but she trusted this man.

The rest of the Earth team gathered closer. Ria quietly explained the situation to Gina and Battista. They might have been wearing formal attire, but they looked ready for a fight.

Mara instructed a servant to add another place setting to her right, away from Rucon who stood still as a statue. A very tense statue.

Councilman Prayda acted conciliatory, but it was an overly-played performance. He rubbed his pudgy hands together and glanced about the room. He nodded in their direction and Mara escorted him over.

"Everyone, I would like to you meet Councilman Gordat Prayda. He was taking a walk up the hill here and just happened to notice our gathering. Isn't that fortunate?" Mara continued with the introductions, the EPs first, then the humans.

Prayda barely acknowledged the three humans but instead turned a lecherous eye on Dani. "Very nice to meet you all." He licked his already wet lips. "Rucon's Earth team is somewhat legend. Such a wonderful and prosperous little planet." He didn't wait for a reply from anyone. "Yes, yes indeed. It's been awhile since I've enjoyed the company of this lovely woman." He patted Mara's hand, his rheumy eyes lingering too long on her chest before turning back to Dani. "When I saw the activity on your little hill here, I decided to come see if I could join your party. It's a perk we council members enjoy, isn't that right Balastar?"

"Indeed, however I had no need to crash this evening's event."

The two councilmen locked eyes, neither willing to speak. Mara jumped in to smooth the moment. "Ria and Dani are our newest Earth Protectors. They're really quite talented."

Prayda released Balastar's gaze and scanned Dani's body from head to toe and back again. "I'm sure she is."

I don't care who you are. I don't have to take this shit. "Excuse me?" Dani said.

Prayda gave a chuckle that made her skin crawl. The man's breath reeked of something foul. "I simply meant that you'd have to be talented to be selected as an EP, my dear."

Yeah right, you fat toad. "Oh look, they're bringing out soup. I hope you'll forgive us, Councilman Prayda, but I'm starving."

"Of course, dear. Of course," he said, not moving. He studied Dani's face for a long moment before he turned and took Mara's arm. "Come Mara, you must fill me in on what you've been doing these last few months." The sweaty little man led Mara to her seat and settled in next to her.

Balastar leaned close to Dani and said in a low voice. "Use caution, Dani. You must always show a council member due respect. Even a repugnant reptile like that one."

"And what of you?" Dani asked as he pulled out her chair. "Must I always show you respect?"

He paused before replying, "I'd prefer honesty over respect if you don't mind." A grin pulled at the corner of his mouth, and she couldn't help but smile. Just being in his company relaxed her. She was glad that Ian and Armond were at the other end of the table.

Balastar sat to her left and Ria took the seat on her right.

Ria repeated Balastar's warning. "Watch your temper with that councilman, Dani."

"I know, I know," Dani said. "Seriously though, he truly reeks of evil."

Ria laughed. "Well said. I don't know whether to be happy or offended that he didn't even acknowledge my presence."

"Don't worry. I'll always acknowledge you," Dani said.

"Awww. Thanks."

Before long, their end of the table had warmed to the charismatic Balastar. Jared chimed in with questions at every chance while Gina and Battista made a show of telling Dani how much they enjoyed having her on the team. Balastar winked at her while Gina rattled on.

Dani glanced at Ian who sat talking to someone she'd never seen before. He was unreadable but Armond, who sat on the other side of him, appeared hostile. The look he gave her bordered on disgust.

She flashed him her best smile. There was only so much a girl could do to keep everyone happy.

Balastar remained a perfect gentleman throughout the evening. He was an intelligent, funny man with a boyish grin. What was not to like? Those nearest him laughed constantly. Marco acted like he'd found a new best friend and waived his bulbous hand demanding more stories.

Dani nudged Ria and motioned to the other end of the table. Prayda pelted Mara with question after question. The poor woman hadn't been able to touch her food. Probably didn't want to, given the man's breath.

Ria nodded. "Rucon looks like he's about to kill the snake. What's he playing at?"

The minutes ticked by, and Rucon became increasingly agitated. Negative energy filled the room and even Balastar quieted. Rucon made it midway through the main course before losing control. He stood and slammed his palms down on the table, causing the dishes to jump.

Ignoring Rucon's display, Prayda stood, folded his napkin and placed it next to his plate. "I want to thank you all for a wonderful evening, but I am afraid I have other pressing matters to attend to." He took Mara's hand and pressed his wet lips against it.

Ew. Dani admired Mara's ability to maintain composure and not wipe the slobber off.

"It was most enlightening, as always," Prayda said, loud enough for all to hear.

Rucon stood, red-faced, frozen to the spot. Prayda nodded in his direction and left the dining hall without a glance back.

Rucon's shoulders relaxed slightly. "Ladies and gentleman, if you will excuse us for a moment. I'd like a word with my team. Continue eating, we'll be back shortly." Rucon motioned for them to follow. Dani sat and waited until Ria nearly knocked her off the chair.

Oh, right. I'm on the team. She chose to ignore the amused look on Balastar's face when she followed Ria out of the dining hall and back to Rucon's library. Once everyone was assembled, Rucon closed the doors and addressed them. "Prayda is planning something. His entire conversation with Mara was a series of veiled threats. Does anyone have any idea what he's doing?"

Armond was the only one to answer. "There's only one thing I'm aware of that he could hurt you with." He didn't say anything further. He simply looked directly at Dani.

Dani wanted to call him out, but it was probably true.

Rucon nodded. "If he knows about her, he could convince the emperor we're lying. Which we are. There's nothing we can do till he makes his move."

"With all due respect," Armond said, "having her here is too dangerous. She isn't worth the risk, your lordship."

Dani stared at the albino. *What the hell does he mean by that?*

"That," Rucon said in a low voice, "is not your call to make."

"Yes, sir." Armond said.

"Until Prayda tips his hand, we must appear to be operating as usual. And Dani, watch what you say to Balastar."

"I will, but…"

Rucon frowned. "What?"

"He knows." Dani sensed a barrage of emotions from around the room, but the look on Armond's face was truly disturbing.

"He what?" Ian said.

Dani held up her hand. "Hold on. I know you're all worried about him, but I don't think you need to. I don't get any kind of negative feelings from him. He wants to help."

"I agree," Ria said. "I don't think he's a threat. More like an ally." She looked at Rucon who nodded slowly. "Maybe it's time I have another talk with councilman Balastar Alder. For now, I want everyone on guard."

Back at the gathering, Prayda's place setting had been removed and Rucon rejoined his wife.

The rest took their seats and listened to Balastar finish a story about diplomatic negotiations with a race that had a very different view of what he politely referred to as "relations."

"They were fornicating all over the place," he said in his deep voice, careful not to let more sensitive ears overhear. "Everyone just carried on like it was nothing. Once they'd finished, and it didn't take long, they'd get up and go about their business. Truly memorable."

Listening to the story, Dani found herself watching his lips. *Maybe he can break the bond I have with Ian.* Her body involuntarily tensed. Did she want that?

Balastar was easygoing and genuine. He cared and made no secret of it. Unlike the slime Prayda, he treated everyone as equals, including the wait staff. He was one of only a few who bothered to thank them. *He's a good man.*

"Dani."

Ian's voice startled her. *"What do you want?"*

He looked at her in a brutal moment of honesty. She caught her breath as his desire for her, along with the impossibility of their being together, hit her. Dani desperately wanted, maybe needed, to ignore the way the thought made her heart ache.

The connection closed and his face slid back to a mask of indifference. *"You can't trust him."*

Dani toyed with her fork. *"Are you listening to my thoughts?"*

"No. It doesn't work that way. I'm observing. You're staring at him."

Dani turned her attention back to Balastar, who watched her now as he finished his story.

"I told you. I think we can trust him." Ian's frustration echoed through her like it was her own. That man whipped her emotions like an egg beater. She thought about his parents and all they were doing for her. They didn't have to do any of it and she didn't want to put them in any danger. But she was right about Balastar. He could be trusted, she was sure. *"It's going to be okay, Ian."*

He held her gaze a moment longer, then she could sense him no more.

The rest of the meal was uneventful and Balastar kept them laughing.

After dinner, the staff brought around dessert trays filled with stunning edible confectionaries. Brightly colored figurines and miniature flora and fauna decorated the trays. They looked more like an alien form of chess than dessert.

Dani selected a teddy bear–like creature and a purple flower. She bit into the flower and her mouth exploded with the most incredible flavors. "Wow," she mumbled, the amazing sweet melting away.

Next to her, Ria popped a winged creature into her mouth. Her eyes slid shut as she savored the flavor. "Morvian chocolate," she sighed. "The same planet the material from your dress came from. I haven't had this stuff in months." She snatched a small tree off a passing tray and bit it in half.

Once the meal was at an end and coffee served, Rucon and Mara excused themselves and wished everyone a good evening.

A few of the couples moved to the dance floor. Dani didn't recognize the music but it was something like a waltz. A breeze blew in from the open doors, and she wanted some air. And some distance from Ian.

Balastar nodded in the direction of the patio. "Care to join me? Perhaps we can squeeze in some alone time after all."

His cool blue eyes held her captive. She'd talk to him tonight, then if need be, she'd go to Rucon tomorrow and explain Balastar was on their side.

"Love to." She told Ria they were stepping out for a bit. Ria checked her watch. "Storms coming. Forty-five minutes, maybe an hour."

"Don't worry, we'll just be on the patio," Dani said.

"All right, I think I'll call it a night." Ria stood and turned to Balastar. "It was nice getting to know you tonight." She extended her hand. "You're not what we expected."

He took her hand and kissed it. "Pleasantly surprised, I hope."

"I think so," Ria said. "Time will tell."

No one missed the serious undertone of the exchange.

Balastar handed Dani her drink. "Time will tell a great number of things in the coming months."

Dani and Ria exchanged glances before Ria departed.

Outside the wind toyed with Dani's hair. The room had become quite warm and the cool breeze was delicious on her skin.

"How did you know?" She asked without preamble. She rested an elbow on the balustrade, enjoying the city view below.

Balastar leaned his back against the stone. He swirled the wine in his glass and scanned the balcony. "The first time I saw you fighting with Ria, I was mesmerized. You were absolutely captivating, but I couldn't figure out why." He took a sip of wine. "One of my abilities, Dani, is being something of an empath. I watched. I opened my psi like a sponge, and imagine my surprise to experience your amazement and glee at psi itself. Something we live with our entire lives, yet there you were—all grown up and psi was brand new to you. Amazing. Your sense of being the outsider was very strong. Given the Cavacent's relationship to Earth, it didn't take much to surmise your origin."

The wind kicked up, whipping Dani's hair across her face.

Balastar reached up and swept it off her lips. Her psi pulsed against his. So very different from Ian yet so very nice. And safe.

"I wasn't certain, of course, till tonight. All I knew for sure was you weren't Sandarian. Jared sealed it. You have a sense of belonging with him."

Dani nodded, letting it all sink in. "So, you don't so much read people as…"

"Get impressions of emotions. Feelings."

"That must come in handy," she said.

"It does, but I would ask a favor of you."

Dani tilted her head to the side.

"Aside from my mother, no one knows of this."

Dani studied Balastar's face. It was a huge risk for him to tell her. He'd asked her earlier for honesty, and she decided to take him seriously. "I will never volunteer that information, but…"

"But," he continued for her, "if you feel I am a threat to your people—Cavacents, humans, then you will do what's necessary."

"Exactly." Dani was relieved he didn't appear angry.

"I can live with that. I assure you I have no intention of working against any of you. It is intriguing, though. There are rumors of psi emergence on non-psi planets. Oddly enough, one of them is your supposed home world of Mitah."

Dani didn't know what to make of the information.

"Well, I'm glad to hear you want to help." Ian's voice made them both jump. He and Armond approached, and as usual, Armond looked like he wanted to throttle her.

"You two," Ian said, low enough not to be heard by others, "should be more careful. Unless I'm mistaken, neither of you knew we were so close."

Dani glared at Ian. That was not the way to address a councilman. "Ian—"

"No." Balastar raised a hand. "He's right. We were careless. It's just that I find this one"—he motioned to Dani—"truly captivating. I will be more cautious in future."

"Thank you, councilman, for your graciousness." Ian said. "We have a great deal at stake here. Such a slip could be deadly." Ian appeared tense, every muscle wound tight.

"Agreed," Balastar said.

"We didn't come out here to listen to a private conversation," Ian said. "My father and I would respectfully request a meeting with you, councilman."

Balastar sounded relieved. "I am of the same mind. I'll contact you in the morning and we'll set a time."

"Good. Now, I have work to do. Please, stay as long as you like."

Dani watched him leave with Armond a few steps behind, then turned back to Balastar.

He rubbed the stubble on his chin. "You have a complicated relationship with Ian."

Dani burst out laughing. Too loud. She stifled it. "You have no idea."

"I enjoyed tonight very much," he said.

"As did I. You're a funny man, Balastar."

He bowed. "I do my best. Can I see you again?"

Dani thought about Ian, about Rucon, about the crumbling empire and Gordat Prayda. Ian may desire her, and she'd be lying if she said it wasn't mutual, but the intensity scared the shit out of her.

"You should know, I don't want to cause trouble with Ian, but—" He swept an errant strand of hair behind her ear. "I will not let this go until we find out where it leads."

Pleasure and anticipation rippled through her. Nice, normal, uncomplicated attraction. "I'd like that."

"Good, I'll pick you up tomorrow morning and have you back by two."

The air around them seemed to flicker, and a blast of wind whipped Dani's dress around her ankles.

"Time to go inside," Balastar said. "The storm is coming."

Dani had the impression those words had more meaning than the obvious.

* * * *

Ian stood in his dark bedroom watching the storm rage outside. Lightening tore through the upper atmosphere. With each strike, the green and purple clouds were visible. Swirling around in a violent mix that never blended, an appropriate metaphor for him and Dani. For now.

He wore nothing but cotton pants and found a perverse pleasure from the ice cold of the marble window frame he leaned against. It helped ground him. Another flash, closer this time. *The storm is here.*

He remembered Balastar's finger on Dani's lips. It took everything he had to maintain his air of calm. Watching her with him, easy, relaxed, laughing. It should be him.

He forced his thoughts to the other problem of the night. Prayda's behavior had surpassed any previous insult. His confidence and arrogance didn't bode well. When the emperor fell, they needed to get off Sandaria quickly. And what then? Ian pondered the blue planet that would be their home, far away from the politics of this world. He closed his eyes, allowing an image of him and Dani together. She laughed like she did with Balastar tonight. He ached at the thought. But, he had to wait. Wait till they were out of reach of Prayda. *How long?* Would it be too late? Would a partial bond fade? Could he even fully bond with a human? What if she was able to bond with Balastar?

Frack. He didn't know what was possible. Ian let out a growl and downed his drink. He turned and went to pour himself another.

Chapter 15

The next day Dani stepped outside into the sun. She let the heat warm her a moment before following Balastar. She wore a blouse with shorts and strappy sandals. After weeks of standard EP gear of boots and jeans it was odd to have so much skin exposed.

Balastar also looked out of character. In Bermuda shorts and a pressed white shirt, he was ready for a cruise. She smiled at him. The man was uncomplicated and gorgeous. It was a good combination.

"What is that?" she asked, coming to his side. In front of them stood, or more accurately, hovered, a vehicle that appeared to be made of glass. "Ah, like your mega structures. It bends light."

"Yes, and then some." He opened a door for her. "Get in."

"Whoa." The interior features, such as seats and a control panel, were outlined in a faint blue light, but you could see through everything. She stepped in and moved to the far side. She sat slowly, unable to squelch the fear of falling through. The cushion held and she let out a breath of relief. Unlike the cruisers on Earth, this had soft plush seats, more like a sports car than a bench.

"It's a sightseeing pod," he said, taking the seat next to her. "Very fast and perfect for our day," he said, closing the clear hatch. "Cameras on the exterior project the view inside. We have until two. My mother is leaving at two-thirty. I want to see her off, then I have the meeting with the Cavacents."

"Where is she going?" Dani heard the sadness in his voice.

"She's from Dirkon, and has chosen to move our entire estate there. I, on the other hand, have decided to see what life on Earth is like." He looked at her with a disconcerting mix of sadness and desire.

"It must be difficult to pack up and leave like that." She placed a hand on his arm.

"It sucks, as you would say." He waved his hand and the vehicle rose into the air.

She looked around the small, perfectly clear space. *It's a bubble. We're in a fricking bubble.* "This is a little disorienting," she said, running her hands along nearly invisible seats. They had the same texture as leather. Were it not for the iridescent outlines, she wouldn't know where anything was. She glanced down to the ground beneath her feet. "I mean, logically, I know it must be safe and all. I just don't feel it in my gut. My gut thinks, sixty seconds from now when we're a hundred feet in the air, it's going to be having a panic attack for all the world to see. Not my world maybe, but a world none the less."

Balastar flashed his million dollar smile and waved a hand toward the console. "It's perfectly safe, and don't worry. If you do panic, no one will see. Except me." He winked at her. "We have a three-sixty degree view out, but no one can see in. Best to keep you out of sight."

"O—kay," Dani squeaked out the last bit when the bubble shot straight up into the air.

Balastar gave her a funny look and slowed their ascent. "Oh. Of course."

"Of course?" Dani asked.

"You don't have gravity modulators on Earth."

Dani nodded, starting to get the hang of it. "Yeah, so when we go really fast, we feel it. It's the whole inertia thing."

Balastar grinned and flicked a finger. The bubble dropped, but again, there was no sense of free fall. No sense of any movement. Except the mind expected it, like the feeling you got stepping onto an escalator that wasn't moving. You know it's not in motion, yet somehow when you hit that first step, your body wants to respond like it is.

Dani laughed. "This is really weird. If it's an antigravity field, why aren't we floating around inside here?"

"Good question. Gravity isn't totally blocked. We're in a bubble. A gravity bubble. Constant force on the inside, not the out."

"So we're in a gravity bubble, inside a bubble car. Most excellent."

Balastar guided the craft out into a gorgeous sunny morning sky.

"We can get around the entire planet in this, Dani. There's a list of places and animals I want to show you."

"This is awesome." She knew the Cavacent compound was large, but this view gave her a whole new appreciation for it. "Thank you so much for doing this," she said, locking eyes with Balastar. His eyes so much like her own—it was like looking into a mirror. Dani sighed. She wasn't sure what she was doing with Balastar. Ian was a constant background noise in her head and her heart. She reminded herself Ian freaked her out and Balastar felt normal. Safe. She returned her attention to the surroundings and soaked it all in. "God, I wish I had a camera."

"You've got your com, right?" Balastar asked.

"Yes."

"Well?"

"Of course, it's a camera too, right?"

Balastar didn't respond.

Dani laughed and reached for her com. "If you give me another 'she's the stupidest being I've ever seen' look one more time today, I'm going to have to hurt you. Not from here, remember?"

"It's charming. Here, let me show you how to use the camera."

They spent the next three hours covering the planet. Literally. With no gravity to slow them down and a serious propulsion device, they moved. Fast. Dani saw beasts and plants that blew her mind. Sandaria was a great deal like Earth in terms of air and gravity, so many forms were familiar, but the abundance of violet and the purple and green clouds made it undeniably alien. In the farming regions, Balastar pointed out massive herds of Sandarian Boorgs. They were the local version of cows, only larger, short-tailed, and maned. Most were a light brown, but some had pale white patches covering their bodies. Balastar took them down for a closer look.

Dani leaned against the side. "Are they hairy? I can't tell."

"More like fuzz. A very fine, soft fuzz."

"Temperament?"

"Totally docile. Sounds harsh I guess, but they're bred for food and hides. They have a good life till their death."

"I hope it's better than on Earth. Our meat industry is known for some pretty horrific practices."

"Sandarians are nothing if not compassionate toward animals, especially their food sources. These guys are genetically bred to die a year after reaching maturity, or earlier if they have an untreatable illness. When it's time, their brains simply stop. No pain. No violence. They drop. The farmers are alerted by chips in their bodies and harvest them immediately. Most of them."

"Most?"

"As you can see there're no fences. There are also wild animals here that need to eat as well. The farmers are tasked with feeding not only our people but balancing the local wildlife. Farming on Sandaria entails a bit more than on Earth."

Dani nodded, seeing the wisdom of the practice.

Next, he took her to the Surfran region. Mountains over sixty thousand feet high breached the stratosphere. Barren and beautiful, the peaks reminded her of Mt. Everest on Earth. Her parents had taken her to Nepal when she was twelve. She'd never forget how stunning those peaks were. An echo of that trip played in her mind, making her both happy and sad.

The pod shot up into the air, skimming the mountain side. "See over there?" Balastar pointed to what looked like a metal igloo close to the tallest peak. "It's a pressurized camp. A couple hundred hearty souls make the trek every year from the bottom to the top. Midway, they switch from hiking gear to a rugged equivalent of a space suite and spend the night at the top where decreased gravity makes for a unique experience."

They headed down to a more tropical region next with stunning waterfalls and purple lagoons. Dani's head swam and she only hoped her captured images would do justice to the incredible sights.

Balastar landed the craft in a small grassy glen. "Hungry?" he asked, setting them down.

She looked at her watch and was surprised to find it was after twelve. "Starving, actually."

The interior of the craft shifted and the bottom half became visible. Dani shook her head.

"What?" Balastar asked with a smile.

"I just keep seeing my life now like it's a movie. Science fiction, of course."

"Of course." He opened a door and pulled out a large picnic basket. The smell of something delicious filled the cabin.

Dani inhaled deeply, her stomach growling. "What is that?"

"An old family recipe. I hope you like soup," he said, opening another cabinet where a loaf of bread and a bottle of wine resided.

The butterflies in her stomach fluttered about. "Quite the spread. If it tastes half as good as it smells, we're good to go."

"Excellent. Grab a blanket from inside the door there and join me." With that, Balastar opened the hatch, grabbed the basket, bread and wine, and stepped out onto the grass.

Once Balastar opened the pod, Dani went into sensory overload. The sound of the waterfall, splashing over the cliff and into the pool below, set an undertone for the experience. The air was slightly damp and smelled of moss and something more floral.

Dani inhaled deeply and followed Balastar outside. "I hadn't realized how quiet it was in the bubble," she said, shaking out the blanket and laying it at Balastar's feet.

He placed the basket in the corner and sat down.

Dani sat next to him and peeked inside. The smell again, mixed with the glen's own aroma. "It's beautiful here."

"Stunning." He wasn't looking at their surroundings.

She met his gaze, full of intensity like charged air before a storm. "You should know, I'm not really a long term relationship kind of person."

Balastar frowned briefly and seemed to consider this. "I'm okay with that. For now. Perhaps I can change your mind."

Dani grinned. "You can try."

He leaned in and she met him halfway for a kiss. His lips were soft and the smell of his cologne mixed with the grass and plants nearby. His psi brushed against hers, but there was nothing more than a pleasant sensation. Unlike Ian, with whom she was terrified she'd lose all control, this she could handle. A pang of guilt stabbed her chest when she thought of Ian, which made her angry. She had no reason to feel guilty. Balastar broke off abruptly when his com emitted an unusual sound.

He groaned and straightened up. "Sorry, I have to take this."

"No problem." She reached over and tore off a piece of bread to quiet the rumbling in her stomach.

Whoever was on the other end did all the talking. Balastar shook his head with a look of amazement on this face. "Thank you for this. I'll go and see her safely off the planet now. I'll be in touch."

"What's happened?" Dani said.

"It's begun. The GTO is about to announce dissolution of the Sandarian Empire. We need to go. Now. My mother needs to get off planet. The Cavacents as well."

They gathered up the lunch items in silence and returned to the pod. Once inside, Balastar set their destination and turned to her. "Sorry about our picnic. Rain check?"

"Sure."

Balastar made an adjustment to the console and they shot forward with insane speed. "I'm taking you back to the compound. I'll take care of my mother and come straight back. I need to convince the Cavacents I'm on their side."

"Sounds good."

Balastar was distracted on the way back. They traveled in silence, getting there in less than twenty minutes. He landed at the main entrance and gave her a brief kiss before taking off again, the pod blinking invisible a few feet off the ground.

Dani sighed. He was a good man. A good, uncomplicated, man. So why did she have to keep reminding herself of that?

Chapter 16

Ian leaned against a small metal trailer that temporarily housed the portal on Cat Island. A recycle crew salvaged as much of the original materials from the villa as possible, but it would be another month before they would finish rebuilding. He couldn't complain. Human technology would take at least a year to rebuild. 3D printing was in its infancy on Earth. In the meantime, he lived in a large RV next to the trailer. He took a sip of his coffee and listened to the sound of the waves lapping on the beach below. He pondered the dark liquid. He liked coffee. Liked the caffeine buzz and the ritual of making and drinking the brew. The human brew. Ian cursed silently as his thoughts returned to Dani. He should be glad she was occupied with Balastar, but he wasn't. Instead, anger and jealousy flowed through him. He shouldn't blame her, but he did. At times it seemed his desire for her was matched only by his anger at her. Completely irrational. It wasn't her fault she was human and the perfect mate for him. He sighed and resisted the urge to fling his coffee to the ground.

A muttered curse preceded Armond as he emerged from the portal shed. The tall blond rubbed at his neck with an uncharacteristic display of emotion.

"No luck, I take it?" Ian said.

"Depends on how you define luck. The device appears to locate the resonant frequency of objects and blasts them with an impressive amount of directional sound waves. It's not an elegant solution for smashing in doors so I'm inclined to think it is more of a by-product of its ability to either produce or amplify psi."

"You're joking, right?"

The trailer door opened again before Armond answered and Mordo stepped out. "Excuse the interruption. I wanted to see how it's going with our mystery device."

Armond repeated his guess.

"Is that even theoretically possible?" Ian asked. "Creating psi?"

"Psi is an energy, like any other. Some Portal Masters believe that Sandarian's innate ability to use psi could someday be artificially duplicated. We know this device can generate sound waves and block an active portal. We don't know what else it can do."

Ian reached out and took the device, turning it over in his hands. "This doesn't look like Torog technology."

"Almost certainly not," Armond said. "It's perfectly suited for our physiology. I'm guessing the Torogs have only a limited understanding of it themselves."

"Any thoughts on where it came from?" Ian asked.

"None," Armond replied.

Mordo took a turn inspecting the black device. "Have you told any of the Portal Masters about this yet?"

"No." Armond hesitated. "I thought I'd leave that up to your discretion."

"Under the circumstances, I think it would be best to keep this to ourselves," Mordo said. "Are you...comfortable working with it?"

"Yes, sir," Armond said.

The exchange between Mordo and Armond hinted at a hole in Ian's knowledge regarding the two men. Mordo had been the one to recommend the albino, and although he had no complaints regarding his service, it was time to find out the whole story. Not just Armond's, but his uncle's as well. "Armond, I need you to fill me in regarding your relationship with the Portal Masters. If we're going to be based here, defending this planet, and you're the only one who can use that device, I need to know your story. All of it."

Armond glanced at Mordo who inclined his head.

"I trained with the Portal Masters for three years." Armond paused and let out a deep sigh. "It turns out my abilities are somewhat sporadic. My attempts at creating portals caused the deaths of two men. The masters decided I would not make a good fit, but found my unique skill set and insights too tempting to completely ignore. Much like our toy here, I appear to have a different kind of psi. So yes, we work together."

"How about the rest of your family? Same abilities?"

"The guild wondered the same thing. They were never able to locate my birth parents."

"Birth parents?" Ian said.

"I grew up in an orphanage."

Ian took a moment to absorb the information. "Okay. You said your abilities with portals are sporadic. Are you sure you want to work with that?" He motioned to the device his uncle held.

"I'm sure. I need to do some further testing, but it appears to have a stabilizing effect on my abilities."

"Use caution," Ian said.

"Of course."

Ian addressed Mordo. "And you, Uncle?" He'd never asked. He figured if Mordo wanted him to know, he would. But the stakes had changed, and it was time.

Mordo took a long breath. "I won't pretend I don't know what you're asking. I also trained with the Portal Masters many years ago. I found the guild to be a harsh mistress. They take their power seriously. I worried then about their sense of entitlement and decided to get out before I knew too much. I was lucky. Had I not been a Cavacent, they most likely would have prevented me from leaving. They warned me never to speak of it, and until now, I've kept my word. During my years there I developed friendships. Boys who believed, whether or not they spoke of it, as I did. One of them, Durgan Serred, became a dear friend. We remain...close." Mordo wiped his brow with a cloth from his pocket.

"Durgan rose through the ranks over the years and is one of the most powerful Portal Masters. Last night he called me. A serious rift has formed within the guild. There are those hoping to expand the role of Portal Masters. They feel their importance in the universe is underappreciated and under-rewarded. I don't know what is going to happen, but we need to be extremely cautious. In the hundred-plus years of their existence, they have never divided. Times are changing, and it's not only the empire that is falling."

"Hence your desire to keep this device a secret from them," Ian said.

"Whatever this is, it may help us protect Earth." Mordo handed the black box back to Armond. "Balastar contacted your father," he said to Ian. "We're meeting with him in twenty-five minutes. I'm inclined to believe Dani and Ria. I don't think he is a threat. Councilman Prayda is another story." Mordo looked out upon the water below. "His behavior last night was too bold, even for him. Something has changed."

"I agree," Ian said.

"I think it would be best if we keep Ms. Standich out of sight," Mordo said.

Anger rose in Ian. "Balastar took her sightseeing this morning. They're in a view pod and won't be seen."

"Good," Mordo said.

"We could bring her back to Earth," Ian suggested.

"I'd rather keep her close to us until we can lock the portals," Mordo said.

"If Gordat finds out she's human"—Armond shoved the device into his pocket—"it won't matter where she is."

Ian didn't like his tone of voice, but he couldn't argue the point.

Mordo didn't comment and turned back to Ian. "How are the property acquisitions going?"

"Good. We've selected an area near Lago Como for our new compound. We're buying property and shielding a large section where we can build."

"Excellent." Mordo wiped his brow again. "I don't see how you put up with this humidity."

"You get used to it," Ian said.

Mordo checked his watch. "Twenty minutes. Why don't you come back home with me now. I'd like to talk to your father before Balastar arrives."

"Sure." Ian took a last drink of his coffee and set the mug down.

"If you don't mind," Armond said to Ian, "there's something I need to take care of on Sandaria."

"No problem," Ian said. "Come with us. We'll still have two ports left for the hour."

* * * *

Dani waived goodbye to Balastar and turned around to go find Ria or Ian when she plowed into Armond.

"Sorry," Dani said. "I wasn't paying attention."

"Do you ever?"

She shifted her weight. "What are you doing here? I thought you returned to Earth."

"Change of plans. Are you busy?" Armond asked. "I'd like to see what you've learned. Ria says you're quite extraordinary."

"I think I should find Ian first, Balastar just got word about the empire and—"

"It can wait."

"But—"

"Ian is prepping for a meeting with your Balastar, and evacuations are well underway. Go change and meet me in the arena."

It sounded as though everything was under control. She didn't like the tone of his voice, but if it helped them get along better, she was game. Besides, she needed the activity. "Fine. I'll be there in five."

It took her more like ten minutes to get ready, but she found him waiting for her on the arena floor.

He didn't waste any time when she approached. "Have you run the sims yet?"

"Sure, started last week with Ria. I love the different worlds. Makes it kind of surreal."

"You need to practice on Earth. It could be useful."

Armond flicked his hand and they were standing in a mountainous terrain. The light of Earth and the heat of the sun induced a surprising nostalgia after her time on Sandaria. It was good terrain for practice, large boulders and fat pine trees dotting the landscape.

"Who are we after?" she asked.

"Each other. You have fifteen seconds. I suggest you run."

Something in his voice made her do exactly that.

* * * *

Rucon disconnected from a call just as Ian and Mordo entered his library.

"Something wrong, Father?" Ian asked.

"Unless I'm mistaken, I've just received a not-so-thinly veiled threat."

"Prayda?" Mordo asked.

"Even more disturbing than that," Rucon said getting up from his desk. He walked around and leaned against it, facing them with a puzzled look.

"Who could be worse than Prayda? Surely not Emperor Korzan?"

Rucon shook his head. "The guild. That was the head Portal Master."

"Might I hazard a guess as to why he called?" Mordo asked.

"What do you know?" Rucon asked.

Mordo crossed his arms. "Was it to do with Armond?"

"Yes. It was an odd conversation. In short, they want him back. I pointed out that although he's taken an oath to protect this family, he is, at the end, a free man. They wanted me to send him to the headquarters and implied that it would be a one way trip. I'm fairly certain there was a threat in there for us as well. What's going on, Mordo?"

"I got word last night from my old friend, Durgan. There is a serious divide in the guild. Between the empire and the Portal Masters, order is crumbling all around."

Rucon looked around his plush library and sighed. "I'll send word. All families coming with us will board my ships tonight after dark. We leave first thing tomorrow."

"I take it you heard?" Balastar said from the doorway. "Sorry, I'm a few minutes early. Samuel said you were expecting me and to come on in."

"Yes, come in." Rucon stood to shake hands.

Ian and Mordo greeted the councilman and they took seats around the fireplace.

Balastar didn't waist time. "I assume your accelerated move schedule is due to the emperor being dethroned?"

Rucon began to respond when his com let three loud beeps. "One moment." He answered the device with a curt "Rucon." He listened for a few moments. "Thank you, my friend. We'll see to the details after I get everyone to Earth. You should know, there is trouble in the guild. I suspect you'll be hearing from them before long. I'll contact you when we're safe. Good luck." He turned to Balastar. "I've heard now. That was Admiral Macon. The military and GTO are moving forward with a coalition. Effective immediately, the emperor's authority is no longer recognized. The Cavacents have also been granted planetary rulership over Earth. You must have some good sources to hear before me," he told Balastar.

"Mine is on the GTO side. Old family friend. He knew my father and welcomes this day. I hadn't heard about your confirmation for Earth. That's great news. Congratulations."

"Thank you. Now what's on your mind?"

Balastar paused. "My father had a great deal of respect for you, Rucon. I want you to know that I do as well. I'd like to join forces. My mother is on her way to her home world. I would like to go with you to Earth. You'll have my full loyalty, of course."

"We'd be happy to have you, son. Mind if I ask why Earth?" Rucon said.

"Two reasons. One, as I'm sure you're aware is Dani Standich."

The increasingly familiar turmoil raged through Ian at the mention of her name, but he managed to remain still.

"The other," Balastar continued, "is a desire to enter the shipping business. My father was a tremendous statesman and managed our family's fortunes as best he could. I'm afraid I have no desire to follow in his footsteps. Now that the council is no longer relevant, it seems a good time to make a change. I've already purchased a modest transport ship. I was hoping I could learn the business from the best."

Rucon laughed. "You have the personality for a trader. I'd be honored."

The two men shook hands.

"Now," Rucon said, "what else needs to be moved on your end?"

"I've got—"

Help!

It was Dani's voice, broadcast louder than anything Ian had ever heard. "What the hell?"

The others heard it too, but Ian was in her head, like the Torog attack on Como. She was terrified. She was in the arena and Armond was going to kill her.

"The arena, now!"

*   *   *   *

It didn't take long for Dani to figure out that Armond was serious. At first she thought he was just testing her limits, but the burn on her left thigh said otherwise. A reflex move took her just far enough to survive.

"Armond! What are you doing?" Dani called out before rolling away. She ran a few paces up the hill.

"You're a problem, Dani Standich. I'm simply providing the best solution. Nothing personal," Armond called back. The spot she'd occupied a moment before exploded into a mass of leaves and dirt.

"Why, are you doing this?" Dani sprinted away, favoring her left leg.

"Because you're poison to the Cavacent family. Ian is tied to you in an unfortunate manner and Rucon, for reasons I can't fathom, would risk his life and fortunes to protect you. He may feel honor bound, but I am not so affected. Your death will free the family I'm sworn to protect."

The trees overhead disintegrated. She covered her head as debris rained down on her.

"What are you talking about?" *Shit. I can't keep this up.* "Help!" She didn't know who she was calling, but she wasn't going to last much longer. Almost instantly, images of her and Ian flashed in her mind. Together on Como, the glow in his eyes. She pressed against her temples, willing it to stop. "Armond, I didn't know what was happening with Ian—what it meant. He didn't tell me."

"You lie. I've been watching. You're tormenting Ian, weakening him, little by little until he gives in to you."

"Like hell, you've got it all wrong." Dani's anger flared and she moved behind a new group of boulders. Sweat poured down her face, stinging her eyes.

"And Balastar," Armond called out, moving. "Are you trying to make Ian jealous?"

"Hell, no." Dani realized she'd stayed motionless too long when Armond's psi gripped her waist and flung her through the air. She slammed into a tree, her head, shoulder, and back exploding in pain. *"Help!"* Dani's psi pulsed with her cry. She didn't know what it meant and had no time to figure it out. She scraped across the rough bark and fell to the ground. Armond lost his grip as soon as she landed. *Get up, get up.* Dani ignored the pain assaulting her body and half crawled, half slid down a slope. She aimed for a large mass of boulders, hoping for a place to hide.

"Come now, Dani. No sense drawing this out." His voice echoed in the desert landscape.

She slid behind a large rock and tried to calm her breathing. "Armond, when we get back to Earth, I'll leave Cat Island and never see Ian again. The Cavacents will be safe. Please don't do this." She bolted to the left. The rocks where she'd been a moment ago rattled and moved. He used his psi to find her.

"Not good enough, Dani. As long as you live, he'll be connected to you," Armond said.

He's playing with me. The bastard could end the sim anytime. "You can't be sure of that. I'm human. It's probably different." Dani moved left again and tripped over a rock. *Shit.*

That was all he needed. He had her pinned tight. No matter how hard she tried she couldn't focus her own psi. Her head pounded. She couldn't concentrate. And there were voices, too many voices.

He lifted her with his psi and brought her closer to where he stood until he stared into her eyes.

He's going to kill me! An odd pulse of psi had her head banging. The voices got louder. Ian, Rucon…screaming at her. Balastar? She tried to look around to see if they were there, but Armond had her immobilized. Another onslaught of images, memories of her and Ian ricocheted around her head.

"Say goodbye, Dani," Armond said, raising his laser.

Ian's voice tore through her fog. *"Tell him 'sleeping beauty.' Now."*

"Sleeping beauty," Dani said. Each word sent a searing pain through her head.

"What?" Armond asked.

"Sleeping beauty," Dani said it louder. And then she heard the voices, for real this time.

Armond swore under his breath, but he didn't fire.

Bet you're sorry you played with me now, aren't you? Dani wanted to smash his pretty albino face in.

"You heard the code, put her down," Rucon's voice boomed through the arena.

Footsteps from different directions echoed around her head.

"Kill the sim, Armond. Now," Ian called out.

The boulders and trees melted away.

Armond set her down none too gently.

More footsteps and Dani blinked in disbelief. Rucon and Ian weren't alone. Mordo, Marco, Ria, and Balastar were all there as well. Mara stepped out from behind Rucon. They all had their weapons and psi focused on Armond. Ria and Balastar hurried to Dani's side.

"How did you all know?" Dani asked.

"Are you kidding?" Ria asked. "Girl, when you broadcast, it's like a Ternian Zook."

"A what?"

"Remind me to show you a vid. They're pretty amazing. And loud. Really loud. It's so cool you can do that. Yet another super power. What's next?" Ria placed her hands on Dani's shoulder and leg and closed her eyes. "Hold still a minute."

Ria's psi poured over her like a soothing compress, rippling inside her body. Images of damaged tissue and broken bones flashed in her mind.

Ria opened her eyes and addressed Rucon. "She's got a couple of broken ribs, a small fracture in her skull and a nasty burn on her leg. Nothing we can't take care of. This will hold her for now." She turned to Armond. "What in Goddess' name were you doing, you arrogant, pompous ass?"

Armond ignored her and addressed Rucon. "With all due respect, I was taking care of the most imminent threat to the Cavacent family."

Everyone spoke at once.

"Killing her isn't going to solve anything," Ria said.

"She can't be the only human with psi," Marco added.

"It's not your place to make decisions for this clan," Rucon said.

Armond showed no trace of emotion. "It is my belief that your judgment has become clouded. You cannot harm the human because of the connection that has begun between her and your son. I can take care of this for you now." Armond took a step toward Dani and everyone reacted. Balastar and Ria stepped in front of Dani and the others raised their weapons.

"Stop," Rucon barked. "Attempt to exceed your authority one more time, and I will end your life, regardless of your abilities with portals. Do not make it necessary."

Mara paled, her hand covered her mouth. "What connection?" She asked it quietly at first, then shouted it. "What connection?"

Dani had never heard her raise her voice, but she had a set of lungs on her, that was for sure.

"Your son is bonding with a human," Armond said. "If they were to produce a child and the emperor were to find out—"

"The Cavacent clan would be cast out, penniless and powerless," Rucon finished for him. "You think this didn't occur to me?"

Mara turned to Ian. "Is this true?"

Ian glanced at Dani. He ran a hand through his hair and let out a breath. He smiled at her then. A full-blown smile. Something she hadn't seen since their night together. No. It was the storeroom. The memory of his voice shocked her. *You're beautiful when you're angry, luv.*

"It is true, Mother," Ian said. "But she's human. I knew the rules. I knew I couldn't let it happen. We don't even know if the bond could be completed."

Dani's breath caught, and Balastar put a hand on her shoulder.

"But that's—" Mara stammered. "You can't—I—" She spun around and stared at Rucon, fists balled at her side. "You knew," Mara said. "You knew and you let it go on. How could you do that? To your own son?"

"Enough!" Rucon said. "He has it under control. With the empire destroyed and our move to Earth, soon it won't matter. They can do what they choose."

"What?" Multiple voices said in unison.

"It's true. We just got word. Evacuation starts now."

Mara glared at him.

"I did what I thought was right," he said to her with a tight jaw.

"Right? Rucon Cavacent, you hypocrite. He needs to know. Everything. They both need to know so they can stop this farce and finish their bond."

"Like hell," Dani said. Judging by the other's reactions, she wasn't the only one confused here.

Ian approached his mother. "What are you talking about? What do I need to know?"

The look of fury Mara threw her husband made them all wince, including Rucon.

"Rules can be broken, Ian," Mara said. "And your bond can be completed. Your father knows that better than anyone. He wasn't capable of denying our bond even for a moment. You can't ignore it. You two"—she looked from Ian to Dani—"belong together."

"Excuse me?" Dani sat up straighter, biting back a groan as pain shot through her ribs. "Get me up, now." Balastar and Ria helped her to her feet.

The thought of giving in to the bond, to Ian, sent panic coursing through her. "I don't care about this psi bonding…" Dani scoured her brain for the right word and gave up. "This thing. I don't care. No one and no *thing* is going to decide my fate for me. You got that? My future. My choice."

"Wait a minute," Ian said. "What do you mean father wasn't able to deny your bond? Why would he?"

Mara relaxed her fists and stood up straight. "You all need to hear this." She looked around, making eye contact with each person there. She inhaled deeply. "Earth isn't just Dani's home. It's mine as well."

"Uh, oh," Ria mumbled.

She's human? Dani didn't bother hiding her surprise. "You're human?"

Marco startled everyone with a loud noise, something between a yell and a laugh. "You mean to tell us, he's half human?" He nodded to Ian. "Strongest psi in generations and it's because he's half human?" Marco laughed now. "That's awesome!"

"Shut up, Marco." Ria glared at him.

"Right," he said, still clearly amused.

Ian stared at his mother, her words sinking in. "Were you planning on sharing this information with me?" The tension in his body was palpable. He was completely absorbed in what she'd said. The shock and disbelief on his face quickly turned to anger. He was pissed.

Rucon took over for the distraught Mara. "I decided it would be best to keep it from you. Your mother wanted to tell you when you were old enough, but I convinced her not to. You couldn't divulge that which you didn't know."

"It would seem," Armond said, interrupting the tension between father and son, "I operated without all the facts." He appeared shaken and even paler than usual.

"Damn right, you did," Rucon said.

Armond knelt down and bowed his head at Rucon's feet. "Please accept my apology, your lordship."

Rucon eyed Armond. "Does this information change your desire to serve my family?"

Armond didn't hesitate. "No, sir. It does, however, present a new sense of urgency in getting everyone safely to Earth."

"Agreed," Rucon nodded. He looked at Balastar next. "And you councilman? Does this change your desire to align forces?"

"Not in the least," Balastar said. "If possible, it has increased my respect for you. We need to finish our meeting. There are logistics to discuss."

"Get up," Rucon told Armond.

Armond rose to his feet.

"Do I have your word you will never again act without authority?"

"Yes, your lordship."

Rucon nodded.

Armond next approached Dani who stood flanked by Balastar and Ria.

"I am glad you possess such ability. If you had fallen sooner, this would have ended very differently. For all of us."

Dani threw him her best "don't bullshit me" look. "You played with me. You could have killed me sooner."

Armond searched her face. "You are correct. Perhaps I was guided by some intuition. It's not like me to delay."

Dani waited for more, but that appeared to be it. "Is that an apology?"

"If you like," Armond said. "I now consider you one of the people I am sworn to protect. You need never fear me again." He bowed low to Dani.

"Ria,"—Ian's voice was quiet—"you and Marco take care of Dani. Armond, go find Samuel. We're coordinating the move with him. Father, Uncle, Balastar, shall we continue our meeting?" Ian was all business. No sign his life had just been rewritten.

"Back to the conference room," Rucon said.

"But—" Mara looked from Dani to Ian.

Dani shook her head. "Sorry, Mara. Like I said, my future, my choice."

Balastar searched her face. "I knew your relationship with Ian was complicated, but I didn't know how complicated."

Dani tried to suppress the feeling that her fate was already written. It scared her and pissed her off in equal measure. "Go on. I'll catch up with you later, okay?"

"Okay." He squeezed her arm and joined the Cavacents.

Marco used his psi to move Dani back to her room. Ria plumped the pillows on the couch and they laid her down in a half reclining position.

"This should keep the pressure off your ribs till I can get them sorted."

"Thanks," Dani said. The adrenaline had worn off and the pain from Armond's attack set in.

"You got this covered?" Marco asked.

"Yep," Ria replied.

"Good. I'm going to go find Armond. Rucon may be okay with this, but I'll never trust him again."

"Great. Another reason for you two to argue. Just remember, Rucon cleared him so don't go making trouble where there isn't any."

Marco grunted and gave Dani a nod before leaving.

Ria pulled up a chair and placed a hand on Dani's leg and another just below her ribs.

Dani settled in the pillows and closed her eyes. She didn't know what to think. Mara was human and Ian was half. She couldn't wrap her head around it. She let out a deep breath. *My choice.* Her mind flashed back to her mother and father. The pain of their death had never left her. Ria's psi worked its magic, sending soothing waves over her. She relaxed deeper, and without intention, found her psi connecting with Ian. It came so easily. Before she closed the connection, pleasure flooded into her. *Oh, God.* Nothing felt this good. She pulled away, slower than she would have liked and wondered if "her choice" was really only so many words.

"You okay?" Ria brought her back to the present. She'd finished and sat watching her.

Dani sat up cautiously, feeling immeasurably better. "Yeah. Much better, thanks."

"You're going to be sore for a few days. Just take it easy, all right?"

"Yeah, okay." She ran a hand through her hair. "This whole thing is such a mess."

"Which part? Armond trying to kill you, being partially bonded with Ian, or Balastar falling for you?"

Dani laughed in spite of it all. "Yes, to all of the above." She rubbed at her eyes. "Balastar took me on a picnic today. Or at least he tried. We were interrupted."

"Oh, please."

"What? It was beautiful. A secluded glen. A waterfall…" Dani replayed the day in her mind.

"You didn't." Ria searched her face.

"What?" Dani said.

"Did you?"

"No!" Dani smacked her on the arm. "We did sort of kiss, though."

"Damn girl, I haven't so much as had a date in months and you've slept with one, and been kissed by another, of the hottest men I know." Ria reached out and put a hand on her knee. "You know what this means, don't you? About you and Ian?"

"Do not go there. I meant what I said. My life, my choice."

"Okay, okay." Ria put her hands up in surrender.

"Sorry, didn't mean to snap at you. This is just so confusing. Balastar is wonderful. He's kind and really seems to care."

Ria gave her a questioning look.

"And he's funny, right?"

"Yes, he's funny. But, Ian—"

"Ian. I'll be honest, he scares me. It's too much with him. Too intense. And now, he's human? That's just crazy." Dani swung her legs off the couch. "And Mara. She thinks the whole thing with Ian is a forgone conclusion. That really freaks me out."

Ria sighed. "I don't know what to say. I'm here if you need me. I'm going to go find out what the plan is. I'll let you know when you're going home."

"Thanks." Dani gave her best friend and alien a hug, then went to get cleaned up.

* * * *

Back in Rucon's library, Ian only half listened to the others discuss the move to Earth. They'd allowed all family and any trusted friends access to the planet. Each household signed a contract relating to confidentiality and fealty to the Cavacent family. At some point, the humans would discover their existence, it was inevitable, but for now they planned to stay as low profile as possible. Low profile to hide from the humans. *His* other half. His mind reeled from the revelation. How could he not have known? And if his mother had psi as well as Dani, how many more were there?

Ian thought back to the day at the pool. If he'd known about his mother, about being half human, then…he and Dani would be together now. His gut tightened along with a pull in his psi. He should have been the one to teach her about that part of herself and about their bond.

Our bond. He allowed himself to think about her. About them being together. A weight lifted from his shoulders. Shame washed over him when he thought of the way he'd treated her. He had to make it up to her. Make her forgive him, and win her back from Balastar.

He stilled as Dani's psi washed over him. He let her. No response, just let her be. A breathtaking blast of pleasure, and then she was gone. Ian sat up straighter. This was a new game. She belonged to him.

Chapter 17

Later that night Dani surveyed her room. She'd collected a surprising number of clothes and a few souvenirs from her time on Sandaria. Her bags sat packed by the door, and they were heading home in the morning. Balastar had left to get his affairs sorted. Moving vans were taking entire households to the space port for transport to Rucon's merchant ships. Dani shook her head. How cool was that? An actual space port. It was all happening incredibly fast, as they had decided speed beat stealth. The move to Earth was on.

She sensed Ian's presence a fraction of a second before the knock at the door. An insane mix of emotions flooded through her.

"Come in." She remained standing when he entered the room, not sure what to expect.

Ian closed the door, hesitating before turning to her. "Do you have a minute?"

Dani folded her arms across her chest. Her heart pounded wildly in her chest. "Why? Figure out another way to treat me badly?"

Ian frowned. "I deserved that."

Despite herself, she buzzed with his proximity. "Yes, you did. What do you want?" She clenched her fists, trying to maintain control.

"To talk. Dani, I'm sorry about the way I've been acting. It was the only way to keep you at arm's length. I had to keep you away. To protect my family. Problem is, staying away from you is getting harder and harder. It's making me crazy and fidgety and I'm carrying around energy I can't expend."

Dani was having the same problems and now, with him just feet away, she was terrified she would lose it.

"I've been doing everything I can to keep our distance. I had no choice. I'm sorry."

"You already said that." She welcomed the anger coursing through her. It gave her control. " So, what? Now you know everything. Your mother. You. You've decided to play nice?" Her anger slipped and her heart ached as she lost herself in his eyes.

"We're moving to Earth. It won't matter there." He opened up then, his psi enveloping her. She nearly dropped to the floor with the impact of pleasure, but he caught her in his arms. The physical contact caused some weird morphing of psi as they joined.

"I'm not playing, Dani. This is real." His lips met hers, his tongue probing her mouth. The pleasure from psi was one thing, one mind-blowing fucking amazing thing, but combined with his touch, it consumed her. He wasn't holding back this time. Not like on Como. When she reached up to wrap her arms around his neck, they were already on her bed. Her body and psi were alive with staggering sensations, every cell buzzing with his energy. Her hands explored as the intensity grew. Suddenly, she was ripped by pleasure so intense, she cried out. Fear exploded. She was losing herself.

"Stop!" Dani blindly flung her body away from him, rolling over the edge of the bed and landing in a heap. "Arg." She rolled onto her ass and backed away, trying to clear her head.

Ian, still on the bed, swung his legs over and stepped toward her.

"No! Don't come any closer." Her heart pounded as she tried to regain control of her psi and the pleasure invading it. She pulled herself to standing and held out her hands. "What the hell was that?"

"We need to finish bonding. It's all right." Ian was out of breath as well.

"That was not all right. Nothing about this is all right. I think I nearly died just now." Like someone about to overdose, Dani grabbed her chest, willing her heart to slow down. She quickly buttoned up her shirt. *When did that happen?*

"Dani," Ian said, keeping his distance. "You don't understand. You belong to me. You're mine."

"I what?" Dani couldn't see straight she was so angry. How dare the arrogant bastard! Thinking he could walk in here and *own* her? "Get out. Now."

"Dani." Ian took a step forward.

"Get out!" she screamed and flung him into the wall next to the door. Her psi pulsed with pleasure at the contact, but her anger gave her control. "Get out," she said again, quietly.

Ian held his hands up in surrender. "I'm sorry."

"You. Already. Said that." Dani pointed to the door.

Ian started to say something but closed his mouth. He looked like he was barely in control. His eyes flashed green.

"Don't even think about it. Get. Out."

He turned and left her alone.

Dani spun around, her back to the door, and grabbed fists full of hair. She tried to take deep calming breaths, but she was shaking and angry as hell. And scared. What happened when they were together... Saying she felt like she'd lose herself wasn't a figurative statement. It was literal. This bond thing... She dropped her hands and managed to breathe deep. This bond wasn't something she'd come back from. Ever. And it scared the shit out of her.

* * * *

The next morning Ian stood by while loaders moved the containers into the ship's bay. All told, they were moving thirty-two households and over five hundred people to Earth. For safety sake, Rucon had ordered the Sandarians on the first two ships. They'd boarded overnight and left before the city woke. They would be docking at Earth's cloaked station in three day's time. His mother and a number of the household staff that had opted to relocate, had ported over earlier that morning. Their belongings would remain on Rucon's ships, cloaked in near Earth orbit until they were ready. Ian checked the roster. Another five to eight hours and they should have everything loaded. They planned for the EPs, his uncle, and his father to leave the planet last.

"That's the last of our belongings." Rucon approached from the rear of the hangar.

"What's going to happen to the compound?" Ian said.

"Once they realize we've gone, someone will snatch it up. Probably Prayda. If he can. There's no telling what will happen with the local power structure. He may lose everything of his own, can't say."

"So, no coming back."

Rucon shrugged. "I don't know what's going to happen now. Where's your team?"

"Armond is with Mordo in your library working on the portal. Marco is on Earth, overseeing operations there and Ria is at the compound."

"And Dani?"

Ian hesitated before answering. He'd completely screwed up last night. Saying she belonged to him was a colossal mistake. He knew better, but being with her, so close to her and no reason to fight it any longer was too much. He'd snapped. "She was with Ria this morning. I don't know about now. She knows we're leaving soon so she won't go far."

Rucon swallowed hard. "Look son, I should have told you the truth sooner."

"Yes. You should have."

"I couldn't do it, you know, all those years ago."

Ian looked at his father. He seemed to have aged in just the last few days. "Do what, father?"

"Deny the bond. When I saw Mara, that was it. I had to have her. I risked it all, but not you. You somehow fought it. Even after the portal move on Earth and her healing you. I'm amazed at your strength. And sorry I made you feel it was necessary."

Ian couldn't remember his father ever apologizing. "Thank you."

They saw the last of the Cavacent belongings lift off. The transport would offload to the starship, then return for more. Although one of his ships could have easily held all the belongings they were moving, Rucon spread it amongst the three already scheduled. His ships never stayed in orbit long and it would have aroused suspicion if one lingered. There were going to be a lot of unhappy Sandarians when they discovered their precious cargo wasn't coming and going as planned.

Ian called the ships captain and instructed him to head to Earth as soon as the transport was unloaded. The third of Rucon's ships waited its turn.

* * * *

Gordat Prayda paced in the den of his mountain side home. Two of the most powerful, known Portal Masters sat on his couch and waited for his response.

"Are you sure?"

"Quite, councilman," the taller Portal Master replied. The other pale, fragile-looking man, hadn't muttered a word.

"And why is this so important to you? Surely, you could move the guild to another planet?"

"That doesn't concern you. Suffice it to say, we are determined to stay on Sandaria and have agreed you are the best candidate to provide leadership and control over the population. That is, of course, if you are interested."

"Of course I am. It's just…well, we've all known the empire was falling apart. This just seems so soon. And what of the emperor?"

"He has been apprehended by the military and will get what he deserves."

As the words sunk in, a smile spread across Gordat's face. "The emperor isn't the only one who's going to get what he deserves when I'm running this place."

"We have no concern with your personal affairs as long as you keep them quiet. It wouldn't do to have the new leader coming across as a tyrant. You must assume the role of a pragmatic politician, willing to take control in time of crisis. We feel it would benefit you to tell the population you have our support. Tell them a committee will be formed to design a new governing body and that elections will be held once said government is defined. This should give you ample time to both achieve your personal goals and win over the favor of your population."

"My personal goals?"

"It is no secret you covet the planet Earth and have, shall we say, issues with Lord Cavacent. Publicly, we will neither support you nor oppose you."

Gordat was giddy. Earth would be his. He would see to it. "But privately?"

"There is something we can do to assist you with the downfall of Lord Cavacent."

"Yes. By all means." Gordat clasped his hands together. "What did you have in mind?"

Gordat couldn't believe his luck, but then he deserved this. He'd waited long enough. It was his turn.

* * * *

Dani sat across the table from Balastar. He held her hand in his, caressing her palm with his thumb. The intimate touch was soothing, grounded.

"Are you okay?" Dani asked.

"Five generations lived in that house. I wish I'd taken you there."

"How about your mom?"

"She's a strong woman. She'll be fine." He smiled. "She's happy to be close to her sisters again."

Dani squeezed his hand. She liked the fact that she could touch him without losing control. And yet…

"Hey, you two." Ria approached the table. "Mordo says Armond is getting close to being able to lock the portal. We should be leaving soon. You won't believe the house. It's empty. Nothing in it." She looked around the nearly deserted dining hall. Only a skeleton crew remained. "This sucks."

"Well put," Balastar said.

"Grab a seat." Dani slid out the chair next to her.

Before Ria had a chance, every com in the room went off. Staff and EPs alike checked their displays. The room was eerily silent as everyone read the emergency broadcast message.

"It's official," Ria whispered. "It's finally happened."

Dani read the message.

To all citizens of the Sandarian Empire. The Galactic Trade Organization and former Sandarian Military have formed an alliance.

Emperor Korzan Sandar is no longer recognized as a sovereign ruler and has been apprehended.

Communications between all member planets and the GTO have already begun.

Sandarian Portal Masters have appointed Councilman Gordat Prayda to serve as president during this time of change.

We urge all governments to continue commerce as usual.

All grievances regarding the emperor's rule, military actions, and membership in the GTO should be directed to the communications division of the trade organization.

More information will be forth coming. For now, we welcome you to a new galaxy.

—Sr. Director of Communications, Wallis DurMichal

"Prayda?" Dani asked. She and Balastar got to their feet. The staff in the kitchen and a few other people gathered around. They all turned when Ian and Rucon rushed into the room.

"That's it," Rucon said. "Prayda isn't going to waste time. We need to get to Earth." He walked over to the cook and two remaining servers. He took the older man's hand and shook it. Then clasped him on the shoulder. "You have served us well all these years. Are you sure you want to stay?"

"I'm sure. For now."

Rucon nodded. "You and the rest of the staff will be taken care of. I'll be in touch in case you change your mind."

"Thank you, your lordship." The man bowed slightly.

Rucon shook hands with the other two and dismissed them.

"Ladies," Rucon said, addressing Dani and Ria. "I need a word with Balastar and Ian. You two go ahead. We'll wrap up here and meet you at Ria's villa."

Dani met Ian's eyes. As angry as she was with him for last night, it broke her heart knowing how difficult it was to leave everything you've ever known behind. She couldn't look at him without feeling the pull of their bond.

Passing through the common, Dani scanned the lonely area and took a deep breath. She wanted to remember this place, the smell, the colors. Everything.

Mordo poked his head around the door as they approached. "Ah, good. We were about to call you."

Their boots echoed in the empty halls. Ria was right, the Cavacent's home was a sad, empty space.

In Rucon's study, Armond stood silent next to the portal. He held the black box which seemed to accompany him everywhere these days. He nodded as they approached.

"How's it going?" Ria asked.

"In theory, I should be able to lock the portals on Earth once everyone is across."

"In theory?" Dani asked.

"It's a good theory," Armond replied.

"Right then," Dani said. "We'll see you on the flip side."

"The what?" Mordo asked.

Dani smiled. "Never mind. See you in Italy. We good to go?" she asked Armond.

He motioned for them to go ahead and she and Ria stepped into the portal. Dani looked back at an odd sound, and caught a brief glimpse of Armond's surprised face before they passed through.

* * * *

The moment Ian entered the library with his father and Balastar, he knew something was wrong. "What's happened?"

"The portal was redirected," Armond said as though he didn't believe it.

Fear gripped Ian's heart. "Redirected where?" A muscle twitched in his neck.

Armond shook his head. "No idea."

"Find out." Ian fought for control.

"Easy, son," Rucon said. "Explain, Armond. What does that mean?"

"It means the Portal Masters have taken control of this portal and changed its destination," Armond said.

"It's been done from time to time," Mordo added, "but it's officially strictly forbidden. Few people even know it's possible. You said they threatened you?" he asked Rucon.

"Yes, and we know they want Armond."

"This portal is compromised." Armond pocketed the device. "The Portal Masters did this intentionally, and short of going through ourselves, we have no way of knowing where it will lead. We should leave here."

"Agreed." Rucon turned to go.

"Wait." Ian took his father's arm. "We have to find the women."

"We have to get to safety first and make a plan," Rucon said. "Then, we find Dani and Ria."

His father was right, but it killed him not knowing where they were. His gut wanted to follow, but training said otherwise.

Mordo pulled out his com and placed a call while they headed for the cruisers. He spoke a few minutes before disconnecting. "We may be in luck. Durgan and some others managed to get away from the guild and out of the city. They are in jeopardy, as are we. I think we can help each other. They're at his family's old estate."

"How many Portal Masters are with your friend?" Armond asked Mordo.

"I didn't ask. Why?"

"If there are enough, with their added energy, we might be able to create a portal of our own. Without being involved with the creation of that portal, the others would have no way of tampering with it."

"How many does it take to create a portal?" Rucon asked.

"With standard psi, approximately twenty-five. It depends upon their individual strength. To do what they did here, however"—Armond motioned back toward the library—"only three to five of the Portal Masters that created it originally."

"But you haven't tested your own portals with a human."

"Correct. However, everything I've tried thus far indicates it will work."

Ian shook his head. "Okay then. We have no choice."

Chapter 18

Dani crashed into Ria from behind. "Ooph—" They stood in a large room with a wall of windows overlooking a lush purple-tinged lawn and a city in the distance. Definitely not Earth. She turned around and discovered five armed men with weapons trained on them. They bore the insignia of the Sandarian Empire. *Shit.* Seated around a table next to the space they'd entered were four robed men who watched them silently a moment, before launching into a quiet but energetic discussion. Stretched across a plush leather couch sat Gordat Prayda. He made her think of Jabba the Hut drooling in his lair.

"Well, well, well, what do we have here," Prayda said, licking his lips.

"What are you doing, Prayda." Ria turned half her back to Dani.

They stood in the defensive stance and waited. They were outnumbered.

"That's President Prayda now," Prayda said smugly.

Dani snorted. "Says who?"

"Says my friends in the guild. Rucon's days are over, ladies. It would be wise for you to reconsider your loyalties."

"What?" Ria asked. "And serve someone like you?"

Dani smiled despite their situation. "Not likely, Prayda."

Prayda sat up, angered. "Well then, we'll just have to wait and see who we capture next. Meanwhile, I'm afraid I don't have time for worthless traitors such as yourselves. Lock them up. Oh, and let's make sure they stay put." He waived to the guards.

Three approached and instructed them to hand over their weapons.

They had no choice but to do as they were told. When Dani handed her laser over to the waiting guard, something stung her neck. "Ow." She spun around and saw another guard with a pen like device. He jabbed it into Ria's neck.

"You bastard," Ria said, rubbing the injection spot.

The guards led them out a side door, down the purple tinged lawn to a long, narrow building.

"This is cozy," Dani said, as the guards led them into a small cell. It was one of many.

The metal clanged loudly as the door slammed shut. Dani's head spun. She was dizzy but in a way she'd never experienced before. "What was that, Ria?" Dani rubbed her neck. She wasn't seeing right. Like frames deleted in a film, leaving a movie that jerked and sputtered.

"Psi suppressant," Ria said. "That shit's not legal. It's dangerous."

"How so?"

"It can cause permanent damage to your psi." Ria came over and put a hand on her arm. "In our third year at academy they gave us a small dose so that we'd know what to expect. This is gonna suck, Dani. Every emotion you ever had is going to be wide open and raw. You're going to feel crazy. Do not try to use your psi. Do you understand?" Ria squeezed Dani's arm. "It will hurt like no pain you've ever experienced. Just remember it wears off with the drug. Keep reminding yourself that. It's going to be okay. Rucon wouldn't leave us here. Come on." She sat on a bench against the wall, the only furniture in the room. "We need to sit before we hit the floor." Ria leaned forward, head in hands.

Dani sat next to her. Ria's words bounced around her head. She knew what they meant but couldn't repeat them if she had to. Her psi was like a weight tied to her. It swayed from side to side, pushing and tugging. It made her nauseous. Thoughts and images flashed through her mind. Each item brought a blast of emotion, much greater than it should have. She saw Ian's face smiling down at her from the bed in Como. *Ian.* She called out to him and a searing pain shot through her head, then nothing.

* * * *

Pain shot through Ian's psi, coming to a point in his head. *Dani.* He knew it was only a shadow of what she was experiencing.

"What is it?" His father sat next to him in the cruiser.

"Dani. She's in serious pain. I think the *crags* used suppressant."

"You can feel it?" Rucon whispered.

Ian didn't bother answering.

"You're farther along the bonding process than I thought. We'll get her back."

I'll get her back or die trying.

"We're nearly there," Mordo said.

They flew over a small village, circled to the west and set down outside a large country estate.

"This is the village of Springrun," Mordo said. "Durgan grew up here."

A tall, pale man emerged from the house. He wore slacks and a sweater, and walked with natural authority.

Mordo stepped out first and the two greeted, clasping arms tightly around each other. "My good friend. I feared I'd not see you again."

Ian noted an unusual level of emotion in his uncle.

"That was nearly the case." The man with speckled gray hair spoke with a deep voice.

The others gathered around and Mordo made introductions. "I'm sure you've heard of Councilman Balastar Alder," he said.

They shook hands. "And this is my brother Rucon and his son, Ian."

"It is good to finally meet you."

"And this, as you remember, is Armond Nolde, now one of Ian's Earth Protectors."

Intros done, they went inside. Durgan instructed the cruiser to be parked in the garage and took them to what was once a spectacular library. The ceiling was easily thirty feet tall. Midway up was a one-sided catwalk that circled the room. Wheeled ladders provided access to any book, anywhere. Now however, the shelves stood bare.

In the center of the space, a long wood table ran three-quarters the length of the room. At one end mingled a group of men. Ian counted eight, nine including Durgan. Although none wore the Portal Master's robes, they all carried the same air of quiet authority. As far as Ian knew, it was unprecedented to have so many Portal Masters outside of the guild's grounds, not to mention their lack of robes. Nine Portal Masters. Ten if you counted Armond and perhaps eleven if you stretched and added Mordo. Was it enough?

* * * *

Gordat Prayda was enjoying his little coup. His first catch wasn't disappointing. There was something about the blonde that intrigued him. He clasped his hands together. The Portal Masters had indeed managed to hijack the Cavacent's portal. The thought made him giddy. Power was an intoxicating mistress, and he loved her. The Portal Masters he'd been assigned were having some kind of disagreement in the corner where they sat. He wished they didn't need to be so close, but he had no choice. So stay they would. He was about to tell them to quiet down when the leader—he supposed that's what he was as the others never spoke—got up and approached him.

"Mr. President," the man said.

Gordat smiled. "What is it?"

"We detected an anomaly with our interception of the portal."

He resented the way Portal Masters spoke, as though they were superior to everyone else. It angered him. "What does that mean?" Gordat scowled.

"We are not entirely sure."

"Then why are you bothering me with it? Figure it out. You're the Portal Masters, not me."

A beat passed before the man spoke again. "I thought, perhaps, you would want to know. It appears likely someone knows the portal was, shall we say, tampered with. Presumably someone at the Cavacent's compound, which makes it likely to be someone with reason to alert Rucon."

Gordat clamored up from the couch. "How is that possible?"

"We are not clear on that," the man replied, as though it was somehow Gordat's fault.

"Imbecile." Gordat's anger flowed through him. The plan was to capture Ian or Rucon himself. He wanted to see the look on their faces when they realized his new position and control over the Portal Masters. He would arrest them and confiscate their lands and Earth as well, but he wasn't an unreasonable person. He'd let the lovely Mara live. Perhaps he'd keep her for himself. He paced and searched for a solution. "Guards."

"Yes sir." The senior officer stepped forward.

"Go to the Cavacent's compound. Arrest any Cavacent you find."

"Yes, sir." The guard left the room.

No matter about the portal. He'd still have his rewards.

Chapter 19

Prayda stood, mouth ajar, before he gathered his wits. "What do you mean it's empty?"

"The compound is deserted. Old Samuel was the only one there. Said they packed up and left days ago. We searched some of the buildings within and they were, in fact, empty."

"Empty of people?"

"Not just people. Empty of everything. It has been abandoned."

"No!" Gordat pounded a fist on the back of the couch. "Where are they? I want them. Put out a sweep, Captain. I want them brought here. Call the space port. Find his ships and you'll find him." Five minutes later the captain returned and reported that the Cavacent's ships were listed as being on their regular trade routes, but there was a problem.

"What is it?"

"The port authority is in an uproar. The cargo that was supposed to be on those ships is taking up all his storage and transfer areas."

Gordat let the thought sink in. "Goddess, would he dare?" He whirled on the Portal Masters in the corner. "Rucon's portal, does it go anywhere but Earth?"

"No sir," the short one said.

Gordat laughed out loud. "I'm stunned. The nerve. He's taken his entire following *to Earth?* That planet is mine. How could he possibly think to get away with this? He's killed all his lovely followers for they are now officially traitors."

"Do you think perhaps," the taller one asked, "you might have a problem taking possession of Earth under the new galactic ruling body?"

Gordat scowled at the insolent man. "I believe once I prove Rucon has been breaking the laws of our planet, any reasonable court would concur that I am the logical one to take control."

The Portal Master shrugged but said nothing.

Gordat desperately wanted to hit the man. "Those two EPs. They were going to Earth. They can't have been the last to go. Rucon would see to the safety of everyone first. No. He's still here." He clasped his hands together. "He's here. Now we just have to find him."

The captain cleared his throat.

"Did you want something?" Gordat spat.

"You captured two of his people. His sense of honor is well known. Have you tried calling him?"

* * * *

Purple-tinged dust filtered through the rays of sun that came through the windows of the empty library. Ian rubbed the back of his neck, anxious to get started and do something to find Dani and Ria. He paced behind the table where the rogue Portal Masters and the others sat. They questioned Armond at length about the mystery device, what he'd accomplished with it, and the redirection of Dani and Ria. Passing around the box, they were shocked to discover Armond was the only person in the room who could accomplish anything more than a directional power burst. No one else could establish anything remotely close to a portal using the device. However, Armond's theory seemed to be holding up. With their help, he was able to establish a portal to Earth. It was untested, but they all agreed it appeared to be a functioning gateway.

"The implications are staggering," Durgan said. "A technology built around an alternate form of psi—I don't know what to think. It implies an entire race with powers similar to our own that we've never encountered."

"Or never knew we encountered," Ian said.

"Indeed," Durgan nodded, his enthusiasm increasing. "Armond, your origins are a mystery, yes?"

"Yes." Armond said.

"Extraordinary." Durgan rubbed his chin. "That might explain your sporadic abilities with the guild. You're clearly very powerful, and as I recall, could in fact manipulate the portals."

"Yes, sir," Armond said quietly. "With deadly results."

"But, now, with this…" Durgan indicated the box.

"Obviously I haven't tried any live subjects, but I have been successful in manipulating portals."

"All by yourself?"

"My experimentation has found no limits as yet. And now, with help, it appears I can create them too."

"Never," Durgan said, pacing the room, "has a portal been created with less than nineteen portal masters. We barely have eleven."

The implication of the statement wasn't lost on Ian. The ability to create portals would be an advantage for them on Earth of unimaginable importance.

"We'll need to determine the new rules," Durgan said. "Will it drain us more each time since there's fewer of us creating it? Is four trips still the max per hour? So many questions."

"Armond"—Mordo folded his arms across his chest—"do you think it would be best to have Portal Masters on Earth to anchor this portal?"

"Since we don't know how many of the normal rules apply, that would make sense."

"All right, for now we will assume the same rules. That means four transports in one hour. No more than six hundred pounds each transport…"

"We're going to need to test it with a live being."

That brought a halt to the conversation.

"I'll go," Durgan said.

"No," a number of the other Portal Masters said at once.

A short, balding man stood. "You're the strongest among us. One day we can create our own guild, but we need you. Besides, everything about this portal looks and feels right. I'll go."

The rest of the Portal Masters agreed. In the end, they decided to send the first four immediately and they went through without incident.

"Well?" Mordo asked when they were done. "I didn't detect any unusual drain. Any of you?"

"I detect nothing out of the ordinary," Durgan said.

The others nodded agreement.

"Which is odd," Armond said, "given there are so few of us."

"The limits could be different." Durgan leaned over the table toward Armond. "Mother Goddess, this could rewrite portal theory entirely."

"Indeed," Armond said. "If the energy dispensation is significantly different—"

"Hold on," Ian interrupted. "Let's stay focused for now. We have ten of us left here and Dani and Ria at some unknown location. Possibly suppressed, which means it will be hours before they can use a portal."

Rucon's com chimed. He retrieved it and glanced down. "It's Prayda." He connected. "What do you want?" Rucon listened. "I should have known. I'll come, but you release them." He disconnected without another word.

"Prayda has Dani and Ria at his estate on the other side of Ardos," Rucon said. "He's going to kill them if I don't go to him."

"He'll never let them go," Balastar said. "It's not in his nature. Torture, killing, that's more his style."

"Why isn't he at the emperor's palace?" Durgan wondered.

"Probably too visible," Armond said. "If he's torturing them and willing to kill, he's going to do it quietly."

"You can't go, Father," Ian said.

"I won't leave any of our team behind, but"—he turned to Mordo—"you need to get to Earth. If we don't make it, I want you there to take care of Mara and establish our base."

It made sense. His father wouldn't leave anyone behind anymore than he would. The GTO granted the Planetary Rulership to the Cavacents. Mara being married to Rucon wouldn't be enough. It had to be a direct descent.

"All right, Mordo is in the next group. I would suggest Durgan and two additional Portal Masters."

Mordo didn't look happy but he agreed.

"That leaves us with eight people and two moves within the hour," Armond said. "However, if you are correct and Dani and Ria have been given suppressant, it will be hours before they can port. Since we know suppressant affects the reliability of standard psi-based portals, we must assume it can do the same with mine as well."

"How does that work?" Ian asked. "Back in the academy, we had to take a small amount of suppressant so we could be prepared, but they never told us how it affected portals," Ian said.

"It's a good question," Armond said. "It works on portals in two ways. First, it makes it difficult for an active portal to 'hold on' to its travelers, and second, the destination can shift unpredictably. Between the two, it is extremely dangerous to attempt."

"Interesting." The intricacies of portals never ceased to amaze Ian. "Armond, you need to stay safe to control the portal. Portal Masters aren't trained for combat. These two should go to Earth as well. They won't do us any good here. That leaves my father, me, and Balastar to get Dani and Ria. We need to get them out and hole up someplace safe until the drug wears off."

"What if we bring one of our transport ships back?" Rucon asked. "We just need to get them off world to be safe from Prayda."

"We can use mine," Balastar said. "Prayda is going to do everything he can to stop you. No one knows I've purchased a transport. It's being refurbished at the Montag station. All we have to do is get a shuttle and bypass security to get there."

"That could work," Rucon said. "And I think I know just the man. He's a little rough around the edges, but I served with him and would trust him with my life. And yours. I'll see if he's still on Sandaria."

A few minutes later Rucon disconnected. "When you're ready, call him. His name is Trulass. He wants to meet near the transport station. He said you might not be vertical but that he'd get you off planet without detection."

"Do I want to know what 'not vertical' means?" Ian asked.

"Probably not." Rucon grinned, sending the contact info to Ian's com.

"All right," Ian said. "Balastar and I will get the women off planet. Mordo will go to Earth with the rest of the Portal Masters."

"What we need," Rucon said, "is time. I want you all off world before I leave."

"Balastar, you know anything about Prayda's home?" Ian asked.

"No. Never been."

"Here." Durgan expanded a visual from his com. "It's cloaked now, but this was taken before he bought the place." The hologram showed a large property nestled halfway up one of the closer mountain ranges. It sat on the edge of a field. Downhill from the main house stood a small, squat, rectangular structure.

Ian pointed to the small structure. "I'd put them there."

"It's worth a look," Balastar said.

"I'll go to Prayda," Rucon stood. "That will buy you time."

"You can't," Ian said.

"Maybe he can." Armond flipped the box from hand to hand.

"What do you mean?" Rucon asked.

"When I was experimenting with this device I used focal points." Armond reached into his pocket. "They allowed me to target items for practice. In theory, we could use one to locate you and port you directly to Earth once we have Dani and Ria."

"We'll simply move this end to Rucon," Durgan said. "It should work."

"You and your theories," Rucon said. "All right. We have a plan. Such as it is."

"Here." Armond handed Rucon a focal point, then gave one to Ian and another to Balastar. "Just in case. I can keep track of all of you this way. If at any time you're in trouble just press the button. I'll port you out."

Rucon turned to Mordo and the two embraced. "I hope to see you soon, brother."

"Goddess willing, you will," Mordo said. "You will."

Moments later, Ian assessed what was left of their group. Himself, Balastar, Rucon and Armond. And two women in need of rescue.

* * * *

Ian gave his father a quick embrace before he left for Prayda's. "We'll contact Armond as soon as we have them. Don't let Prayda goad you into losing your temper."

Rucon huffed. "Be careful. I want all of us back on Earth as soon as possible."

They gave his father a few minutes lead before following after. Twenty minutes later they parked outside the Purple Ranges Inn. Armond would check in under an alias and wait to hear from either Ian or Rucon. They only had one move in the next twenty-eight minutes. If a focal point flashed, it meant someone was in trouble and needed extracting.

"You sure you don't want me to come?" Armond asked.

"I'm sure. You're our safety net."

Ian and Balastar had their usual laser guns and that was it. It would have to be enough. They left the cruiser nestled under thick foliage far off the road and hiked up to the small building from behind. It had rained the night before. The ground was damp with no dry leaves to give them away. Ian inhaled the smell of decaying plant matter and fresh leaves that filled the woods. Muted sounds from what he hoped were animals drifted through the damp. They made their way in silence.

Waves of raw emotion assaulted Ian as they approached. Dani was broadcasting straight into him. She must be thrashing around in her own private Hell. Only it wasn't so private. Ian fought to stay closed off but the closer they got, the more difficult it became. He slowed as an image of two adults, husband and wife, *her parents,* flashed across his mind. He stumbled as the pain of their loss ripped through him.

Balastar placed a hand on his shoulder. "What's wrong?"

Ian straightened up. He'd reflexively stopped and grabbed his head trying to shake the attack. "It's Dani. She's definitely suppressed."

Balastar frowned. "And you're feeling what she is?"

"Yes."

"How about Ria?"

"Nothing from Ria."

Balastar dropped his hand.

"Look," Ian said, "we've avoided this but you need to know. Dani and I are partially bonded and I intend to finish it." He held up a hand at Balastar's expression. "With her permission."

Balastar's expression turned cold. "Good luck with that," he said, leaving him behind and heading back up the hill.

"I don't need luck," Ian growled. He didn't waste any time catching up to Balastar.

The intensity of the connection eased off. He didn't know if it was because the drug was wearing off or simply his connection to Dani wavered. They approached the back of the structure silently. Ian signaled to Balastar. They each went a different way around the sides of the building. They would round the corner to the front at the same time and see what they found. He gripped his laser and another crippling wave of emotion hit him. This time the image was of himself, getting out of his bed after Dani saved his life. Her pain and confusion when he looked at her like she was dirt seared through him. He'd left her there and gone to take a shower. Now it was her shame and humiliation as his father stared at her. *Frack.* Ian shook his head, then rubbed his face trying to focus. He stepped forward and turned the corner to see a guard's back to him, a weapon trained on Balastar. He fired and took the man out. Stunned, not killed. Not unless necessary. Balastar stood there, hands out as if to say "what took you so long?"

No other guards were evident. They moved to the center of the building and found two closed double doors.

Ian moved to open the door with his psi, but stopped. Given the open connection between him and Dani, it could injure her. He nodded for Balastar to get it instead. They stood clear as the doors opened and waited. Nothing. They stepped inside to find cells running left and right. Something pulled Ian to the left. Balastar followed after. They found Dani and Ria in the last cell. Their tense bodies curled into balls on the floor.

Balastar blasted the door open with a laser. Ian couldn't handle touching Dani right now. They were both being affected by the suppressant. He motioned for Balastar to take her and picked up Ria.

Voices came from outside. They rushed back to the door.

"We may have to take our chances with a move," Ian said, "get your focal point ready."

Three guards burst through the door, lasers aimed and most likely set to kill.

"Look what we have here," the shortest guard said. "You just hold still boys." He spoke into a device on his wrist. "We got ourselves a councilman and another male here, boss. Looks like they're trying to make off with your catch of the day."

Gordat Prayda's voice replied. "The other male, he wouldn't be tall and blond would he? Boy by the name of Ian Cavacent?"

"You're out of line, Prayda," Ian said.

"You've made this so much easier," Prayda's voice cackled. "Kill the men."

Ian squeezed the focal point.

Chapter 20

The room blinked out and Ian hit the ground hard. Fortunately, soft purple grass caught their fall as he rolled sideways, trying not to crush Ria. Only it wasn't Ria next to him. It was Dani.

The movement jarred her awake and she reacted by stumbling unsteadily to her feet, ready for an attack.

"Stay calm, Dani. You're safe." Ian scanned the area, hoping he was right. There was no sign of Balastar or Ria.

"What are we doing here?" Dani turned in circles. She held a hand to her head and stared at a spot on the grass.

"Are you okay?" Ian tried to put his arm around her for support.

"Stop!" Dani stumbled backward. "What are we doing here? Why would you do this?"

"Do what?"

"Bring us here. That's sick."

"I didn't bring us here. Gordat ordered us killed. We had to signal Armond to pull us out. Suppressant affects the portals. We had to take a chance on a move. I've never been here before. When were you—"

He saw Balastar leaning in to kiss her. Here, in this glen. She was still projecting. Not as strongly as before, but enough.

A primal growl ripped out of him. He spun around and stomped away from her. *I did not need to see that.* Jealousy and anger filled him. He heard Dani cry out and turned to find her on her knees. She leaned forward till her forehead rested on the grass and cradled her head with her arms.

"I can't do this," she said. "I can't do this, Ian."

He heard her sobs and her anguish wrenched his heart. Every part of him wanted to go and comfort her, but he was having enough trouble of his own. Every pulse from her psi filled him with random thoughts, memories, and such intense emotion it was as though he'd taken the suppressant himself. He clenched his fists and forced himself to stay calm. Dani was awash in paranoia.

"You're going to be okay, Dani. It's going to wear off."

"No. What if it doesn't?" Her voice was muffled as she spoke into the grass.

"Suppressant always goes away."

Her body relaxed as the wave passed. She sat up, tears streaming down her face. "Why are we here? Why you?"

"I can't answer that. Like I said, it affects the way portals work. We're lucky we didn't end up in an ocean. Or orbit." What he didn't say was that he suspected she'd done it. Somehow she'd directed them here. Not Balastar. Him.

His com chimed and he answered.

"Thank the Goddess. Are you okay?" Balastar's concern obvious.

"I'm fine. Do you have Ria?" Ian asked.

"Yes. We're at the Inn with Armond. You have Dani?"

"Yes. She's getting better, but slowly."

"Ria too." Balastar's voice had an edge to it. "Ian, after Ria and I got here, Armond decided he had to get your dad out."

Ian checked the time. It was still three minutes before the hour was up. "That's five moves under an hour."

"I know. He's passed out, but breathing. I don't know if he's okay or… if your dad even made it to Earth."

There was nothing he could do but hope for his safety. Right now, they needed to get to the space port.

"Call the cruiser back, then come and get us."

"Where are you?"

Ian had to laugh at the absurdity of it all. "You're not going to like it. Here, I'll send you the coordinates on my com."

Balastar coughed on the other end of the line. "What in the Goddess' name are you doing there?"

"No idea," Ian said.

"We'll be there as soon as possible." Balastar disconnected.

"They're coming to get us," he said to Dani.

Dani flinched. "Balastar is a good man."

"Yes, he is."

"He's nice. And funny." Dani looked at him. "Why are you here?" Her shoulders slumped but she seemed more stable.

"I don't know. Balastar had you and I had Ria. It must have to do with our…relationship. It's a good thing we're together, though. We'd never have found you if you ended up here alone."

She shook her head, not understanding.

"Armond gave us focal points to track us and to signal if we needed help. A lot has happened since you left. He's making portals with that box we found at the villa. Portal Masters are helping him."

"No! Ian, they're helping Gordat."

"Not all of them. Some are coming with us to Earth. Already there, actually. We'll fill you in later. You okay?"

Dani wrapped her arms around herself and rocked back and forth. "It comes and goes now."

"It's going to stay gone eventually. Hang in there." The only reason he didn't go to her is because he'd been inside her head. She was truly conflicted where he and Balastar were concerned. Which was entirely his fault, given the way he'd treated her. "Let me know if there's anything I can do."

Dani just nodded. She looked around the glen, her gaze stopping at a flattened spot.

Her anger and confusion rippled through him. She was ashamed of the way she was dealing with the suppressant.

"You're handling this as well as anyone could, Dani."

"How do you know what I'm feeling?" Frustration clear in her voice.

"Our connection. I'm getting hit with your emotions. Comes and goes. I'm a sponge where you're concerned and I can't block it very well."

"You're getting all of this? Everything?"

Ian nodded. "Images too."

"Well that's just great." She hugged herself harder and put her head back on the ground.

Images of Balastar and himself flashed across his mind. She was trying not to think of them, but it just made it worse. She groaned and tilted slightly side to side.

He spun back around. He needed some space. He headed toward the waterfall, hoping the noise would drown out her anguish and his own emotions.

* * * *

Dani desperately wanted to hold onto the clarity that came more frequently now, but each time, the onslaught of pain and memories washed over her again. Every painful event she relived amplified a hundred times. Even the good stuff with her parents was awash with the pain of their loss. Every time she thought it was over, more surfaced. Finally, after what seemed like days from the time she'd been injected, but probably only hours, the intensity subsided. Each attack had caused her body to tense, and now she sat up, her muscles were sore and stiff.

"It's getting better," Ian said from behind her. He came around and crouched a good ten feet away. "I can't feel much anymore."

The reminder of how much he probably knew brought a flush of embarrassment. It was surreal sitting in the glen with Ian. She nodded slowly. "Every muscle in my body hurts."

"Going to be that way for awhile." Ian picked up a pebble and hurled it across the grass to splash into the stream. "I'm really sorry about your parents, Dani. I know exactly how much you loved them. And I'm sorry about the way I treated you. Sorry I pushed you away. Right into Balastar's arms."

Ian grabbed another rock and stood, this time hurling the thing into the waterfall three hundred feet away. He kept his back to her, the muscles on his neck bulged with tension.

Dani watched him throw rocks into the falls. His movements were stiff. *Thank God, Balastar and I didn't do anything more than kiss.* "I'm sorry you had to see that," Dani said.

"Don't be. It was my fault."

"True." Dani struggled to stand but knew she wasn't going to make it. "Ian, I need help."

He hurried to her side and helped her to her feet, wrapping his arm around her waist. Her legs trembled with the effort. She feared she might collapse at any moment, but the warmth of his touch and the support he provided were a little slice of heaven.

"I need to get my legs working again. Don't let go."

"Never." His voice was almost a whisper.

"Over there." She indicated a boulder next to the water. "I'm seriously thirsty."

He held her tight as they made their way, step by step. Each step hurt, but it was so good to be moving she didn't care.

Ian helped her sit on the rock and looked around. He walked over to a large tree with massive purple leaves and pulled down a branch. He pulled off a leaf and returned to the stream. Folding the leathery surface, he bent down and filled it with water.

She took it gratefully. "Nice trick."

He refilled it when she finished.

"I think I cried every ounce of water out of me." She set the leaf aside. It uncurled and dripped the last bit of liquid down the rock.

The surface of the pool rippled. The sound of the idyllic waterfall and the stream emptying off to the left was perfect. She thought of her parents, without pain this time. Just the sadness she was used to. She remembered the love they shared, the intensity of their relationship. Losing them had torn her apart, and she'd spent her life avoiding any such entanglements. Until now. She met Ian's gaze. He searched her face, looking for what, she didn't know. She took a slow deep breath. "That stuff makes it pretty hard to hide. Even from yourself."

"What do you mean?"

"It means I found some clarity among all that pain. Once you realized who you were and stopped trying to fight the bond, I fought it harder." She turned her body to face him, wincing with the ache in her muscles. "I took every nasty thing you did to me and held tight to it. Even after, when I knew why you did it. I held tight to the anger because it protected me."

"From what?"

"From you. From everything you represent. Being with you isn't normal." She tried to run her hand threw her hair but it was a tangled mess. *I must be something to look at right now.* She started separating the strands. "It's not normal. Not like—not like being with Balastar."

Ian shifted his position. "Normal is highly overrated."

She'd always thought so too. "What happened the other night, in my room—"

Ian started to speak but she waved him off.

"No, don't. It wasn't your fault. I was right there with you till…"

"Till the end. What happened at the end?"

"I panicked. I was mad at you for getting close to me again, but I also freaked out. I lose control with you. I feel like I'm sinking underwater and I'll never find my way back to the surface. Never be me again. I know this bond thing is permanent and it scares the hell out of me."

Ian inched a little closer. "I get that. Makes sense. I think that feeling was, in fact, the beginning of the last phase of bonding. I can tell you, from what I've heard, you do lose control. In a way. It's more of a focus on our psi and losing touch with our bodies for a while. I can also tell you no one has ever complained."

Dani couldn't help but smile. How could anyone complain about that kind of pleasure? Pleasure because of her psi. Her smile slipped. He'd touched her just now and her psi hadn't responded. "What if it's gone? My psi. Or damaged. Ria said that could happen."

"She was right. We won't know till the suppressant is out of your system, and probably not for hours after that. Don't even think about using your psi till we know it's safe. It would be acutely painful and you'd have no control of it."

Dani toyed with the leaf in her hand. What if her psi was gone? She'd never bond with Ian. The thought of making love to Ian and having normal sex, like any other man, sent fear through her. For the first time, she wanted to finish what they'd started. Her feelings for Balastar were strong, but she couldn't see her future without Ian. Her emotions were a wild mix of highs and lows. Could she really handle a relationship? Would it work? Another stab of fear. She pictured them lying in bed late on a Sunday morning. Absolute joy washed over her. What if he left her, or died? Her heart pounded with the thought. *I am such a mess.*

"Easy. Just breath through it. Let it pass. You've got a weird mix of emotions here."

Ian rubbed his hand up and down her back. It was heaven. Pure heaven. *Shit. Now, I've gone and fallen in love.*

Ian's hand froze.

She cast a sideways glance at him.

"I got that one," Ian said. "Do you mean it?" His voice held such hope.

She tore the leaf in half and inhaled the odd citrusy scent. "What if my psi is gone?"

He lifted her chin to face him.

"Don't care. I love you with or without psi."

Chapter 21

The trill of a cruiser horn made them both jump. Dani groaned when she saw Balastar at the controls. He looked so happy.

Ian stood and helped her to her feet. He looked happy too, and more than a little smug.

"Be nice," she said.

"I've never been this happy in my life, Dani. I'll be nice."

He smiled and her heart melted. She loved that smile. She loved him. Her legs were coming back to life and she easily made it to the cruiser.

Balastar hopped out but remained by the door. He watched them, noting Ian's possessive hand on the small of her back. His jaw clenched when he opened the door for them. "You okay?" he asked.

"Getting there," Dani said. She reached out and put a hand on his arm. She glanced between the two men. Both of whom she loved on some level, but only one of whom she couldn't live without. Ian slid into the cruiser, giving them a moment of privacy.

Balastar shifted his weight to the other foot and looked inside the cruiser. Ian sat next to a shaky-looking Ria. They talked quietly. Armond lay sprawled on the rear facing bench seat, looking deathly pale.

"I take it the bond wins, huh?" Balastar asked.

"I never meant to hurt you."

"I know." He gave her hand a quick squeeze. "I wouldn't want to deny anyone their psi-mate, even if I could. Get in. We need to move."

She climbed in and sat between Ian and Ria. "How you holding up?"

Ria managed a lopsided grin. "Not as good as you from the look of it." She nodded toward Ian. "'Bout time you stopped fighting it."

The cruiser lifted off and swung around the way they'd come. Sunlight glinted off the stream that fed the waterfall.

"You were right," Dani said to Ria. "That really sucked."

"Yeah. If I ever see Gordat again, he's a dead man."

"How's he doing?" Ian asked, checking Armond for a pulse. It was weak, but steady.

Ria brushed some stray hairs off Armond's face. "Balastar managed to get some protein concentrate in him, but that's all. He's got to be drained. He needs healing and food. I wish I could help him."

"Don't even think about it," Ian said. "Not till you're clear."

"I know."

Ian sat back and put his arm around Dani's shoulders, pulling her close. She shut her eyes, comforted by his touch and Ria's presence. Since her parents had died, she hadn't belonged anywhere. Now, with these people, she was home. It didn't matter what planet they were on. With Ian by her side and Ria, Jared, Marco, all of them. She was home. Almost.

* * * *

Nearly twenty minutes later they landed outside a dingy-looking warehouse. Ian had explained the plan and it sounded as good as any. A scruffy-looking man who had to be Rucon's old friend, Trulass, guided them into a hanger bay.

"I hope your dad was right about this guy." Dani squeezed his hand. *And I hope your dad is okay.* How horrible would it be if the day they got together was the day his father died?

He kissed her hand and led them out of the cruiser.

Trulass was thin and scrappy, quite the opposite of Rucon. Physical appearance clearly wasn't a priority with this one, and if she had to guess, she'd bet he cut his own hair.

He stepped up, hand extended. "You must be Ian. Spit'n image of your da'. Though I'd guess you have a good head on him, ya?"

"About five inches, yes." The men shook hands.

Dani climbed out and shook his hand next. Rough and callused. A working man's hands.

"Rucon described you all so there aren't no mistakes. You'd be Dani, then."

"Thanks for helping us out," Dani said.

"Glad to do it. Ah, and this wee lass here, that'd be Ria. And you I recognize," he said as Balastar stepped up. "Nice to meet you, councilman."

Balastar shook hands. "Just Balastar now."

"Aye. Interesting times these." Trulass looked into the cruiser. "Wasn't expecting five. Who's that?"

"That's one of my Earth Protectors. He's a Portal Master and pulled a fifth port getting my father away from Gordat."

"A fifth?" It was clear he knew the dangers and the chance of failure. "Right, since when does Rucon have 'is own Portal Masters?"

"It's a long story," Ian said. "Let's get him loaded and get out of here. He needs help. Balastar has a medic on his transport."

"Let's do it then," Trulass said, leading the way.

Balastar used his psi to move the large man into the shuttle. Ria followed behind and climbed in.

Ian took Dani's hand. "Hold on." He pulled her toward him and kissed her. "I just want to say I'm sorry, one last time. And to let you know, I'll never hurt you again."

Dani place her hand on his cheek. "I know. I trust you more than I ever thought possible." The extent and truth of the statement amazed her.

He grinned. "As soon as you're clear, there's something we need to finish." Ian trailed his thumb over her lips.

"I'm impressed with your restraint," she said, giving his thumb a teasing nibble. "I haven't sensed your psi since we landed in the vale."

"That's because one slip and you could be set back for days. That would be torture on a whole new level."

She didn't want to think where they would be if the bond couldn't be finished. She took his hand and kissed it. "I don't think I've ever been this happy. I was thinking about it in the cruiser. It's like—"

A bright red beam ripped through Ian's chest. Later, she'd wonder if she really did see *through* his body before he staggered against the cruiser.

Balastar roared with anger and fired back at the guards by the hangar door.

"Get in the shuttle now," Trulass shouted.

Ria braced herself by the door and fired over their heads providing cover.

Balastar rushed over to Ian and hoisted him up with psi.

Dani had her hands over his wounds but, there was no stopping the flow of blood.

A beam of laser buzzed next to Dani's ear.

"Move it, guys," Ria shouted and took out the source of the fire. She and Trulass covered them while they got Ian through the door of the ship and placed him on a cot near Armond.

Dani was shaking, her hands and arms covered in blood.

Ian's face was getting paler by the second and his breathing more rapid and shallow.

"Get me something to stop the bleeding," Dani yelled.

Trulass jumped inside and grabbed a first aid kit from the wall.

Ria slowly backed up toward them, keeping the door covered.

"Get in lassie," Trulass said. "We're leaving here now." He punched a few buttons on the console and a solid door slid across the entire side of the hangar.

"What are you doing?" Ria said. "We have to leave through those doors."

"Not to worry. I'm just buying us a few minutes." Trulass closed the door of the ship and rushed to Ian, rolling him on his side. From the kit he pulled out a flat package. He ripped it open and unfolded a piece of material twelve inches across. He slapped it over the bleeding wound and rolled Ian onto his back. He quickly pulled out another package and did the same to the front wound. The material morphed. It formed itself to Ian's body with a one- or two-inch indent where the hole was.

Dani was sick at the thought of what was missing from that hole, then realized she didn't know for sure which side his heart was on. "His heart," she said aloud.

"Left. Just like yours," Ria said, strapping Ian into the bed below where Armond lay.

"Why are you doing that? You have a Gravity Modulator, right?"

Trulass laughed. "Not on this old boat. We have dampers and shields, no GravMod. Now everyone buckle in. It's going to be a rough start." He headed to the controls and strapped himself in.

Balastar and Ria did the same.

Dani remained standing, not wanting to leave Ian's side.

Ria pointed to a jump seat at the head of the bed.

Dani pulled it down and strapped in.

"Reclining," Trulass called from the cockpit.

Dani's heart skipped a beat as her seat slid forward and her back and headrest assumed a near forty-five degree angle. She looked out a window above Ria's head. This wouldn't be good for Ian. She put a hand on his shoulder.

Ria shook her head and showed Dani how to place her hands on the grooves of the arm rests.

"Where you goin' Trulass?" Ria called out.

"Don't worry sweetheart, just a little back door I was hoping I'd never use. Hope I can get someone to send me my stuff, cuz they're not going to let me come back here after this." His voice rose as he flipped a series of switches.

The light in the hangar changed.

He opened the roof. Dani gripped the arm rest.

A siren blared throughout the cabin and Trulass let out a crazed "Whoooo Yaaaa! Let's go, baby. Say goodbye to Sandaria!"

Gravity pressed her against the seat back. She fought for each breath as the sky outside paled from blue to black. Spots danced in front of her eyes. Just when her consciousness was slipping away the weight lifted and she was slammed to the left as the craft shot out of the atmosphere. Now she weighed ounces. Ian barely touched the bed as his body pulled against the restraints. His chest rose and fell sporadically.

The crushing weight on her chest had nothing to do with gravity. *You can't die. Not now.*

Ian's chest stilled.

Dani waited.

He wasn't breathing.

"He's dying!" she screamed as she pulled at her buckles.

"Hold up there, girl," Trulass said. "We just broke every airspace rule in existence. I'm hoping they have more on their minds right now than a rogue shuttle. Here, that should help."

Partial gravity returned and Dani leapt to Ian's side. "You can't do this, Ian." She started chest compressions. "It's a hundred beats a minute, right?" she asked through her tears to no one and any one.

"Yeah. A hundred," Ria said at her side.

"Get the shocker from the cabinet above the jump seat," Trulass called out from the cockpit.

Balastar grabbed what looked like a round clothes iron with a cord. "Step back, Dani."

Ria ripped his shirt aside and Balastar placed the iron over his heart. "Now," he said before pressing the button.

Ian's body convulsed, then collapsed back down.

"Come on Ian, we have unfinished business, remember?" Dani shook him.

He didn't move.

Balastar shocked him again with no effect.

Dani stared at Ian's lifeless body. *This can't be happening. We just got it right.* She grabbed Ian by the shoulders and shook. "We just got it right," she screamed at him. Anger flared through her and she shook harder. "Damn you, Ian." She stopped and he just lay there. *No. No. No. No. No. No!* Her psi exploded. She flew away from Ian and slammed into the wall behind. Searing pain shot through her head as she slid to the floor and everything went black.

Chapter 22

The little men were back. Banging on her brain with their hammers. They'd been worse before. She blinked her eyes and winced at the bright light. Her eyes stung and her vision blurry, but she could tell someone sat in a chair next to her. She pulled herself up and leaned against soft pillows, blinking until her vision cleared.

Ria's small form curled up nicely in the uncomfortable looking chair. A background hum and vibration filled the room. She looked at Ria, her mind a blank. She struggled to remember how she got here. *Where is here?* She was forgetting something. Something important. Fear. She was terrified but didn't know why. Then it came back. Gordat. The drug. Ian.

Oh, God, Ian. She struggled to breathe. She tried to swallow but her mouth was impossibly dry.

Ria woke and came to her side. "Hey. Glad to see you're awake. It's been over a day."

Dani looked at her friend. How could she be so upbeat at a time like this? She didn't want to be here. Didn't want to be anywhere. She tried to tell Ria, but she only coughed.

"Here." Ria handed her a cup with a straw.

Dani took it but just looked at it. What did it matter? She should stop. Stop drinking, stop eating.

Ria lifted the cup to her lips.

A tear slid down her face as she drank. Slowly at first, then more quickly.

Ria smiled at her, then looked perplexed. "What gives?"

"What gives?" Dani managed.

"Girlfriend." Ria set the cup down and put her hand on Dani's. "Did you forget?"

"Don't forget." It was Ian's voice. Dani shook her head. *Still forgetting something.*

The door to the room swung open and Ian stepped inside. Tall, strong, and sexy as hell.

She swung her legs off the bed and he met her halfway. She flung her arms around his neck and buried her face in his chest.

His arms grabbed her and held tight.

"You forgot, didn't you," Ian said, placing a kiss on her head.

"Apparently. I only remember…" She couldn't finish. She remembered him lying on the bed, not breathing, and there was nothing she could do.

"It's all right. I'm here. I'm fine. Once again, you saved me." Ian pulled back to look at her. "It seems to be something of a habit with us."

Dani was strung out from losing him all over again and getting him back. "That's three you owe me." She looked around. "So, where are we and what happened? You stopped breathing." She placed a hand over his chest to feel his heartbeat.

"We're on Balastar's transport ship," Ian said. "About two days from Earth. As for what happened, Ria's the better person to ask."

"Wait," Dani held her hand up. "We're on a ship. In space?"

"You got it," Ria smiled.

"That is so cool. Okay, tell me how I got here."

"I'll tell you what I know," Ria said, coming around the bed. "Never seen anything like it. We both still had suppressant in our systems. And, yeah, you stopped breathing." She poked Ian in the ribs. "Balastar tried to jump start your heart, but it didn't work. Dani, you started screaming "no, no, no" over and over and something happened. Balastar says it was a shockwave. A psi shockwave. Your psi, Dani. It blasted all of us, but Ian's body pulsed. Five or six times, I'm not sure, but he started breathing again. You on the other hand"—Ria gave Dani a playful push—"passed out cold. Been that way for nearly a day.

"Now we had three unconscious bodies, two beds, and no way to tell who was going to live. We stuffed you in the bed next to Ian, made it here, and let the healer do his thing. Ian first, then Armond. He's back to his arrogant self, by the way. But you, we couldn't do anything with. No telling what that blast did, given your drugged state. We've just been watching and waiting."

"You woke up once," Ian said. "I was here. I told you we were going to be okay and not to forget."

Vague memories floated past. "I kind of remember that. It's fuzzy. What about my psi? Is it okay to use?"

Ian and Ria exchanged a look.

"We don't really know," Ian said. "The ship's healer said to wait and see what happens naturally. He recommended not forcing any psi connections."

"Huh," Dani said. "What about your dad?" She remembered Rucon's unknown fate.

"He's fine. Looks like we'll make it to Earth with everyone intact."

Dani wondered about that. She didn't feel quite right, but she was going home. With Ian. She glanced down at the white medical gown she wore. Given the coolness of the room, she was glad they'd included socks. "All righty then. I need a shower and I need clothes."

"If you're up for it, I can show you to our cabin," Ian said, looking adorably sheepish. "I've got your clothes there."

"And your boots," Ria added. "Can't forget the boots."

"Thanks, guys."

"You can thank Balastar. When we decided on this plan he had a couple of days worth of our stuff sent to the transport. Everyone except Armond, of course."

Ian and Ria shared a laugh.

"What?" Dani said.

"Just make sure you compliment him on his fashionable attire," Ria said. "As soon as possible."

"Can't wait to see that," Dani said, taking Ian's arm. "Lead the way, good sir."

"M'lady." Ian nodded and led her out.

The cabin wasn't large but it was perfectly adequate. A bed, dresser, a couch, and a decent-sized bathroom.

"I didn't visualize a transport ship having cabins like this. Don't know why, really. Just didn't picture it this way."

"People frequently want to travel with their stuff. Not all transports have the option but this one does. It has six cabins and the captain's suite."

Dani walked over and peered out a rectangular window. It was the perfect height to place her fingers on the sill and rest her chin. "Space, the final frontier," she said, her breath fogging the glass. "Dad would have loved this."

Ian joined her. "I wish I could have met your parents."

"Me too."

He turned her toward him and stared into her eyes.

The love she saw there made her uncomfortable. She wasn't ready to voice her deepest fear so she pulled away and grabbed the clothes he'd placed on the bed. "I can only imagine what I must look like. Time for a shower."

Ian pulled a new com unit out of his pocket and set it on the bedside table. "Call me when you're ready. I'll give you a tour of the ship."

"Great, thanks."

He didn't say a word as she stepped into the bathroom and closed the door.

Being clean again felt downright sinful. Which made her think of Ian and their grand finale, yet to come. Her gut clenched. She had no sense of her psi and was terrified to try anything. Ian said he'd love her without it, but she wasn't sure about how she would feel. She looked at herself in the mirror. She couldn't remember the last time she'd done her hair properly. She pulled it into a ponytail, put on some eye shadow and mascara and looked, to her at least, worlds better. *When we get home, I'm getting my hair cut, my nails done and having a two-hour massage.*

She put on her boots and grabbed the com Ian had left for her.

He must have been near because he was at the door in seconds. The man radiated happiness.

Dani wanted to feel the same.

He wrapped his arms around her. "You look beautiful."

"You're easy to please," she said.

"When it comes to you, I am." He kissed her, gently, not forcing anything.

The touch of his lips sent chills down her spine but nothing else. "Okay," she said, stepping back. "Don't want to start something we can't finish. Where's that tour you promised?"

Ian hesitated a beat then stepped aside. "After you, m'lady."

Dani slid past and out into the hall, trying to hide her devastation. *It's gone.* The kiss had been just that. A kiss. She barely heard Ian's explanation of the areas they passed. She was pulled from her morose state when he led her into the viewing deck.

It resembled a home theater except, instead of a TV, it had a floor-to-ceiling window. An irrational stab of fear shot through her when she approached the wall.

She gave a halfhearted laugh, then reached out and touched the glass. They approached Saturn with the rings clearly visible. "Oh my God. It's incredible. I feel like I'm going to fall."

"Don't worry. I'll be there to catch you if you do."

Her stomach tightened.

"Don't shut me out." He stroked her cheek and pulled her close. "We're in this together, remember?"

She didn't want to say it but she had to. "I don't want you to feel obligated. This isn't what you bargained for. Just me. Just a human."

"Gods, Dani. Do you think there is so little between us?"

"It's not fair to you."

"What? Finding the woman I want to spend my life with? How is that not fair?"

"You know what I mean, Ian."

"Yes, I do. So what if your psi is damaged or gone? I thought you loved me."

It occurred to her then that the word "heartbreak" wasn't just a metaphor. "I love you with every fiber of my being." She couldn't stop the tears.

"Thank the Goddess," he said, taking her in his arms. "Now stop this nonsense. Just love me. That's all I ask."

Joy and relief spread through her. She laughed as he wiped her tears away. The happiness she saw in his face reflected her own. He bent down and kissed her. No gentle touch this. As their lips met, she grabbed his hips and pulled him closer. She ran her hands up his chest and snaked them around his neck. Their tongues caressed as he probed deeper. A thrill started in her loin and rippled up her torso and in a silent explosion their psi collided. Dani sucked in a breath as the pleasure took over. *Yes.* She held still, reveling in the experience.

Ian's laughter brought her back to the present. Before she knew what was happening he had her in his arms and was heading to their cabin.

"We finish this now," he said, his eyes glowing green.

Ian set her down inside the cabin and waved the door closed with a flick of his hand. They tore off their clothes. Ian's eyes gleamed with desire that matched her own. A primal growl rose from within her. Gone was the terror she'd experienced that night in her room. The night before she and Ria were captured. She was fearless, and she'd never wanted anything more in her life.

There was nothing but this man before her. She pressed herself against him. With the touch of his skin, the buzz that only Ian caused ran through her. Cupping his balls with one hand she took hold of his erection. A groan escaped his lips as she stroked him up and down. Her own desire growing beyond anything she'd ever known. She rubbed the tip of his cock against her clit, sending thrills out in every direction. He nipped and kissed a trail from her shoulder to a spot behind her ear, causing her body to shudder. Their psi intertwined, bending, folding, caressing. Each twist and turn causing a wave of inhuman pleasure. He scooped her up and took her to the bed. She gazed into his glowing eyes and it was pure joy. He lay her down and positioned himself next to her, running his fingers across her skin. He leaned down and kissed her nipple, circled it with his tongue, and pulled it into his mouth.

"Oh, Ian," she sighed as she let the intense sensation wash over her.

Any place he focused his attention became a center of pleasure all its own. His hands roamed her body whipping her into a near orgasmic frenzy.

"Ian, I need you inside me. Now," she said, winding her fingers through his hair to guide him up.

He let go her breast with a last kiss and moved over her. When his gaze shifted to her face, he sent a wave of euphoria to her. "Your eyes are glowing, luv."

"Seriously?" She lifted her hands to her face and smiled at the luminescence that reflected on her skin.

He moved his hips, rubbing his shaft against her clit.

She growled and pulled him down, wrapping her legs around his waist. His erection pressed against her wetness. The orgasmic pleasure built, but a sense of joy existed that hadn't been there before.

He swayed his hips, rubbing her into a frenzy.

She shifted, trying to make him enter.

He moved again, brushing around where she needed him most.

She pushed against his shoulders. "I believe you missed."

"I never miss," he said as he pulled back and entered her fully.

The psi-body connection exploded inside them. With each thrust, the feeling crested and rolled back as he withdrew. Dani moaned, unable to fathom how this was possible.

He raised his upper body.

She looked down. The sight of his massive cock sliding in and out mesmerized her. Each thrust brought her body closer to the moment she craved.

His eyes blazed green. "Are you ready?" His voice rumbled low and deep, like that first night, so long ago. So long, only weeks, a lifetime.

She didn't answer. She pulled him down and kissed him hungrily. Their psi whirled. The pleasure took over. The edge that had terrified her before approached. She didn't fear it this time. She craved it. Needed it on a level she didn't understand. Over they went. She knew he'd stopped kissing her but couldn't tell where she ended and he started.

She moaned, her psi pulsed, the pleasure increasing with each beat. Faster and deeper his psi caressed hers. The sensation was overwhelming. Then a change. Something shifting. Faster and faster. Far away, she heard her body inhale. Normal senses ceased functioning. Her psi took over and the pleasure left her speechless. Dani blinked. It was as though her eyes stopped working, as a world of green and blue colors engulfed her.

"Ian . . ."

"It's all right."

A vague sensation of his face nuzzling her neck permeated the fog. It thrilled her body, and reminded her of the two distinct realms of pleasure that engulfed her. Joy, that matched her own, radiated from Ian. She tried to concentrate enough to focus her eyes, but still her world was green and blue. *"Why can't I see?"*

"We're experiencing the world purely with our psi now. This is our bond. Our psi are no longer unique entities, but part of a whole. This is us. Bonded."

Another thrust and another thrill, like free fall, so intense and hard to describe, as the feeling was outside her body and yet...it was her. Pleasure rippled through her, but this... The psi equivalent of bodies locked in the ancient act of mating caused all thought to cease. Pleasure was all that existed as Dani let go completely.

* * * *

Dani came to her senses piece by piece. Like sliding into her favorite jeans and shirt, she settled into her body. Her psi was calm, and Ian's warmth radiated through her. His chest pressed against her back, his arm around her waist. The stillness contrasted with the frenzied pleasure of before. A kiss, below her ear, let her know he was awake as well. She opened her eyes, her vision back to normal, and rolled to her back.

"Wow," she said.

"Eloquent as always."

She punched him in the shoulder. "There are no words to describe that." She traced the line of his jaw with her finger, loving the way the sensation trickled up her arm. She got to his lips and slid her finger across.

An image of the party. Her standing with Balastar, his fingers at her lips flashed in her mind.

She looked into his eyes with a question, but he smiled at her and winked.

"Mine," echoed in her head.

She returned his smile and answered back. *"Mine."*

* * * *

Later that night Dani and Ria were having far too much fun with Armond. The two women, Ian, Balastar, and Armond sat in the ship's kitchen-lounge area. Due to Balastar's forethought everyone had spare clothes except Armond, who wasn't supposed to be there. Because of that, laundry day had high entertainment value. Ian was the closest in size to Armond, but the shirt hugged his body and the pants only came to the ankles. It wasn't very flattering. After what they'd been through, they needed a good laugh, and his superior attitude dressed like that was the funniest thing Dani had seen in a long time.

"Hold on, just one more vid for Jared. He'd kill me if I didn't document your fashion statement."

"I'm glad you find me so amusing." Armond flipped the black box over and over. Apparently, portals required stationary end points so he was stuck with the rest of them until they reached Earth. Still, he never let the device out of his sight.

"Can I see that?" Dani asked Armond.

He shrugged and handed it to her.

"What do you call it?"

"It doesn't have a name," Armond said. "Perhaps we should find a term for it."

"Well, in the mean time, I'm going to call it…Bob."

"Bob?" Armond asked.

The others laughed.

"Unless someone has a better name, it's Bob." Turning it over she studied the small silver-buttoned keypad. "You say the Torogs still have one of these? Another Bob?"

"At least one," Ian said. "All we know is they had the two on Earth when they attacked. Question is, where did they get them?"

"Yeah. And how did they block the portal?" Ria asked.

"I have not been able to answer that." Armond leaned in, taking interest. "I can create portals with the assistance of Portal Masters using this, but they cannot. We believe it is because of the subtle difference in my psi."

"Not so subtle when you use *Bob*," Ria said, emphasizing the name.

"Indeed." Armond tugged at the ill fitting shirt.

Dani tilted her head. "And there were rags with Ian's blood when you guys found it."

"Given that he was the only one who'd been injured, that is my assumption," Armond said. "However, we were never able to test it as the villa was destroyed."

"And you can't use it?" Dani looked to Ian.

"Of course not," Ian said. "I'm not a Portal Master."

"Neither is he, technically." She motioned to Armond who saw where she was going.

"You should try it." She handed the device to Ian. "Give old Bob here a go. Can you show him how?" she asked Armond.

She'd never seen the albino so animated. He explained how Portal Masters learned to create portals. Next, he walked them through the process he'd devised using the black box. It wouldn't do anything in space, but they'd be able to tell if Bob responded at all.

"Portal Masters guard their secrets closely," Armond said. "I wasn't fully initiated so I can't say for sure, but my theory now is that they use something similar to this when they create portals."

"They use technology?" Ian asked.

"Possibly." Armond held his gaze.

"Why is that important?" Dani asked.

"Because it might mean the guild is built on a lie. They've always said it was an innate ability that only they could wield."

"It does require someone with substantial psi. We gathered around a pedestal when we trained. It could have contained something similar to this."

"Wow." Ian reached for the box. "Let's try it."

Armond walked them through what to do, and within a minute the buttons on the device were back lit.

"Mother Goddess," Ria said, "let me see Bob." She took the box from Ian.

Neither she nor Balastar could use it. Dani was the last to try. She focused as instructed and the force within instantly hummed inside her. The buttons lit.

"Fascinating." Armond was downright animated. "I would wager that your mother can use it as well, Ian. I must do further testing when we reach Earth. It could be the Torogs were able to use enough of your residual psi energy from your blood to create a block in the portal. Once established, it would require virtually nothing to maintain." Armond tapped the table rapidly. "Yes, normal psi cannot be used in this manner. It never occurred to me. I'll need your blood."

Dani nudged Ian, grinning. "He's gonna need your blood."

Ria made a face like a vampire and leaned closer to Ian.

"Very funny." Ian pushed Ria back with psi and kissed Dani's head. "I wonder if this is how we moved the portal. It never made sense that we pulled that off."

"Sounds logical," Armond said.

"So what does all this mean?" Dani asked.

"It means," Armond said, "that me, you, Ian, and possibly Ian's mother, share a common trait. One different than that of the vast majority of Sandarians. How that is possible, I have no idea."

* * * *

A late summer breeze toyed with Dani's freshly-styled hair. Classical music drifted across Ria's outdoor patio, providing background for the dinner party. They were all there, her new "family." Rucon sat at the head of the table with Mara at his side. Ian was at the other end next to her. The others filled the space between. Mordo and Durgan were deep in conversation as usual.

Dani whispered into Ian's ear. "Is it me, or is there something going on between your Uncle and Durgan?"

Ian took a moment to observe Mordo and shrugged. "He's always kept his private life private. You could be right."

Balastar and Marco sat on either side of Ria, who was enjoying the attention. Jared and Balastar continued to hit it off and Armond, as usual, seemed lost in his own world.

Gina and Battista came out with the last of the food dishes and joined the group. Rucon waited for them to get settled before calling for everyone's attention. The conversations tapered off and all eyes were on the head of the Cavacent clan.

"I want to start by thanking Gina for cooking another amazing meal."

Murmurs of agreement sprang from around the table. Jared raised his glass and the rest followed suit.

Mara put her hand over Rucon's and spoke next. "I want to thank my future daughter-in-law for suggesting we replace one of our meetings every month with a casual meal." Mara had taken a more active role with the EPs since their move to Earth. She was also heavily involved with the planning and development of the new compound going up in the hills above the lake.

Dani bowed her head. "My pleasure." She and Mara were getting to know each other better and it was wonderful having a mother figure in her life.

Mara started off the informal meeting with a status of the construction of the compound and a brief report of how the other Sandarian families were faring.

Rucon went next with the numbers for the carnium mines and finishing with the latest status on the Torogs. "The last jump within our perimeters was over two weeks ago. The pattern suggests they were determining the extent of our protection. If that's the case, they now know they can't enter undetected. At this point, it's a wait and see proposition. I've talked with Supreme Commander Macon and he's willing to assign resources if necessary to protect the mines. Our ships can handle anything less than a full blown assault, which I don't think they'll do."

Everyone paid attention while passing bowls and plates of food around the table.

"Any further information on why they're doing this?" Ian asked.

Mordo answered. "We still think they want Bob back." Dani loved the fact that everyone had accepted her nickname for the alien device.

"It's the best theory we have." Rucon passed a plate of roasted potatoes to Jared.

"Speaking of Bob," Mordo said. "Durgan and I have an interesting development on that front."

Armond nodded, apparently already in the know.

"Earlier today we were evaluating Armond during the creation of a portal to see if we could detect any anomalies. We used our combined psi to effectively blanket him and discovered there was, in fact, a clear foreign signature."

Durgan leaned in, excitement on his face. "Yes, and even more astonishingly, we can detect that anomaly even when he's not projecting. It's always present."

Rucon put his drink down. "Have you tried it with the others?"

"Not yet," Mordo said. "We thought we would do so this evening, with your permission, of course."

"By all means."

The two men got up and stood behind Mara. After a moment Dani saw a fine green mist envelop her. It looked almost the same as when Rucon projected. Mordo and Durgan nodded simultaneously. It was there. They next moved to Ian and finally her. They all had the signature. For good measure, they tested Ria and Balastar to confirm they lacked the telltale sign. They did.

They returned to their seat and Mordo reached for some salad. "We thought perhaps we would make regular forays on Earth to see if we could detect any others."

"It is somewhat draining," Durgan said, "but we should be able to work for an hour at a time."

Dani passed on the Brussels sprouts. She couldn't stand the little green balls. "What will you do if you find someone?"

"Nothing for now. We're simply curious to see how prevalent the alternative psi might be."

There was a lull while everyone finished filling their plates and dug in. It was a perfect evening and they ate in companionable silence for awhile.

Ian's psi brushed over her. *"Eat up, luv. You're going to need your strength when I get you home."*

Dani looked at him while she took a large bite of potatoes. *"Promises, promises."* It was more, and they both knew it.

Balastar broke the silence. "I wanted everyone to know, I've discussed with Rucon, and I'll be heading out next week. I intend to learn the transport business inside and out. I'll be living on my ship for the next year at least."

Dani sighed. It was the right thing for him to do, but she would miss him. They'd talked after getting back to Earth. It was hard for him to see her and Ian together, and he needed to move on.

Mordo and Durgan were in a hushed discussion before Mordo spoke up. "Balastar, would you be agreeable to taking Durgan and I with you for a few months?"

"What are you thinking?" Rucon asked.

"That it might be a good idea to search other planets for the alternate psi form. We very much want to know where it comes from."

"Yes," Durgan said. "It's such a fascinating mystery."

"Perhaps I should go as well," Armond said.

"No." Rucon put his fork down. "I want you and Bob to stay put. You don't leave this planet without at least two security personnel." He leaned back and crossed his arms. "It does present a problem however. The Portal Masters are not happy with you, Durgan. Their alliance with Prayda concerns me greatly. I don't know how far they will go to punish you for deserting with so many of the guild's members. You may go, if Balastar is willing, but you need protection."

Balastar had no problem with taking them. While they discussed possible guards, Marco spoke up and surprised them all.

"I'll go."

"Why?" Ian asked. "Are you not happy here?"

"Oh no, boss. I'm fine. It's just that I've been here on Earth for five years now. A little break and some travel to other planets will be good."

Dani got excited thinking about the idea. She whispered to Ian. "Could we do that someday?"

"Don't see why not. After the Torogs are dealt with and the galaxy stabilizes." He smiled at her. "In the meantime, maybe we can do some planet-hopping on our honeymoon."

She loved her life and this man. Suddenly anxious to get home, she caressed him with her psi. *"Eat up big boy."*

* * * *

The following day the sound of hammering and drills echoed down the hallway. The villa on Cat Island was completed from a structural standpoint, but workers still labored at the finishing touches on crown molding, cabinets, and paint.

"I can't stand this noise any longer," Dani said, getting up from the couch in their bedroom. "Let's go see Ria and your folks."

Ian stood as well. "We just saw them. I have a better idea. Get your swimsuit on."

Thirty minutes later, they were in water up to Ian's chest. She had her hands on his shoulders with her legs wrapped around his waist. "I feel like an exhibitionist."

"No one can see what's happening with our psi." Ian kissed her, then gently bit her lower lip playfully.

The water was warm and the yellow sun beat down from above. No more purples.

"You have a pool of your own, you know," Dani said.

"We have a pool," Ian said, nibbling on her neck.

Dani ran a hand through his wet hair. "We have a pool."

"Yes," Ian said. "We have a pool with lots of carpenters and painters surrounding it."

"Good point."

"I wanted to come here today. Back where it all started."

A couple walked up the path from Jared's place but they were too engrossed with each other to pay much attention.

"You could argue that it started at the warehouse. You, watching me fight."

"I could, but that didn't seem very romantic. And besides, they don't serve mixed drinks there."

"Ah. Priorities. Well played." Dani sipped her drink. "What do you think it means? Mara and I with psi. No other humans we've tried can use Bob."

"We've only tried three humans, but the implication is that we have different origins than most Sandarians. Think about it. You and my mother's families could be descendant from aliens who came here hundreds of years ago."

Dani thought of the irony. Either her father had alien origins, or he married a woman who did.

"Different than Sandarians. That's crazy." Dani twirled a finger through his hair. "And what about this GTO military alliance?"

"It will probably be years before order in the galaxy settles down. There are planets that have been repressed for generations. Not allowed to develop space travel. They now have that freedom. Other planets were forced to join with the emperor's military even though they had no interest in doing so. That's one reason this coup worked. There were enough dissatisfied elements within the military to make it happen. Now, their primary focus will be what it was supposed to be. Protecting weaker planets and enforcing fair trade within the GTO. The alliance has its work cut out for it. The good news is that they've abandoned the psi superiority complex. Beings, including humans, will be treated as equals. In theory anyway. There will be worlds that will fight the change, but it's a start."

"And what of our dear Portal Masters? Have they chosen a location yet?"

Ian smiled. "They'll stay close. Durgan is dropping the whole secretive, restrictive stance. These men will be allowed families and freedom. They won't know if they can create portals of their own away from Sandaria for some time. They need to increase their numbers and train the new members as best they can. It's a long road."

"A long road. I like the sound of that." She leaned forward and kissed him deeply. He tasted of rum and pure Ian. She moaned as the passion rose.

"You picked a hell of a time to join the Cavacent family. It's going to be a wild ride, if nothing else."

Dani ran her palms up Ian's chest. "I think I can handle a wild ride or two."

He nibbled on her neck and she let the pleasure flow. She sighed and whispered, "Or two thousand."

Meet the Author

Geek. Mother of teens. Wife to her very own alien. Lover of sun, sand, science, and the stars. Sabine lives in Florida with her husband, kids, cats and whole mess of characters in her head.

You can visit Sabine at www.SabinePriestley.com, or tweet her @ SabinePriestley. She would love to hear from you!

Preview

Enjoy this preview of Rebellion by Sabine Priestly!

Ria Montori is no stranger to kicking ass. Despite her petite size, she's a former Sandarian military officer currently serving the Cavacent clan and adjusting to life on a strange planet called Earth. She has no time to search for her psi-mate, the one being who could bring her pleasure beyond any mere physical intimacy. Which doesn't explain why she's bonding with a Curzan native who just killed a government official.

Ty Sordina hates Ria's kind. The Sandarians enslaved his people and murdered his parents in front him when he was a child. He has sought revenge ever since, and nothing will get in his way. Especially not a feisty redhead who challenges his every instinct and calls to his psi like no other.

But there is a war coming. And the two beings who want nothing to do with each other hold the fate of an entire planet in the heat of their undeniable desire . . .

Chapter 1

Ria Montori leaned against the transparent panel with arms crossed, enjoying the view of Earth below. It was good to get off-planet, if only to the Cavacents' cloaked base station. The little blue planet hung suspended in space, so different from the purples and greens of Sandaria.

Times like these gave her a chance to reflect. She was proud of what she'd accomplished. Because of her small size, she'd had to work twice as hard as anyone else to be taken seriously. Graduating second in her class in the military academy had helped. After her obligatory three years of service, she'd signed on with the Cavacent clan and now had a coveted spot as an Earth Protector, EP for short. But things were changing in the Sandarian Empire, and her world along with it.

She and Dani Standich, the newest member of the EP team, were overseeing the arrival of supplies from Sandaria. EPs had a wide range of duties outside of protecting Earth. The Cavacent clan had escaped Sandaria during the fall of the old empire in such a hurry, many things had been left behind. Due to the animosity of both the new planetary ruler and the Portal Masters' Guild, they might never be able to return, but with the help of those still living there, things were working out. They had been able to recover a large percentage of belongings they'd been forced to leave behind, and most of Rucon Cavacent's shipping business had survived intact.

"You okay?" Dani asked. "You look sad."

Ria regarded the tall blonde. She was a stark contrast to her own petite build and fiery red hair. Where Ria's world had shrunk, Dani's had exploded—other worlds, aliens, empires, all laid bare to her. She blew out a breath. "I'm okay. Glad we pulled this duty today. I don't know if this will make sense to you, but I'm feeling a little claustrophobic on Earth."

"How can you be claustrophobic on a planet?" Dani asked.

She tried to find the words to explain. "Because Sandaria is home to the Portal Masters, it's probably the most connected planet in the galaxy. You could request travel to at least a dozen planets. Starships are constantly coming and going." Both women wore the standard EP attire of black button-up shirt, black jeans, and boots. Ria turned to face Dani and shoved her hands in her front pockets. "I spent three years cruising the stars in the military before I hired on with the Cavacents. And now, with the fall of the emperor, that little ball out there is all there is. Does that make sense?"

Dani squeezed her arm. "It does. I mean, it's kind of weird for someone like me who never knew anything but Earth, but it makes sense." Dani bounced up and down on her toes. "I still get goose bumps being able to see Earth from out here. Don't you?"

Ria gave her a smirk. Her friend radiated a disgusting amount of happy. She'd recently bonded with Ria's boss, Ian Cavacent, and there were times Ria wanted to smack the happy out of her. She was glad for them, of course, but one could only take so much sunshine.

It was a calm day below, with few clouds to hide the surface.

"I still can't believe it," Ria said, tucking a strand of hair behind her ear. "A few months ago Earth was just a job. Now it's home."

Dani huffed. "A few months ago, I didn't know aliens existed or that I had super powers."

Ria smacked Dani on the elbow. "Psi isn't super powers."

Dani gave her a look.

"Yeah, okay. From a human perspective, maybe it is," Ria said. "We're Supergirls."

Ria's com started screaming like a teenager, making both women jump. Dani's com followed a moment later with the atmosphere breach alert.

Ria wasn't sure what surprised her more, the screaming or the breach. "Harvey, silence the alert," Ria said. "And stop screaming." She'd modified her com on Earth, giving it access to the Internet. Over time and with some tweaking on her part, it was developing a personality. The results so far had proved amusing. She never knew what Harvey would do.

"Yes, ma'am," her com said, sounding miffed.

Dani shot her a what-the-fuck look as they bolted for the portal. "That scared the crap out of me."

"Sorry." Ria stifled a laugh. "I've been playing with the interface. Screaming female wasn't exactly what I was going for."

Ria pulled up the status of the six cloaked transport ships that currently surrounded Earth. Two of them were picking up an alien signature on the planet. *How is that even possible?* They stepped through the portal together. Ria felt the familiar pull on her body and tingle of her psi as they were transported from the station to Earth. They emerged in Ian and Dani's study on Cat Island in the Bahamas. The portal exited through the fireplace and onto woven grass rugs. White floor-to-ceiling bookcases covered the walls, and a massive desk sat near a window overlooking the cliff and water below.

"What gives, Ian?" Ria said. "How could we have an atmosphere breach without an approach from space?"

Ian ran a hand through his wavy blond hair. It was obvious that he and Dani were communicating telepathically via their bond.

Dani's face paled.

"Your ships picked up alien signatures on the planet," Ria said. "Who is it, and how did they get here?"

The shock was evident in Ian's voice. "They exited hyper-space inside the impact zone."

"Frack me," Ria said as the meaning sunk in. *Who would do that?* Inside the zone meant it was pure luck they didn't exit partially or fully inside the planet. Earth could have been destroyed today. A cold sweat formed on her skin as the horrific scene played out in her mind.

The fourth EP currently on Earth at the moment entered the room from the hallway. The arrogant albino, Armond, had arrived from the tunnels and looked as shocked as the rest of them.

The final EP, Marco, was on a mission with Ian's uncle and wouldn't be back for a few weeks, at least.

Ian projected the status holo and searched the incoming data.

Armond joined them as information updates came in on the vid. "Identified?"

"Torogs," Ian said, looking puzzled.

"Where are they headed?" Ria asked.

Ian scratched his head. "They were headed straight toward Asia, but they've changed course."

Ria followed the trajectory of the signal. "They're coming here." It was impossible not to remember the last time the Torogs had visited Cat Island. They'd stormed the villa. Their ball-jointed limbs and leathery bodies had half climbed, half fallen through the dining room window. At the same time, they'd smashed in the front door. They'd managed to slice off Marco's hand before he and everyone but Dani and Ian had made it through the portal back to Sandaria. Those two had almost died when the Torogs bombed the tunnel that led from Ian's villa. They'd barely survived by pulling off a nearly impossible portal move and following the others to his home planet. The whole thing had been a mess. "Is this some kind of joke?"

"No joke," Ian said. He brought up the villa's sensors that showed it cloaked and shielded. "They can't get in here. Question is, what do they want? Why did they change course?"

"What if they weren't headed to Asia, but the Maldives?" Ria asked.

The EPs had bases around the globe. Ian on Cat Island, Ria in Lago Como, Marco in New Zealand, and Armond in the Maldives.

Ian raised an eyebrow. "Go on."

"It would explain the change of course if they're tracking Armond. They were headed to his base. Now they're coming here."

"Why would they be doing that?" Armond looked down on her with an air of superiority.

"I don't know. You're the self-proclaimed genius. You figure it out."

They all watched as the Torog signal approached the Island. It hovered around the Cat for nearly ten minutes before blasting out of the atmosphere and setting off another round of alarms. They followed the signature until they were satisfied the aliens weren't coming back.

Ian's com signaled an incoming call. He spoke briefly and disconnected. "My father wants to see us."

A network of subterranean tunnels interconnected by portals existed deep under the Earth's surface. The EPs used them to travel the globe and the Cavacent clan for mining the rare and precious mineral carnium. The trace mineral was a required element in the fuel used by their Faster Than Light, or FTL, interstellar ships. The team filed out of Ian's library and headed for the cruiser. Twenty minutes later, they were gathered in Ria's villa in Bellagio, Italy. Rucon Cavacent, Ian's father, had chosen Lago Como as the location of the new Cavacent compound, currently under construction in the hills above the lake. In the meantime, Ria's villa was the most centrally located and served as temporary headquarters. They gathered around the large dining room table. Ria had instantly felt at home the first time she had seen the marble floors and rich browns and reds of the walls of the ornate Italian villa. She'd inherited it from a previous EP and wouldn't change a thing.

Rucon was not happy as he wrapped up a call to someone on his com. "They must pay for this. They could have destroyed us. Not to mention the entire planet is buzzing with the news of something leaving the atmosphere. Earth is still a dark planet. They don't know about us." Rucon paused, listening before he continued. "Agreed. Thank you, Torril. I'll be in touch."

Torril Anantha. Ria was impressed. Not many people were on a first name basis with the head of the newly formed Galactic Trade Organization.

Rucon tapped his fingers on the tabletop. "He's launching an investigation. Even with the current state of unrest, risking an entire planet warrants the GTO's attention. There will also be a small battleship stationed along with our transport ships. If they attempt this again, we'll be able to hunt them down."

Chasing the Torogs wasn't an option with the transport ships. Although heavily armed, they weren't designed for pursuit.

"For now," Rucon said standing, "we keep all bases shielded at all times."

Rucon was taking this seriously. Full-time shielding meant full-time monitoring as well. The shields prevented anyone and anything from crossing their perimeter. From the local deliveryman to birds and animals. It wouldn't do to have humans walking into an invisible wall.

Rucon interrupted her thoughts before she could ask how long he expected to keep the shields active. "One more thing. Assuming everything remains quiet, Mara and I have accepted an invitation to attend the Summer's Ball on Mitah this year. An old friend of mine lives there." He scanned the faces around the table. "We've all been working hard since coming to Earth. I think it's time for a break. As long as we don't have further complications from the Torogs, I'm extending the invitation to the whole team. We'll make a portal back to Earth as soon as we get to Mitah."

"Excellent," Ria said.

The others were equally excited about the prospect.

Rucon said his goodbyes, leaving the rest to discuss plans.

Dani, who'd never been anywhere other than Earth and Sandaria, was bouncing up and down. "Anyone been to Mitah?"

"I've never been," Ria said, "but I dated a guy from there for a while at the academy. It's supposed to be beautiful." And it would be great to have another world to go to occasionally.

"And you guys?" Dani asked.

Armond shook his head, but Ian nodded. "We've been to the ball a few times. You're going to love it. It's a three-day visual spectacle, complete with a masquerade ball. You two"—Ian nodded to Ria and Dani—"are going to need to go ahead of time for dresses."

Dani clapped her hands like a child.

Ria nearly choked on her water. "Why? We're an hour and a half from Milan. World class designers and all that."

Ian crossed his arms and smiled. "Yes, but you can only get Mitan silk from Mitah, and trust me. You want Mitan silk."

It had been four days since the Torog's return to Earth. There had been no further attempts. Whether that was due to the battleship now orbiting with Rucon's transport ships or not, they had no idea. Ria and the other EPs were forty minutes into a training session in her sim room on Bellagio. They'd chosen a tropical jungle with four different types of alien life forms for variety. Distinguishing between harmless native wildlife and deadly aliens wasn't always easy. It was a team mission, and so far, they hadn't lost anyone. Today's weapon of choice was a small handheld laser called a dart. It worked like a gun on one setting and like a two-and-a-half-foot sword in the other. The training models were designed to deplete rapidly over time until only the sword function remained, and that got shorter until only the casing was left. So far, everyone still had functioning guns.

It was she and Dani's turn to hold their base. Ian and Armond flushed the surrounding area. Ian was ahead in kills, but so far, she and Dani were ahead on team saves. So as usual, the women were keeping them alive, and the guys were shooting things.

Ria wiped the sweat from her eyes. "We need to pick a desert next time. This humidity sucks."

"You get used to it," Dani said.

The bushes to their left rustled, and both women swung their lasers in the ready.

Ian stepped out, and Ria sparked with envy when he grabbed Dani and planted a kiss on her before he disappeared back into the foliage.

"Seriously?" Ria said. "You can't go an hour without locking lips?"

Ian's laughter rippled through the trees.

Dani beamed.

Ria rolled her eyes.

Another rustle, and a four-legged creature with razor sharp teeth launched itself at Ria's chest. "Morits!" Ria called out as she sliced the critter in half.

The sound of Ian and Armond battling away let her know they'd found the nasty critters as well. Six more made it past the men. Dani made easy work of the two that had targeted her. Ria nearly made it unscathed but when four hit her at once from all sides, one managed to latch onto her lower arm. Those jaws had some serious force, and her hand popped off, dropping the creature to the ground with it.

"Aw, come on. Not fair. There were four of them." Ria lifted up her wrist and studied the bloody stump. "Halt sim."

Ian and Armond approached from opposite ends of the clearing, equally covered in sweat.

Dani came to her side and inspected her handless arm. "It would almost be easier if they were bigger. It's hard to keep track of them when they're so small."

"Perhaps your relative height to the ground also contributed to your demise," Armond said.

Ria glared at him. "Are you *seriously* going there?"

"I'm simply stating that you were closer to them than Dani."

"Whatever," Ria said. "Little shits. Reset sim," she called out.

Morit bodies and Ria's hand evaporated. The illusion of a bloody stump did, as well, and her own hand reappeared as they all caught their breath. The jungle around them melted into the floor, and they soon stood in the metal gray of the sim room.

"That wasn't bad," Ian said. "We made it nearly an hour, outnumbered five to one. I'm good with that."

Ria was annoyed by the fact that she'd been the one to go out first. She had a competitive nature and hated losing.

She was still in a bad mood later that night when she sat at the kitchen table with her two Support Agents, Gina and Battista. They lived in a suite of rooms off the kitchen. Together, they cooked, cleaned, and took care of the estate. They looked like a normal, older Italian couple—a bit on the pudgy side, but sprightly enough. In truth, they were both highly trained and fully in the know about aliens. Across the table, they were giggling over a shared joke. Looking at them fawn over each other, you'd think they were psi-mates like Dani and Ian, but they weren't. They were simply humans in love and, at the moment, irritating.

Gina finished a bite of pasta and chuckled at Ria. "Ms. Dani, she tell me you lose today. It's not like you to lose, no?"

Ria bit the side of her cheek, still steaming. "I was being attacked by four furballs with teeth. One of them took my hand off." She shoved a large forkful into her mouth.

Apparently sensing Ria's chagrin, Battista jumped into the conversation. "We ran into the Mancini boy in town yesterday. He said to tell you hello and give him a call someday."

"He likes you, all right." Gina patted her arm. "You should call him. Maybe have dinner."

Ria pulled a strand of hair from her pasta. "If he ever decides to grow up, maybe I will."

Battista burst out laughing. "If he's like his *papi,* that will never happen."

"How about that cook in town?" Gina said. "He always makes a point of coming out and saying hello when you go to his restaurant."

Ria appreciated their concern, but the conversation just made everything worse. She pushed her chair back and grabbed her plate.

"*Bellisima*, where are you going?" Battista asked.

"*Si,*" Gina said, frowning at the food left on her plate. "You have not finished. You don't like it? I can make you something else." Gina moved to get up, as well, but Ria waved her back down.

"No, no. I'm just not hungry right now." She wasn't usually this abrupt, but between spending the afternoon around Dani and Ian and now these two, her single status was starting to annoy her. She thought about walking into town and having a drink but didn't think that would help. With the clan's move to Earth, the constant construction of the compound, and flipping Torogs showing up, dating hadn't been a priority.

At least now, she had something to look forward to. The Summer's Ball sounded like the perfect excursion. "I'll save the rest for later. You two enjoy dinner. I'm going to hit the sim room for awhile before I call it a night." Normally, she wouldn't want a workout this late, but she was feeling antsy. Her psi buzzed with too much energy. In lieu of having a decent male specimen in her life, a match or two in the sim room would have to do.